Scalzi, J.
Lock in.

PRICE: $33.99

MAY 2015

LOCK IN

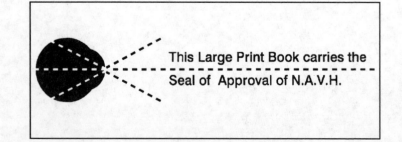

This Large Print Book carries the
Seal of Approval of N.A.V.H.

LOCK IN

JOHN SCALZI

THORNDIKE PRESS
A part of Gale, Cengage Learning

Farmington Hills, Mich • San Francisco • New York • Waterville, Maine
Meriden, Conn • Mason, Ohio • Chicago

GALE
CENGAGE Learning®

Copyright © 2014 by John Scalzi.
Thorndike Press, a part of Gale, Cengage Learning.

Thorndike Press® Large Print Basic.
The text of this Large Print edition is unabridged.
Other aspects of the book may vary from the original edition.
Set in 16 pt. Plantin.

LIBRARY OF CONGRESS CATALOGING-IN-PUBLICATION DATA

Scalzi, John, 1969–
   Lock in / by John Scalzi. — Large print edition.
      pages cm. — (Thorndike Press large print basic)
   ISBN 978-1-4104-7834-4 (hardcover) — ISBN 1-4104-7834-3 (hardcover)
   1. Virus diseases—Fiction. 2. Epidemics—Fiction. 3. Large type books.
   I. Title.
PS3619.C256L63 2015
813'.6—dc23   2014048735

Published in 2015 by arrangement with Tom Doherty Associates, LLC

Printed in the United States of America
1 2 3 4 5 6 7 19 18 17 16 15

To Joe Hill,
I told you I was going to do this.

And to Daniel Mainz,
my very dear friend.

HADEN'S SYNDROME

Haden's syndrome is the name given to a set of continuing physical and mental conditions and disabilities initially brought on by **"the Great Flu,"** the **influenza**-like global **pandemic** that resulted in the deaths of more than 400 million people worldwide, either through the initial flu-like symptoms, the secondary stage of meningitis-like cerebral and spinal inflammation, or through complications arising due to the third stage of the disease, which typically caused complete paralysis of the voluntary nervous system, resulting in **"lock in"** for its victims. Haden's syndrome is named for **Margaret Haden,** the former **first lady of the United States of America,** who became the syndrome's most visible victim.

The physical origin of the Great Flu is unknown, but it was first diagnosed in **London, England,** with additional diagnoses occurring in **New York, Toronto, Amsterdam, Tokyo,** and **Beijing** almost immediately thereafter. A long incubation period before visible symptoms allowed for wide dispersal of the virus before its detection. As a result, more than 2.75 billion people worldwide were infected during the disease's initial wave.

The disease's progression exhibited differently in each individual depending on several factors, including personal **health, age, genetic makeup,** and relative environmental **hygiene.** The first flu-like stage was the most prevalent and serious, causing more than 75 percent of the overall deaths associated with Haden's. However, a similar percentage of the affected presented only the first stage of the syndrome. A second stage of the syndrome, which affected the rest, superficially resembled viral meningitis and additionally caused deep and persistent changes in the brain structure of some of its victims. While affecting fewer people, the second stage of Haden's featured a higher mortality rate per capita.

Most who survived the second stage of Haden's suffered no long-term physical or mental disabilities, but a significant number

— more than 1 percent of those initially infected by the Great Flu — suffered from lock in. An additional .25 percent experienced damage to their mental capabilities due to changes in their brain structure but no degradation of physical ability. An even smaller number — not more than 100,000 people worldwide — experienced no physical or mental declines despite significant changes in their brain structure. Some of those in this latter category would go on to become **"Integrators."**

In the United States 4.35 million of the nation's citizens and residents experienced lock in due to the Great Flu, with other developed nations having a similar percentage of citizens locked in. This prompted the United States and its allies to fund the $3 trillion **Haden Research Initiative Act,** a **"moon shot"** program designed to rapidly increase understanding of brain function and speed to market programs and prostheses that would allow those afflicted with Haden's to participate in society. As a result of the HRIA, innovations such as the first **embedded neural nets, Personal Transports,** and the Haden-only online space known as **"the Agora"** came into being within twenty-four months of the act being signed by **Presi-**

dent Benjamin Haden.

Although the HRIA led to significant new understanding of **brain development** and **structure** and prompted the development of several new industries catering to Haden's-affected individuals, over time many people complained that Haden's-related research was overprioritized and that the intense focus on Haden's sufferers, known as "Hadens," had created a government-subsidized class that despite their "locked-in" status nevertheless had several competitive advantages over the population at large. This led to United States senators **David Abrams** and **Vanda Kettering** sponsoring a bill to cut subsidies and programs for Hadens, tied to a significant tax cut. **The Abrams-Kettering Bill** was initially defeated but was presented again with changes, and passed both houses of Congress by bare majorities.

Despite significant research into the virus that causes Haden's syndrome, and the development of social hygiene programs to minimize its spread, there is still no reliable vaccine for the disease. Up to 20 million people are infected worldwide each year, and in the United States, between 15,000 and 45,000 people suffer from lock in annually. While a vaccine eludes researchers, some progress has been made in after-infection treatment, including promising new therapies for "rewiring" the voluntary nervous system. These therapies are currently in animal trials.

— "Haden's Syndrome" article on
HighSchoolCheatSheet.com

CHAPTER ONE

My first day on the job coincided with the first day of the Haden Walkout, and I'm not going to lie, that was some awkward timing. A feed of me walking into the FBI building got a fair amount of play on the Haden news sites and forums. This was not a thing I needed on my first day.

Two things kept all of the Agora from falling down on my head in outrage. The first was that not every Haden was down with the walkout to begin with. The first day participation was spotty at best. The Agora was split into two very noisy warring camps between the walkout supporters and the Hadens who thought it was a pointless maneuver given that Abrams-Kettering had already been signed into law.

The second was that technically speaking the FBI is law enforcement, which qualified it as an essential service. So the number of Hadens calling me a scab was probably lower than it could have been.

Aside from the Agora outrage, my first day was a lot of time in HR, filling out paperwork, getting my benefits and retirement plan explained to me in mind-numbing detail. Then I was assigned my weapon, software upgrades, and badge. Then I went home early because my new partner had to testify in a court case and wasn't going to be around for the rest of the day, and they didn't have anything else for me to do. I went home and didn't go into the Agora. I watched movies instead. Call me a coward if you like.

My second day on the job started with more blood than I would have expected.

I spotted my new partner as I walked up to the Watergate Hotel. She was standing a bit away from the lobby entrance, sucking on an electronic cigarette. As I got closer the chip in her badge started spilling her details into my field of vision. It was the Bureau's way of letting its agents know who was who on the scene. My partner didn't have her glasses on so she wouldn't have had the same waterfall of detail on me scroll past her as I walked up. But then again, it was a pretty good chance she didn't need it. She spotted me just fine in any event.

"Agent Shane," said my new partner, to

me. She held out her hand.

"Agent Vann," I said, taking the hand.

And then I waited to see what the next thing out of her mouth would be. It's always an interesting test to see what people do when they meet me, both because of who I am and because I'm Haden. One or the other usually gets commented on.

Vann didn't say anything else. She withdrew her hand and continued sucking on her stick of nicotine.

Well, all right then. It was up to me to get the conversation started.

So I glanced over to the car that we were standing next to. Its roof had been crushed by a love seat.

"This ours?" I asked, nodding to the car, and the love seat.

"Tangentially," she said. "You recording?"

"I can if you want me to," I said. "Some people prefer me not to."

"I want you to," Vann said. "You're on the job. You should be recording."

"You got it," I said, and started recording. I started walking around the car, getting the thing from every angle. The safety glass in the car windows had shattered and a few nuggets had crumbled off. The car had diplomatic plates. I glanced over and about ten yards away a man was on his phone, yelling at someone in what appeared to be Armenian. I was tempted to translate the yelling.

Vann watched me as I did it, still not saying anything.

When I was done I looked up and saw a hole in the side of the hotel, seven floors up. "That where the love seat came from?" I asked.

"That's probably a good guess," Vann said. She took the cigarette out of her mouth and slid it into her suit jacket.

"We going up there?"

"I was waiting on you," Vann said.

"Sorry," I said, and looked up again. "Metro police there already?"

Vann nodded. "Picked up the call from their network. Their alleged perp is an Integrator, which puts it into our territory."

"Have you told that to the police yet?" I asked.

"I was waiting on you," Vann repeated.

"Sorry," I said again. Vann motioned with her head, toward the lobby.

We went inside and took the elevator to the seventh floor, from which the love seat had been flung. Vann pinned her FBI badge to her lapel. I slotted mine into my chest display.

The elevator doors opened up and a

16

uniformed cop was there. She held up her hand to stop us from getting off. We both pointed to our badges. She grimaced and let us pass, whispering into her handset as she did so. We aimed for the room that had cops all around the door.

We got about halfway to it when a woman poked her head out of the room, looked around, spied us, and stomped over. I glanced at Vann, who had a smirk on her face.

"Detective Trinh," Vann said, as the woman came up.

"No," Trinh said. "No way. This has nothing to do with you, Les."

"It's nice to see you, too," Vann said. "And wrong. Your perp is an Integrator. You know what that means."

" 'All suspected crimes involving Personal Transports or Integrators are assumed to have an interstate component,' " I said, quoting the Bureau handbook.

Trinh looked over at me, sourly, then made a show of ignoring me to speak to Vann. I tucked away that bit of personal interaction for later. "*I* don't know my perp's an Integrator," she said, to Vann.

"I do," Vann said. "When your officer on scene called it in, he ID'd the perp. It's Nicholas Bell. Bell's an Integrator. He's in our database. He pinged the moment your guy ran him." I turned my head to look at Vann at the mention of the name, but she kept looking at Trinh.

"Just because he's got the same name doesn't make him an Integrator," Trinh said.

"Come on, Trinh," Vann said. "Are we really going to do this in front of the children?" It took me a second to realize Vann was talking about me and the uniformed cops. "You know it's a pissing match you're going to lose. Let us in, let us do our job. If it turns out everyone involved was in D.C. at the time, we'll turn over everything we have and be out of your hair. Let's play nice and do this all friendly. Or I could not be friendly. You remember how that goes."

Trinh turned and stomped back to the hotel room without another word.

"I'm missing some context," I said.

"You got about all you need," Vann said. She headed to the room, number 714. I followed.

There was a dead body in the room, on the floor, facedown in the carpet, throat cut. The carpet was soaked in blood. There were sprays of blood on the walls, on the bed, and on the remaining seat in the room. A breeze turned in the room, provided by the gaping hole in the wall-length window that the love seat had gone through.

Vann looked at the dead body. "Do we know who he is?"

"No ID," Trinh said. "We're working on it."

Vann looked around, trying to find something. "Where's Nicholas Bell?" she asked Trinh.

Trinh smiled thinly. "At the precinct," she said. "The first officer on the scene subdued him and we sent him off before you got here."

"Who was the officer?" Vann asked.

"Timmons," Trinh said. "He's not here."

"I need his arrest feed," Vann said.

"I don't —"

"*Now,* Trinh," Vann said. "You know my public address. Give it to Timmons." Trinh turned away, annoyed, but pulled out her phone and spoke into it.

Vann pointed to the uniformed officer in the room. "Anything moved or touched?"

"Not by us," he said.

Vann nodded. "Shane."

"Yeah," I said.

"Make a map," Vann said. "Make it detailed. Mind the glass."

"On it," I said. My recording mode was already on. I overlaid a three-dimensional grid on top of it, marking off everything I could see and making it easier to identify where I needed to look behind and under things. I walked the room, carefully, filling in the nooks and crannies. I knelt down when I got to the bed, turning on my headlights to make sure I got all the details. And there were in fact details to note under the bed.

"There's a glass under here," I said to Vann. "It's broken and covered in blood." I stood up and pointed over to the room's desk, which featured a set of glasses and a couple of bottles of water. "There are also glass shards on the floor by the desk. Guessing that's our murder weapon."

"You done with your map?" Vann said.

"Almost," I said. I took a few more passes around the room to pick up the spots I'd missed.

"I assume you also made your own map," Vann said, to Trinh.

"We got the tech on the way," Trinh said. "And we've got the feeds from the officers on the scene."

"I want all of them," Vann said. "I'll send you Shane's map, too."

"Fine," Trinh said, annoyed. "Anything else?"

"That's it for now," Vann said.

"Then if you don't mind stepping away

from my crime scene. I have work to do," Trinh said.

Vann smiled at Trinh and left the room. I followed. "Metro police always like that?" I asked, as we stepped into the elevator.

"No one likes the feds stepping into their turf," Vann said. "They're never happy to see us. Most of them are more polite. Trinh has some issues."

"Issues with us, or issues with you?" I asked.

Vann smiled again. The elevator opened to the lobby.

"Do you mind if I smoke?" Vann asked. She was driving manually toward the precinct house and fumbling for a package of cigarettes — real ones this time. It was her car. There was no law against it there.

"I'm immune to secondhand smoke, if that's what you're asking," I said.

"Cute." She fished out a cigarette and punched in the car lighter to warm it up. I dialed down my sense of smell as she did so. "Access my box on the FBI server and tell me if the arrest feed is there yet," she said.

"How am I going to do that?" I asked.

"I gave you access yesterday," Vann said.

"You did?"

"You're my partner now."

"I appreciate that," I said. "But what would you have done if you met me and decided I was an untrustworthy asshole?"

Vann shrugged. "My last partner was an untrustworthy asshole. I shared my box with her."

"What happened to her?" I asked.

"She got shot," Vann said.

"Line of duty?" I asked.

"Not really," Vann said. "She was at the firing range and shot herself in the gut. There's some debate about whether it was accidental or not. Took disability and retired. I didn't mind."

"Well," I said. "I promise not to shoot myself in the gut."

"Two body jokes in under a minute," Vann said. "It's almost like you're trying to make a point or something."

"Just making sure you're comfortable with me," I said. "Not everyone knows what to do with a Haden when they meet one."

"You're not my first," she said. The lighter had popped and she fished it out of its socket, lighting her cigarette. "That should be obvious, considering our beat. Have you accessed the arrest feed yet?"

"Hold on." I popped into the Bureau's evidence server and pulled up Vann's box.

The file was there, freshly arrived. "It's here," I said.

"Run it," Vann said.

"You want me to port it to the dash?"

"I'm driving."

"Autodrive is a thing that happens."

Vann shook her head. "This is a Bureau car," she said. "Lowest-bidder autodrive is not something you want to trust."

"Fair point," I said. I fired up the arrest feed. It was janky and low-res. The Metro police, like the Bureau, probably contracted their tech to the lowest bidder. The view was fps stereo mode, which probably meant the camera was attached to protective eyewear.

The recording started as the cop — Timmons — got off the elevator on the seventh floor, stun gun drawn. At the door of room 714 there was a Watergate security officer, resplendent in a bad-fit mustard yellow uniform. As the feed got closer the security officer's taser came into view. The security officer looked like he was going to crap himself.

Timmons navigated around the security officer and the image of a man sitting on the bed, hands up, floated into view. His face and shirt were streaked with blood. The image jerked and Timmons took a long look

23

at the dead man on the blood-soaked carpet. The view jerked back up to the man on the bed, hands still up.

"Is he dead?" asked a voice, which I assumed was Timmons's.

The man on the bed looked down at the man on the carpet. "Yeah, I think he is," he said.

"Why the fuck did you kill him?" Timmons asked.

The man on the bed turned back to Timmons. "I don't think I did," he said. "Look —"

Then Timmons zapped the man. He jerked and twisted and fell off the bed, collapsing into the carpet, mirroring the dead man.

"Interesting," I said.

"What?" Vann asked.

"Timmons was barely in the room before he zapped our perp."

"Bell," Vann said.

"Yeah," I said. "Speaking of which, does that name sound familiar to you?"

"Did Bell say anything before he got zapped?" Vann asked, ignoring my question.

"Timmons asked him why he killed that guy," I said. "Bell said he didn't think he did."

Vann frowned at that.

"What?" I asked.

Vann glanced over to me again, and had a look that told me she wasn't looking at me, but at my PT. "That's a new model," she said.

"Yeah," I said. "Sebring-Warner 660XS."

"Sebring-Warner 600 line isn't cheap," Vann said.

"No," I admitted.

"Lease payments are a little steep on a rookie FBI salary."

"Is this how we're going to do this?" I asked.

"I'm just making an observation," Vann said.

"Fine," I said. "I assume they told you something about me when they assigned me to you as a partner."

"They did."

"And I assume you know about the Haden community because it's your beat."

"Yes."

"Then let's skip the part where you pretend not to know who I am and who my family is and how I can afford a Sebring-Warner 660," I said.

Vann smiled and stubbed out her cigarette on the side window and lowered the window to chuck out the butt. "I saw you got grief on the Agora for showing up to work yesterday," she said.

"Nothing I haven't gotten before, for other things," I said. "Nothing I can't handle. Is this going to be a problem?"

"You being you?"

"Yeah," I said.

"Why would it be a problem?" Vann asked.

"When I went to the Academy I knew people there thought I was there as an affectation," I said. "That I was just farting around until my trust fund vested or something."

"Has it?" Vann asked. "Your trust fund, I mean. Vested."

"Before I even went to the Academy," I said.

Vann snickered at this. "No problems," she said.

"You sure."

"Yes. And anyway, it's good that you have a high-end threep," she said, using the slang term for a Personal Transport. "It means that map of yours is actually going to have a useful resolution. Which works because I don't trust Trinh to send me anything helpful. The arrest feed was messy and fuzzy, right?"

"Yeah," I said.

"It's bullshit," Vann said. "Metro eyewear feeds auto-stabilize and record at 4k resolution. Trinh probably told Timmons to shitty it up before sending it. Because she's an asshole like that."

"So you're using me for my superior tech abilities," I said.

"Yes, I am," Vann said. "Is *that* going to be a problem?"

"No," I said. "It's nice to be appreciated for what I can do."

"Good," Vann said, turning into the precinct house parking lot. "Because I'm going to be asking you to do a lot."

CHAPTER TWO

"Who's the clank?" the man asked Vann, as he met us at the precinct. My facial scan software popped him up as George Davidson, captain of the Metro Second Precinct.

"Wow, really?" I said, before I could stop myself.

"I used the wrong word, didn't I," Davidson said, looking at me. "I can never remember if 'clank' or 'threep' is the word I'm not supposed to be using today."

"Here's a hint," I said. "One comes from a beloved android character from one of the most popular films of all time. The other describes the sound of broken machinery. Guess which one we like better."

"Got it," Davidson said. "I thought you people were on strike today."

"Jesus," I said, annoyed.

"Touchy threep," Davidson said, to Vann.

"Asshole cop," Vann said, to Davidson. Davidson smiled. "This is Agent Chris

Shane. My new partner."

"No shit," Davidson said, looking back at me. He clearly recognized the name.

"Surprise," I said.

Vann waved at Davidson to get his attention back over to her. "You've got someone I want to talk to."

"Yes, I do," Davidson said. "Trinh told me you would be coming."

"You're not going to be as difficult as she's been, I hope," Vann said.

"Oh, you know I'm all about cooperation between law enforcement entities," Davidson said. "And also you've never crossed me. Come on." He motioned us forward, into the bowels of the station.

A few minutes later we were staring at Nicholas Bell through glass. He was in an interrogation room, silent, waiting.

"Doesn't look like the guy to shove someone out of a window," Davidson observed.

"It wasn't a guy," Vann said. "The guy was still in the room. It was a love seat."

"Doesn't look like the guy to shove a love seat out of a window, either," Davidson said.

Vann pointed. "That's an Integrator," Vann said. "He spends a lot of time with other people in his head, and those people want to do a lot of different things. He's in better shape than you think."

"If you say so," Davidson said. "You'd know better than I would."

"Have you talked to him yet?" I asked.

"Detective Gonzales took a pass at him," Davidson said. "He sat there and didn't say a word, and did that for about twenty minutes."

"Well, he has a right to remain silent," I said.

"He hasn't invoked that right yet," Davidson said. "He hasn't asked for a lawyer yet, either."

"That wouldn't have anything to do with your Officer Timmons zapping him into unconsciousness at the scene, now, would it?" Vann asked.

"I don't have the full report from Timmons yet," Davidson said.

"You're a beacon of safe constitutional practices, Davidson."

Davidson shrugged. "He's been awake for a while. If he remembers he's got rights, then fine. Until then, if you want to take a pass at him, he's all yours."

I looked over to Vann to see what she was going to do. "I think I'm going to pee," she said. "And then I'm going to get a coffee."

"Down the hall for both," Davidson said. "You remember where."

Vann nodded and left.

30

"Chris Shane, huh," Davidson said to me, after she was gone.

"That's me," I said.

"I remember you when you were a kid," Davidson said. "Well, not a kid, exactly. You know what I mean."

"I do," I said.

"How's your dad? He going to run for senator or what?"

"He hasn't decided yet," I said. "That's off the record."

"I used to watch him play," Davidson said.

"I'll let him know," I said.

"Been with her long?" Davidson motioned after Vann.

"First day as her partner. Second day on the job."

"You're a rookie?" Davidson asked. I nodded. "It's hard to tell, because —" He motioned to my threep.

"I get that," I said.

"It's a nice threep," he said.

"Thanks."

"Sorry about the 'clank' thing."

"It's not a problem," I said.

"I'd guess that you'd have less-than-flattering ways of describing us," Davidson said.

" 'Dodgers,' " I said.

"What?"

31

" 'Dodgers,' " I repeated. "It's short for 'Dodger Dogs.' It's the hot dog they serve at Dodger Stadium in L.A."

"I know what a Dodger Dog is," Davidson said. "I don't think I get how you get from us to them."

"Two ways," I said. "One, you guys are basically meat stuffed into skin. So are hot dogs. Two, hot dogs are mostly lips and assholes, and so are you guys."

"Nice," Davidson said.

"You asked," I said.

"Yeah, but why *Dodger* Dogs?" Davidson said. "This is a lifelong Nationals fan asking."

"Got me," I said. "Why 'threep'? Why 'clank'? Slang happens."

"Any slang for him?" Davidson pointed to Bell, who was still sitting there, quietly.

"He's a 'mule,' " I said.

"Makes sense," Davidson said.

"Yeah."

"Ever use one?"

"An Integrator? Once," I said. "I was twelve and my parents took me to Disney World. Thought it would be better to experience it in the flesh. So they scheduled me an Integrator for the day."

"How was it?"

"I hated it," I said. "It was hot, after an

hour my feet hurt, and I nearly pissed myself because I had no idea how to do it like you guys do, right? That's all taken care of for me, and I got Haden's so young that I don't remember doing it the other way. The Integrator had to surface to do it, and they're not supposed to do that when they're carrying someone. After a couple of hours I complained enough that we went back to the hotel room and swapped back out with the threep. And *then* I had a good time. They still had to pay the Integrator for the full day, though."

"And you haven't done it since."

"No," I said. "Why bother."

"Huh," Davidson said. The door to the interrogation room opened and Vann came through it, carrying two cups of coffee. He pointed to her. "She's one, you know."

"She's one what?"

"An Integrator," Davidson said. "Or was, anyway, before she joined the Bureau."

"I didn't know that," I said. I looked over to where she was sitting down and getting comfortable.

"It's why she's got this beat," Davidson said. "She gets you guys in a way the rest of us don't. No offense, but it's hard for the rest of us to wrap our brains around what's going on with you."

"I understand that," I said.

"Yeah," Davidson said. He was quiet for a second, and I waited for what I knew was coming next: the Personal Connection to Haden's. I guessed an uncle or a cousin.

"I had a cousin who got Haden's," Davidson said, and internally I checked off the victory. "This was back with the first wave, when no one had any idea what the fuck was going on. Before they called it Haden's. She got the flu, and then seemed to get better, and then —" He shrugged.

"Lock in," I said.

"Right," Davidson said. "I remember going to the hospital to see her, and they had a whole wing of locked-in patients. Just lying there, doing nothing but breathing. Dozens of them. And a couple of days before, all of them were walking around, living a normal life."

"What happened to your cousin?" I asked.

"She lost it," Davidson said. "Being locked in made her have a psychotic break, or something like that."

I nodded. "That wasn't uncommon, unfortunately."

"Right," Davidson said again. "She hung in for a couple of years and then her body gave it up."

"Sorry," I said.

"It was bad," Davidson said. "But it was bad for everyone. I mean, shit. The first lady got it. That's why it's *called* Haden's."

"It still sucks."

"It does," Davidson agreed, and pointed to Vann. "I mean, she got Haden's too, right?" Davidson asked. "At some point. That's why she's like she is."

"Sort of," I said. "There was a tiny percentage of people who were infected who had their brain structure altered but didn't get locked in. A tiny percentage of *them* had their brains altered enough to be able to be Integrators." It was more complicated than that, but I didn't think Davidson actually cared that much. "There's maybe ten thousand Integrators on the entire planet."

"Huh," Davidson said. "Anyway. She's an Integrator. Or was. So maybe she'll get something out of this guy after all." He turned up the volume on the speakers so we could hear what she was saying to Bell.

"I brought you some coffee," Vann said, to Bell, sliding the coffee over to him. "Knowing nothing about you, I guessed you might want cream and sugar. Sorry if I got that wrong."

Bell looked at the coffee, but otherwise did and said nothing.

"Bacon cheeseburgers," Vann said.

"What?" Bell said. Vann's apparent non sequitur had roused him out of complete silence.

"Bacon cheeseburgers," Vann repeated. "When I worked as an Integrator I ate so many goddamned bacon cheeseburgers. You might know why."

"Because the first thing anyone who's been locked in wants when they integrate is a bacon cheeseburger," Bell said.

Vann smiled. "So it's not just me it happened to," she said.

"It's not," Bell said.

"There was a Five Guys down the street from my apartment," Vann said. "It got so that all I had to do was walk through the door, and they'd put the patties on the grill. They wouldn't even wait to take my order. They knew."

"That sounds about right," Bell said.

"It took two and a half years after I stopped integrating before I could even look at a bacon cheeseburger again," Vann said.

"That sounds about right, too," Bell said. "I wouldn't eat them anymore if I didn't have to."

"Be strong," Vann said.

Bell grabbed the coffee Vann brought for him, smelled it, and took a sip. "You're not

Metro," he said. "I've never met a Metro cop who'd been an Integrator."

"My name is Agent Leslie Vann," she said. "I'm with the Bureau. I and my partner investigate crimes that involve Hadens. You're not typically what we consider a Haden, but you *are* an Integrator, which means a Haden might have been involved here. If there was, then you and I both know this is something you may not be responsible for. But you have to let me know, so I can help you."

"Right," Bell said.

"The police tell me that you've not previously been forthcoming on the whole talking thing."

"I'll give you three guesses why," Bell said.

"Probably because they zapped you as soon as they saw you."

"Bingo."

"Not that it means anything, but I apologize to you for that, Nicholas. It's not the way I would have handled it if I were there."

"I was sitting on the bed," Bell said. "With my hands up. I wasn't doing anything."

"I know," Vann said. "And like I said, I apologize for that. It wasn't right. On the other hand — and this isn't an excuse, just an observation — while you were sitting on the bed with your hands up, not doing anything, there *was* a dead guy on the floor, and his blood was all over you." She moved a single index finger to point. "Still all over you, come to think of it."

Bell stared at Vann, quiet.

"Like I said, not an excuse," Vann reiterated, after fifteen seconds of silence.

"Am I under arrest?" Bell asked.

"Nicholas, you were found in a room with a dead guy, covered in his blood," Vann said. "You can understand why we all might be curious about the circumstances. Anything you can tell us is going to be helpful. And if it clears your name, so much the better, right?"

"Am I under arrest?" Bell repeated.

"What you are, is in a position to help me out," Vann said. "I'm coming into this late. I've seen the hotel room, but I got there after you were taken away. So if you can, clue me in to what was happening in that room. What I should be looking for. Anything would help. And if you help me, I'm in a better position to help you."

Bell gave a wry smile to this, crossed his arms, and looked away.

"We're back to the not talking," Vann said.

"We can talk about bacon cheeseburgers again, if you like."

"You can at the very least tell me if you

were integrated," Vann said.

"You're kidding," Bell said.

"I'm not asking for details, just whether or not you were working," Vann said. "Or were you *about* to work? I knew Integrators who did freelancing on the side. A Dodger wants to do something he can't be seen doing in public. They've got those gray-market scanner caps that work well enough for the job. And now that Abrams-Kettering's passed, you've got a reason to go looking for side gigs. The government contracts are drying up. And you've got family to think about."

Bell, who had been sipping his coffee, set it down and swallowed. "You're talking about Cassandra now," he said.

"No one would blame you," Vann said. "Congress is taking away funding for Hadens after the immediate infection and transitional care. Said that the technology for helping them participate in the world has gotten so good that it shouldn't be considered a disability anymore."

"Do you believe that?" Bell asked.

"My partner is a Haden," Vann said. "If you ask me, it means now I have an advantage, because threeps are better than the human body in lots of ways. But there are a lot of Hadens who slip through the cracks.

Your sister, for example. She's not doing what Congress expects her to do, which is to get a job."

Bell visibly bristled at this. "If you know who I am then you certainly know who *she* is," he said. "I'd say she has a job. Unless you think being one of the prime movers behind the Haden Walkout this week and the march they have planned for this week-end is something she's doing in her *spare time.*"

"I don't disagree with you, Nicholas," Vann said. "She's not exactly working at Subway, making sandwiches. But she's also not making any money doing what she's do-ing."

"Money isn't that important to her."

"No, but it's about to become important," Vann said. "Abrams-Kettering means that Hadens are being transitioned out to private care. Someone has to cover her expenses now. You're her only living family. I'd guess it falls to you. Which brings us back to that hotel room and that man you were with. And brings me back to my point, which is that if you were integrated, or were about to be integrated, then that's something I need to know. It's something I need in order to help you."

"I appreciate your desire to *help,* Agent

Vann," Bell said, dryly. "But I think what I really want to do is wait until my lawyer arrives and let him handle things from here."

Vann blinked. "I wasn't told you'd asked for a lawyer," she said.

"I didn't," Bell said. "I called him while I was still in the hotel room. Before the police zapped me." Bell tapped his temple, indicating all the high-tech apparatus he had stuffed into his skull. "Which I recorded, of course, just like I record almost everything. Because you and I agree on one thing, Agent Vann. Being in a room with a dead body complicates matters. Being electrocuted before I could exercise my rights complicates them even more."

At this, Bell smiled and looked up, as if paying attention to something unseen. "And that's a ping from my lawyer. He's here. I expect your life is about to get much more interesting, Agent Vann."

"I think we're done here, then," Vann said.

"I think we are," Bell said. "But it was lovely talking food with you."

CHAPTER THREE

"So, to recap," Samuel Schwartz said, and held up a hand to tick off points. "Illegally stunning my client when he was not offering any resistance, detaining him without cause in a holding cell, and then two separate law enforcement agencies, one local, one federal, question him without making him aware of his rights and without his lawyer present. Have I missed anything, Captain? Agent Vann?"

Captain Davidson shifted uncomfortably in his desk chair. Vann, standing behind him, said nothing. She was looking at Schwartz, or more accurately, at his threep, standing in front of the captain's desk. The threep was a Sebring-Warner, like mine, but it was the Ajax 370, which I found mildly surprising. The Ajax 370 wasn't cheap, but it also wasn't the top of the line, either for Sebring-Warner or for the Ajax model. Lawyers usually went for the high-end imports. Either Schwartz was clueless about status symbols or he didn't need to advertise his status. I decided to run him through the database to see which was the case.

"Your client never expressed his right to remain silent or his desire for a lawyer," Davidson said.

"Yes, it's strange how getting hit with fifty thousand volts will keep a person from verbalizing either of those, isn't it," Schwartz said.

"He didn't ask for them after he got here, either," Vann noted.

Schwartz turned his head to her. The Ajax 370 model's stylized head bore some resemblance to the Oscar statuette, with subtle alterations to where the eyes, ears and mouth would be, both to avoid trademark issues and to give humans conversing with the threep something to focus on. Heads could be heavily customized, and a lot of younger Hadens did that. But for adults with serious jobs, that was déclassé, which was another clue to Schwartz's likely social standing.

"He didn't have to, Agent Vann," Schwartz said. "Because he called me before the cops stunned him into silence. The fact he called a lawyer is a clear indication that he knew his rights and intended to exercise them in this case." He turned his attention to Davidson. "The fact your officers *deprived* him of his ability to affirm his right does not mean he refused his right, even if he did not *reiterate* that fact here."

"We could argue that point," Davidson said.

"Yes, let's," Schwartz said. "Let's go to the judge right now and do that. But if you're not going to do that, then you need to let my client go home."

"You're joking," Vann said.

"You can't see me smile at that comment, Agent Vann," Schwartz said. "But I promise you the smile is there."

"Your client was in a room with a dead body, the guy's blood all over him," Vann said. "That's not the mark of complete innocence."

"But it's not the mark of guilt either," Schwartz said. "Agent Vann, you have a man who has no previous police record. At all. Not even for jaywalking. His line of business requires him to surrender control of his body to others. As a consequence of that, from time to time he meets clients he does not personally know, who conduct business with others he also does not personally know. Such as the dead gentleman at the Watergate."

"You're saying your client was integrated at the time of the murder," I said.

Schwartz turned and looked at me for what I suspected was the first time in the entire conversation. As with Schwartz's threep, mine had a fixed head, which showed no expression. But I had no doubt he was sizing up my make and model just as I had sized up his, looking for clues as to who I was and how important I was to the conversation. That, and taking in my badge, still in my chest display slot.

"I am saying that my client was in that hotel room on business, Agent Shane," he said, after a moment.

"Then tell us who he was integrated with," Vann said. "We can take it from there."

"You know I can't do that," Schwartz said.

"Vann tracks down creeps with threeps all the time," Davidson said, motioning at Vann. "That's nearly her whole job, as far as I understand it. There's no law against tracking a person back from information on their threep."

Out of reflex I moved to correct Davidson's bad comparison, then caught Vann's glance at me. I stopped.

Schwartz was silent for a moment, then Davidson's tablet pinged. He picked it up.

"I just sent you ten years of case law about the status of Integrators, Captain," Schwartz said. "I did it because Integrators are relatively rare and therefore, unlike Agents Vann and Shane here, who are currently being *wholly* disingenuous, you might be speaking out of genuine ignorance and not just your usual levels of casual obstructionism."

"All right," Davidson said, not looking at his tablet. "And?"

"Superficially, Integrators perform the same role as Personal Transports," Schwartz said. "They allow those of us who have been locked in by Haden's syndrome to be mobile, to work, and to participate in society. But *this*" — Schwartz tapped his threep's chest with his knuckles — "is a machine. Without its human operator, it's a pile of parts. It has no more rights than a toaster — it's property. Integrators are humans. Despite the superficial resemblance to what threeps do, what Integrators do is a skill and profession — one that they train hard for, as Agent Vann can no doubt tell you." He turned to Vann at this point. "Speaking of which, now you can tell Captain Davidson where I'm going with this."

"He's going to argue there's Integrator-client privilege," Vann said, to Davidson.

"Like attorney-client privilege, or doctor-patient privilege, or confessor-parishioner privilege," Schwartz said, and pointed at Davidson's tablet. "And *I'm* not going to argue it, since the courts have already done so, and have affirmed, consistently, that Integrator-client confidentiality is real and protected."

"No Supreme Court cases," Vann said.

"And that should tell you something," Schwartz said. "Namely, that the idea of Integrator-client privilege is so noncontroversial that no one's bothered to appeal it all the way up. That said, please note *Wintour v. Graham,* affirmed by the D.C. Court of Appeals. It applies directly here."

"So you're going to argue your client didn't murder anyone, it was his *client* who did it," Davidson said. "And that you can't tell us who that client is."

"He can't tell you who the client is, no," Schwartz said. "And we aren't saying it was murder. *We* don't know. Since neither Metro nor the Bureau has bothered to charge my client with murder yet, I'm guessing neither do you, at least not yet."

"But you *do* know," Vann said. "Bell said he's been recording everything. He'd have a record of the murder."

"First, if you try to use anything my client

said to you in that illegal interrogation of him in any way, I'm going to make life very difficult for you," Schwartz said. "Second, even if there is a record of what happened in that room, it's covered by privilege. My client's not going to turn it over. You can try to get a warrant for it if you like. All we *will* attest to is that my client was working from the moment he stepped into that room until the moment your goons assaulted him" — Schwartz pointed at Davidson for emphasis — "and dragged him out of there. He's not responsible, and you have nothing. So either arrest him and let me go to work dismantling your case and setting up a *very* profitable suit for police harassment, or get him out of that interrogation room right now and let him go home. These are your options, Captain Davidson, Agent Vann."

"How does he get to have you as a lawyer?" I asked.

"Excuse me?" Schwartz asked, turning back to me.

"You're general counsel at Accelerant Investments, Mr. Schwartz," I said, reading from the data I had pulled up. "That's a Fortune 100 company. It has to keep you busy. I don't suspect you have a private practice on the side, or that Mr. Bell could afford you if you did. So I'm wondering

48

what Mr. Bell has done to deserve having someone of your caliber show up here to spring him."

Another second of silence from Schwartz, and Davidson's tablet pinged again. He opened the ping, looked at it, and then turned it around to show Vann and me. The tablet was open to a colorful site full of baby goats and merry-go-rounds.

"It's called 'A Day in the Park,'" Schwartz said. "Not everyone who's locked in is a lawyer or a professional, as I am sure you are amply aware. Some of those who are locked in are developmentally challenged. For them, operating a PT is difficult or next to impossible. They spend their days under very controlled stimulus. So I run a program that lets them out for a day in the park. They go to the petting zoo, ride rides, eat cotton candy, and otherwise get to enjoy their lives for a couple of hours. You should know about it, Agent Shane. Your father has been one of its co-sponsors for the last seven years."

"My father doesn't outline all his charitable work with me, Mr. Schwartz," I said.

"Indeed," Schwartz said. "In any event. Mr. Bell donates his time for this program. He does more for it than any other local Integrator here in D.C. In return I told him

49

if he ever needed a lawyer, he should call me. And here we are."

"That's a sweet story," Davidson said, putting down the tablet.

"I suppose it is," Schwartz said. "Especially because now I'm going to give my client a happy ending to this particular problem. Which will either be his freedom, or a retirement-level settlement from both the Metro Police Department and the FBI. Your call, Captain, Agent Vann. Tell me what it will be."

"Your thoughts," Vann said, at lunch.

"About this case?" I asked. We were sitting in a hole-in-the-wall Mexican place not too far from the Second Precinct. Vann was plowing through a plate of carnitas. I was not, but a quick status check at home told me that my body had gotten its noontime supply of nutritional liquid. So I had that going for me.

"Obviously, about the case," Vann said. "It's your first case. I want to see what you're picking up and what you're missing. Or what *I'm* missing."

"The first thing is that the case should now be all ours," I said. "Schwartz admitted Bell was working as an Integrator. Standard procedure with Hadens means that the case needs to be transferred to us."

"Yes," Vann said.

"Do you think there's going to be a problem with this?" I asked.

"Not with Davidson," Vann said. "I've done him some favors and he and I don't have any problems with each other. Trinh will be pissy about it, but I don't really care about that and neither should you."

"If you say so."

"I do say so," Vann said. "What else."

"Since the case is ours now, we should have the body sent to the Bureau for our people to look at," I said.

"Transfer order already processed," Vann said. "He's on the way now."

"We should also get all the data from Metro. High resolution this time," I said, remembering Trinh's last bit of feed.

"Right," Vann said. "What else."

"Have Bell followed?"

"I put in a request. I wouldn't count on it."

"We won't put a tail on a potential murder suspect?"

"You might have noticed we have a protest march coming into town this weekend," Vann said.

"That's Metro's problem," I said.

"Dealing with the logistics of the march,

yes," Vann said. "Keeping tabs on the protest leaders and other high-value individuals, on the other hand, is all us. What about Schwartz?"

"He's a schmuck?" I ventured.

"Not where I was going," Vann said. "Do you believe his story about how he happened to be Bell's lawyer?"

"Maybe," I said. "Schwartz is really rich. I checked when I pulled his data earlier. Through Accelerant, he's worth at least two or three hundred million. Really rich folks do a lot of reputational transactions."

"I have no idea what you just said." Vann stuck another piece of carnitas into her mouth.

"Rich people show their appreciation through favors," I said. "When everyone you know has more money than they know what to do with, money stops being a useful transactional tool. So instead you offer favors. Deals. Quid pro quos. Things that involve personal involvement rather than money. Because when you're that rich, your personal time is your limiting factor."

"Speaking from experience?" Vann asked.

"Speaking from very close observation, yes," I said.

That seemed a good enough answer for Vann. "So you think this could be a case of noblesse oblige on the part of Schwartz toward a hired hand."

"I'm saying it wouldn't surprise me," I said. "Unless you think there's something else there."

"I do think there's something else there," Vann said. "Or someone else. Lucas Hubbard."

I sat there, thinking about the name Vann had said. Then it smacked me like a fish across the head. "Oh, man," I said.

"Yeah," Vann said. "Chairman and CEO of Accelerant. The single richest Haden on the planet. Who lives in Falls Church. And who almost certainly uses an Integrator for board meetings and in-person negotiations. You need a face for face-to-face meetings. One that moves. No offense."

"None taken," I said. "Do we know if Nicholas Bell is the Integrator he uses?"

"We can find out," Vann said. "There aren't that many Integrators in the D.C. area, and half of them are women, which rules them out, given what I know about Hubbard."

"I know people who have Integrators tied up on long-term service contracts," I said. "Locks up their use except for NIH-required public service. If Bell's on a contract we could find that out, and for whom."

"Yeah," Vann said. "I hate that shit."

"Abrams-Kettering," I said. "You said it to Bell, Vann. They passed that law and suddenly a lot of folks have to think about where their paychecks are coming from. Everyone around Hadens has to change the way they do business. Rich Hadens can pay for Integrators. Integrators have to eat."

Vann looked grumpily into her plate of food.

"This shouldn't be a surprise to you —" I said. I wanted to segue into asking her about her time as an Integrator, but got a ping before I could.

"Excuse me a minute," I said to Vann, who nodded. I opened up a window in my head and saw Miranda, my daytime nurse. She was in the foreground. In the background was me, in my room.

"Hi, Miranda," I said. "What's up?"

"Three things," she said. "One, that bedsore on your hip is back. Have you felt it yet?"

"I've been busy working my threep today, so I'm sensory forward here," I said. "I haven't really noticed anything going on with my body."

"All right," Miranda said. "I've numbed it

in any event. We're going to have to change your body movement schedule a bit to work around the sore, so don't be surprised if you come home today and you're facedown on the bed."

"Got it," I said.

"Two, remember that at four Dr. Ahl is here to work on your molar. You're going to want to dial your body sensitivity way down for that. She tells me it's likely to get messy."

"It doesn't seem fair I get cavities when I don't even use my teeth," I joked.

"Three, your mother came in to tell me to remind you that she expects you home in time for the get-together at seven. She wanted me to remind you that it is in your honor, to celebrate your new job, so don't embarrass her by being late."

"I won't," I said.

"And I want to remind *you* to tell your mother that it's not my job to forward messages to you," Miranda said. "Especially when your mother is perfectly capable of pinging you herself."

"I know," I said. "Sorry."

"I like your mom but if she keeps up this Edwardian shit, I may have to chloroform her."

"That's fair," I said. "I'll talk to her about it, Miranda. I promise."

"All right," Miranda said. "Let me know if the bed sore starts to bother you. I'm not happy it came back."

"I will. Thank you, Miranda," I said. She disconnected and I reconnected with Vann. "Sorry about that."

"Everything all right?" she asked.

"I have a bedsore," I said.

"You going to be all right?"

"I'll be fine," I said. "My nurse is rotating me."

"There's an image," Vann said.

"Welcome to the Haden life," I said.

"Not to assume too much, but I'm surprised you don't have one of those cradles designed to keep down bed sores and exercise your muscles and such."

"I do," I said. "I just ulcerate easily. It's a condition. Entirely unrelated to the Haden's. I would have it even if I weren't, you know" — I motioned with my arm, to display my threep — *"this."*

"Sucks," Vann said.

"We all have problems," I said.

"Let's get back to Bell," Vann said. "Anything else we should be thinking about?"

"Do we need to consider his sister?" I asked.

"Why would we need to do that?" Vann asked.

"I don't know," I said. "Maybe because Cassandra Bell is the best-known Haden separatist in the country, and currently spearheading a general strike and that protest march you were reminding me about?"

"I know who she is," Vann said. "What I'm asking is why you think it's relevant."

"I don't know that it is," I said. "On the other hand, when the previously under-the-radar Integrator brother of a famous Haden radical is intimately involved in what looks to be a murder, using his body as the weapon, I think we might have to consider all the angles."

"Hmmm," Vann said. She turned back to her plate.

"So," I said, after a minute. "Did I pass the audition?"

"You're a little edgy," Vann said, to me.

"I'm nervous," I said. "It's my second day on the job. The first one with you. You're the senior partner. I want to know how I'm working out for you."

"I'm not going to give you participation ribbons every couple of hours, Shane," Vann said. "And I'm not that mysterious. If you piss me off or annoy me, I'm going to let you know."

"Okay," I said.

"So stop worrying about how you're doing, and just do the job," Vann said. "Tell me what you think, and tell me what you think about what I'm thinking. You don't have to wait for me to ask. All you have to do is pay attention."

"Like when you looked over to me today in Davidson's office," I said.

"When you were going to contradict Davidson about threeps and Integrators being more or less the same thing," Vann said. "Yes, that's an example. I'm glad you caught it. You don't need to be helping Schwartz."

"He was right, though. Schwartz, I mean."

Vann shrugged at this.

"Are you saying I should just shut up every time someone says something stupid or factually wrong about Hadens?" I asked. "I just want to be clear what you're asking."

"I'm saying pay attention to when it makes sense to say something," Vann said. "And pay attention to when it makes sense to hold it in for the moment. I get that you're used to saying what you think to anyone, anytime. That comes from being an entitled rich kid."

"Come on," I said.

Vann held up a hand. "Not a criticism, an observation. But that's not the job, Shane. The job is to watch and learn and solve."

She popped the final piece of carnitas into her mouth, then reached into her suit jacket for her electronic cigarette.

"I'll try," I said. "I'm not always good at shutting up."

"That's why you have a partner," Vann said. "So you can vent at me. Afterward. Now, come on. Let's get back to work."

"Where to now?"

"I want to get a better look at that hotel room," Vann said, and sucked on her cigarette. "Trinh hustled us through it pretty quickly. I'm ready for a slow dance."

CHAPTER FOUR

"This doesn't look like the Watergate," I said, as we entered the third subbasement of the FBI building.

"We're not going to the Watergate," Vann said, heading down a corridor. I followed.

"I thought you wanted to take another look at the room," I said.

"I do," Vann said. "But there's no point going back there now. Metro police have been all over it. Trinh and her people have inevitably messed it up looking at things. And I wouldn't be surprised if Trinh released it to the hotel for cleanup." She stopped at a door. "So we're here to look at the room instead."

I read the placard next to the door. "Imaging Suite," I said.

"Come on," Vann said, and opened the door.

Inside was a room roughly six meters to a side, white walls, bare except for projectors in each corner and a space where a technician stood behind a bank of monitors. He looked over at us and smiled. "Agent Vann," he said. "You're back."

"I'm back," Vann agreed, and motioned to me. "Agent Shane, my new partner."

The technician waved. "Ramon Diaz," he said.

"Hi," I said.

"Are we ready?" Vann asked.

"Just finishing diagnostics on the projectors," Diaz said. "One of them's been wonky for the past couple of days. But I have all the data that came over from Metro."

Vann nodded and looked at me. "Did you upload your scan of the room to the server?"

"I did that before we left the room," I said.

Vann turned to Diaz. "We're going to use Shane's scan as the base," she said.

"Got it," Diaz said. "Let me know when you're ready."

"Fire it up," Vann said.

The hotel room popped into being. The scan wasn't a live video feed of the room but instead a mass of still photos knitted together to create a static, information-dense re-creation of the room.

I took a look at it and smiled. The whole room was there. I had done a good job of panning and scanning.

"Shane." Vann pointed at a curving object on the carpet, not too far from the corpse.

"Headset," I said. "Over-the-head scanner and transmitter for neural information. It suggests that this guy, whoever he is, was a tourist." I figured Vann knew this but was checking to see if I did.

"Looking to borrow Bell's body," Vann said.

"Yeah," I said. I knelt and got a better look at the headset. Like all these sorts of headsets, it was a one-of-a-kind affair. Technically speaking, the only people cleared to use Integrators were Hadens. But wherever there's a less-than-legal demand, there's a black market.

The headset was jammed-together medical equipment designed for early-stage Haden's diagnosis and communication. It was a kludge, but a clever one. It wouldn't give the tourist anything close to the actual, full Integrator experience — you needed a network implanted inside your head for that sort of thing — but it would offer something like high-definition 3-D with additional faint but real sensory perception. It was more real than the movies, anyway.

"This one looks pretty high-end," I said to Vann. "The scanner's a Phaeton and the transmitter looks like General Dynamics."

"Serial numbers?"

"I don't see any," I said. "Do we have the real thing in evidence?"

Vann glanced over at Diaz, who looked up and nodded. "I can take a closer look at it if you want," Diaz said.

"If you don't find anything on the exterior, see if you can scan the inside of it," I said. "The processing chips probably have serial numbers on them. We can see when the batches were sent off, and from there piece together who's supposed to be owning the scanner and transmitter."

"Worth a shot," Vann said.

I stood up and looked over to the corpse, facedown in the carpet. "What about him?" I asked.

Vann looked back to Diaz. "Nothing yet," he said.

"How does that happen?" I asked Diaz. "You have to get fingerprinted to get a driver's license."

"Our examiners only just got him," Diaz said. "Metro took fingerprints and did a face scan. But sometimes they take their time sharing information, if you know what I mean. So we're doing our own and running those through our databases now. We'll be doing DNA too. We'll probably find him by the time you're done here."

"Let me see the face scan," Vann said.

"You want just the face, or the wide-angle shot when they turned him over?"

"Wide-angle shot," Vann said.

The man on the floor instantly flipped. He was olive-skinned and looked mid- to late thirties. From this angle the severity of the cut throat was a whole lot more dramatic. The wound slashed from the left side of the neck, near the jawline, and continued downward, terminating on the right side of the hollow of the throat.

"What do you think?" Vann asked me.

"I think we've got an explanation for the arterial spurts," I said. "That's a hell of a cut."

Vann nodded but was silent.

"What is it?" I asked.

"I'm thinking," Vann said. "Give me a minute."

While she was thinking I looked at the corpse's face. "Is he Hispanic?" I asked. Vann ignored me, still thinking. I looked over to Diaz, who pulled up the face by itself to examine it.

"Maybe," he said, after a minute. "Maybe Mexican or Central American, not Puerto Rican or Cuban, I'd guess. He looks like he might have a lot of Mestizo in him. Or he might be Native American."

"What tribe?"

"No clue," Diaz said. "Ethnic typing's not actually my gig."

By this time Vann had gone over to the image of the corpse and was looking at the hands. "Diaz," Vann said. "Do we have a broken glass in evidence?"

"Yes," Diaz said, after checking.

"Shane got an image of it from under the bed. Pull it up for me, please."

The image of the room spun wildly as Diaz yanked it around, pulling us all under the bed and looming the image of the shattered, bloody glass over us.

"Fingerprints," Vann said, pointing. "Do we have any idea whose they are?"

"Nothing yet," Diaz said.

"What are you thinking?" I asked Vann.

She ignored me again. "You have the feed from Officer Timmons?" she asked Diaz.

"Yeah, but it's pretty crappy and low res," Diaz said.

"Goddamn it, I told Trinh I wanted everything," Vann said.

"She might not be holding out on you," Diaz said. "Metro cops these days let their feeds run their whole shift sometimes. If they do that they use a low-res setting because it lets them record longer."

"Whatever," Vann said, still clearly annoyed. "Put it up for me and overlay it onto Shane's room shot."

The room wheeled around again and went back to its real-world dimensions. "Feed coming up," Diaz said. "It's going to be in bas-relief because of Timmons's position. I cleaned up the jerkiness."

On the bed, Bell appeared, hands up. The feed started running in real time.

"Wait," Vann said. "Pause it."

"Done," Diaz said.

"Can you get a clearer image of Bell's hands?"

"Not really," Diaz said. "I can blow it up, but it's a low-res feed. It's got inherent limitations."

"Blow it up," Vann said. Bell jerked and grew large, his hands racing toward us like a giant trying to play patty-cake.

"Shane," Vann said. "Tell me what you see."

I looked at the hands for a couple of moments, not seeing whatever it was that I was supposed to be seeing. Then it occurred to me that *not* seeing a thing was what Vann was going for.

"No blood," I said.

"Right," Vann said. She pointed. "He's got blood on his shirt and his face but none on his hands. The broken glass has bloody finger marks all over it. Diaz, pull back out." The image zoomed out again, and Vann went over to the corpse. "This guy, though, has blood all over his hands."

"This dude cut his own throat?" I asked.

"Possible," Vann said.

"That's genuinely bizarre," I said. "Then this isn't a murder. It's a suicide. Which would get Bell off the hook."

"Maybe," Vann said. "Give me other options."

"Bell could have done it and cleaned up before hotel security got there," I said.

"There's still the bloody glass," Vann said. "We've got Bell's fingerprints on file. He had to give them when he became a licensed Integrator."

"Maybe he was interrupted," I said.

"Maybe," Vann said. She didn't sound convinced.

An idea popped into my brain. "Diaz," I said. "I'm sending over a file. Pop it up as soon as you get it, please."

"Got it," Diaz said, a couple of seconds later. Two seconds after that the scene shifted to outside of the Watergate, to the hurled love seat and the crushed car.

"What are we looking for?" Vann asked.

"It's what we're not looking for," I said. "It's the same thing we *weren't* looking for on Bell's hands."

"Blood," Vann said, and looked closely at the love seat. "There's no blood on the love seat."

"Not that I can see," I said. "So there's a good chance the love seat went out the window before our corpse cut his own throat."

"It's a theory," Vann said. "But why?" She pointed to the corpse. "This guy contracts with Bell to integrate, and then when Bell gets there he throws a love seat out the window and then commits bloody suicide in front of him? Why?"

"Throwing a love seat out of a seventh-story window is a pretty good way to get the attention of the hotel security staff," I said. "He wanted to frame Bell for his murder and this was a way to make sure security would already be on their way before he killed himself."

"It still doesn't answer the question of why he'd commit suicide in front of Bell in the first place," Vann said. She looked back down at the corpse.

"Well, we do know one thing," I said. "Bell was maybe telling the truth when he said that he didn't do it."

"That's not what he said," Vann said.

"I think it was. I saw the feed."

"No," Vann said, and turned back to Diaz. "Run the Timmons feed again."

The image snapped once more to the hotel room, and the bas-relief of Bell reappeared. Diaz set it running. Timmons asked Bell why he killed the man in the room. Bell responded that he didn't think he had. "Stop it," Vann said. Diaz stopped the feed just as Timmons zapped Bell. He was frozen mid-spasm.

"He didn't say he didn't kill him," Vann said to me. "He said he didn't *think* he killed him. He's saying he didn't *know.*"

A light went on in my head, and I remembered my one personal experience with an Integrator. "That's not right."

"Integrators are conscious for their sessions," Vann said, nodding. "They subsume and stay in the background during integration, but they're allowed to surface if the client needs help or is about to do something outside the scope of the integration session."

"Or is about to do something stupid or illegal," I said.

"Which is usually outside the scope of the session," Vann pointed out.

"Okay," I said, and motioned back to the corpse. "But what does that matter? If this guy is a suicide, then Bell telling us he doesn't think he did it doesn't tell us anything we don't know. Because now we're thinking that maybe he didn't do it, either."

Vann shook her head. "It's not about whether this is a murder or a suicide. It's about the fact Bell says he can't remember. He's *supposed* to be able to remember."

"That's if he's integrated," I said. "But we think he came to the room to pick up this side job, right? In which case, there was no one else in his brain when he allegedly blacked out."

"Why would he black out?" Vann asked.

"I don't know. Maybe he's a drinker."

"He doesn't look drunk on the feed," Vann said. "He didn't smell or act like he'd been drinking when I questioned him. And anyway . . ." She fell silent again.

"Are you going to be doing a lot of that?" I asked her. "Because I can already tell it's going to bug me."

"Schwartz said Bell was working," Vann said. "That client-Integrator privilege applied."

"Right," I said, and motioned to the corpse. "That's his client."

"That's just it," Vann said. "He's *not* a client."

"I'm not following you."

"Integration is a licensed and regulated

70

practice," Vann said. "You take on clients and you have certain professional obligations to them, but only a certain class of person is allowed to be your clientele. Only Hadens are supposed to be clients of Integrators. This guy" — she indicated the corpse — "is a tourist. He's able-bodied."

"I'm not a lawyer, but I'm not a hundred percent behind this theory here," I said. "A priest can hear a confession from anyone, not just a Catholic, and a doctor can claim confidentiality from the second someone walks through the door. I think Schwartz is probably making the same claim here. Just because the dude's a tourist doesn't mean he's not a client. He is. Just like someone who's not a Catholic can still confess."

"Or Schwartz slipped up and let us know that someone was riding Bell," Vann said.

"That doesn't make any sense," I countered. "If Bell was already integrated then why would he be meeting with a tourist?"

"Maybe they were meeting for something else."

"Then why bring that?" I pointed to the headset.

Vann was silent for a minute. "Not all of my theories are going to be gold," she said, eventually.

"I get that," I said, dryly. "But I don't

71

think it's you. None of this makes much sense. We've got a murder that probably isn't, of a man we haven't ID'd, who had a meeting with an Integrator who may have already been integrated, who says he can't remember things he should. That's a mess, right there."

"Your thoughts," Vann said.

"Shit, I don't know," I said. "It's my second day on the job and already it's gotten too weird for me."

"You guys gotta wrap it up," Diaz said. "I've got another agent who needs the room in five."

Vann nodded at this and turned back to me. "Let me put it another way," she said. "What are our action items?"

I looked over to Diaz. "Any matches on our corpse yet?"

"Nothing yet," Diaz said, after a second. "That's a little weird. It doesn't usually take this long to process a match."

"Our first action item is to find out who our dead guy is," I said, to Vann. "And how he's managed not to have any sort of impression on our national database."

"What else?"

"Find out what Bell's been up to recently and who is on his client list. Maybe that'll pop up something interesting."

"All right," Vann said. "I'll take the stiff."

"Oh, sure," I said. "You get the fun gig."

Vann smiled at this. "I'm sure Bell will be tons of fun."

"Do I need to be here while I'm doing this?" I asked.

"Why?" Vann asked. "You have a date?"

"Yes, with a Realtor," I said. "I'm looking at apartments. Federally approved. Technically I'm supposed to have a half day today for it."

"Don't expect too many more of those," Vann said. "Half days, I mean."

"Yeah," I said. "I'm kind of figuring that out on my own."

CHAPTER FIVE

The realtor was a small, elegant-looking woman named LaTasha Robinson, and she met me directly outside the Bureau building. One of her realty specialties was the Haden market, so the Bureau connected me with her to help me find an apartment.

Given her clientele, the chances that she might not know who I was were close to nil, a suspicion that was verified as I approached. She smiled a smile I recognized from years of being trotted out as the official Haden's Poster Child, part of the official Haden's Poster Family. I didn't hold it against her.

"Agent Shane," she said, holding out her hand. "Really lovely to meet you."

I took the hand and shook it. "Ms. Robinson. Likewise."

"I'm sorry, this is kind of exciting," she said. "I don't meet that many famous people. I mean, who aren't politicians."

"Not in this town, no," I agreed.

"And I don't think of politicians as being *famous,* do you? They're just . . . politicians."

"I couldn't agree more," I said.

"My car's right over here," she said, pointing to a relatively unflashy Cadillac parked where it would get ticketed. "Why don't we get started?"

I got into the passenger side. Robinson got in the driver's seat and pulled out her tablet. "Amble," she said, and the car slid out from the curb, just ahead, I noted as I glanced in the rearview mirror, of a traffic cop. We headed east on Pennsylvania Avenue.

"The car's just going to drive around for a few minutes while we get set up here," Robinson said, tapping her tablet. For all her gushing a few seconds before, she slipped into business mode pretty quickly. "I've got your basic request list and personal information" — she looked over as if to acknowledge I was, in fact, a Haden and she knew it — "so let's get a few things narrowed down before we start."

"All right," I said.

"How close do you want to be to work?"

"Closer is better."

"Are we talking walking distance close, or

75

Metro line close?"

"Metro line close is fine," I said.

"Do you prefer a neighborhood that's hip, or one that's quiet?"

"It doesn't really matter to me."

"You say that now but if I get you an apartment over a bar in Adams Morgan and you hate it, you're going to blame me," Robinson said, looking over at me.

"I promise noise isn't going to bother me," I said. "I can turn down my hearing."

"Do you plan on using the apartment to socialize?"

"Not really," I said. "I do most of my socializing elsewhere. I might have a friend over from time to time."

Robinson looked over again at this, and seemed to be considering whether to ask for clarification, and decided against it. It was a fair call. There were threep fetishists out there. They really weren't my thing, I have to say.

"Will your body be physically present, and if so, will you need a room for a caretaker?" she asked.

"My body and its caretaking are already squared away," I said. "I won't be needing space for either. At least not right away."

"In that case I have some Haden efficiency flats on my availability list," she said.

"Would you like to see those?"

"Are they worth my time?" I asked.

Robinson shrugged. "Some Hadens like them," she said. "I think they're a little small, but then they're not designed for non-Hadens."

"Are they close by?"

"I've got a building of them on D Avenue in Southwest, right by the Federal Center Metro," Robinson said. "The Department of Health and Human Services hires a lot of Hadens, so it's convenient housing for them."

"All right," I said. "We might as well check them out."

"We'll go there first," Robinson said, and spoke the address to the Cadillac.

Five minutes later we were in front of a depressing slab of anonymous brutalist architecture.

"This is lovely," I said, dryly.

"I think it used to be a government office building," Robinson said. "They converted it about twenty years ago. It was one of the first buildings redesigned with Hadens in mind." She nodded me into the lobby, which was clean and plain.

A threep receptionist sat behind a desk. The threep was set to transmit ID data over the common channel. In my field of vision its owner's data popped up above the threep's head: Genevieve Tourneaux. Twenty-seven years old. Native of Rockville, Maryland. Her public address for direct messages.

"Hello," Robinson said to Genevieve, and showed her her Realtor's ID. "We're here to look at the vacancy on the fifth floor."

Genevieve turned to look at me, and I realized belatedly that I didn't have my own personal data out on the common channel. Some Hadens found that rude. I quickly popped it up.

She gave me a quick nod as if in acknowledgment, did a small double take, then recovered and turned her attention to Robinson. "Unit 503 is unlocked for the next fifteen minutes," she said.

"Thank you," Robinson said, and nodded over to me.

"Hold on a second," I said. I turned back to Genevieve. "May I have guest access to the building channel, please?"

Genevieve nodded to me and I saw the channel marker pop up in my view. I connected to it.

The lobby walls exploded into signage.

Some of the notes were your basic corkboard notes: people looking for roommates or to sublet or asking after lost pets. At the moment, however, signs about the walkout and march dominated — signs reminding tenants to stay home, plans for walkout activities, requests to let Hadens coming into town for the march crash in apartments, with the sardonic notation that they won't need much space.

"Everything okay?" Robinson asked.

"It's fine," I said. "I'm just taking in the posters on the wall." I read a few more and then we walked over to the elevator bank and took the next lift up to the fifth floor.

"Extra-large elevators," Robinson noted, as we rose. "Hydraulic lift. Makes it easier to bring bodies up to the rooms."

"I thought these were all efficiency apartments," I said.

"Not all of them," Robinson said. "Some are full-sized and have dedicated medical suites and caretaker rooms. And even the efficiencies have cradle hookups. Those are supposed to be used on a temp basis, although I hear some Hadens are using them full-time now."

"Why is that?" I asked. The elevator stopped and the doors opened.

"Abrams-Kettering," Robinson said. She walked out of the lift and down the hall. I followed. "Assistance is getting slashed so a lot of Hadens are downsizing. Those in

79

townhomes are moving into smaller apartments. Those in apartments are moving into efficiencies. And some of those in efficiencies are taking on roommates. They're using the chargers in shifts." She glanced back to me and her eyes flickered over my shiny, expensive threep, as if to say *not that* you *have to worry about that.* "It's been bad for the market, to be honest, but that's good for you as a potential renter. Now you have a lot more options, a lot cheaper." She stopped at apartment 503. "That is, if *this* doesn't bowl you over." She opened the door and stood aside to let me pass through.

Haden Efficiency Apartment 503 was two meters by three meters and entirely bare, save for one small built-in countertop. I stepped inside and immediately got claustrophobia.

"This isn't an apartment, it's a closet," I said, stepping forward to let Robinson in.

"I usually think of it as a bathroom," Robinson said, and pointed to a small tiled area, which had a bank of electrical outlets and a couple of covered drains on the floor, flush with the tile. "That's the medical nook, by the way. Right where the toilet would be."

"You're not exactly giving me the hard

sell on this apartment, Ms. Robinson," I said.

"Well, to be fair, if all you're looking to do is park your threep every night, this isn't a bad choice," Robinson said. She pointed to the back right corner, where grooves and high-voltage outlets were set into the wall, ready to receive inductive chargers. "It's designed with standard threep cradles in mind, and the hardwired and wireless networks are fast and have deep through-put. The space has been designed with threeps in mind, so you don't have ines-sential things taking up space, like closets and sinks. It's everything you need and absolutely nothing you don't."

"I hate it," I said.

"I thought you might," Robinson said. "It's why I showed it to you first. Now that we have it out of the way, we can look at something you might actually be interested in."

I stared back at the spot of tile and thought about putting a human body there, more or less permanently. "These kinds of apart-ments are hot right now?" I asked.

"They are," Robinson said. "I don't usu-ally deal with them. Not enough commis-sion on these. They usually get rented through online want ads. But yes. Right now, this kind of apartment is selling like hotcakes."

"Now I'm feeling a little depressed," I said.

"*You* don't have to feel depressed," Robinson said. "You're not going to live here. You're not going to have your body in here."

"But apparently some people are," I said.

"Yes," Robinson said. "Maybe it's a blessing the bodies don't notice."

"Ah, but that's not true," I said. "We're locked in, not unconscious. Trust me, Ms. Robinson. We notice where our bodies are. We notice it every moment we're awake."

I felt like Goldilocks for the next several stops. The apartments were either too small — we didn't look at any more apartments that were officially efficiencies, but a couple were at least informally around the same square footage — or too large, too inconvenient, or too far away. I began to despair that I would be destined to store my threep at my desk at the Bureau.

"Last stop of the day," Robinson said. By now even her professional cheeriness was wearing through. We were in Capitol Hill, on Fifth Street, looking at a red town house.

"What's here?" I asked.

"Something off the usual menu," Robinson said. "But it's something I think you might be a good fit for. Do you know what an intentional community is?"

" 'Intentional community'?" I said. "Isn't that another way of saying 'commune'?" I looked up at the town house. "This is a weird place for a commune."

"It's not exactly a commune," Robinson said. "This town house is rented out by a group of Hadens living together and sharing the common rooms. They call it an intentional community because they share responsibilities, including monitoring each other's bodies."

"That's not always a great idea," I said.

"One of them is a doctor at the Howard University Hospital," Robinson said. "If there's any substantial problem, there's someone on hand to deal with it. I understand it's not something you'll need, of course. But there are other advantages and I know they have a vacancy."

"How do you know these people?" I asked.

Robinson smiled. "My son's best friend lives here," she said.

"Ah," I said. "Did your son live here too?"

"You're asking if my son is a Haden," Robinson said. "No, Damien is unaffected. Tony, Damien's friend, contracted Haden's when he was eleven. I've known Tony all his life, before and after Haden's. He lets me know when they have a vacancy. He knows I won't bring over anyone I don't think would be a good fit."

"And you think I would be a good fit."

"I think you might be. I've been wrong before. But you're a special case, I think. If you don't mind me saying so, Agent Shane, you're not looking for a place because you *need* a place. You're looking for a place because you *want* a place."

"That's about right," I said.

Robinson nodded. "So, I thought I would let you look at this and see if it's something you want."

"Okay," I said. "Let's take a look."

Robinson went to the door and rang the bell. A threep opened it and threw its arms wide when it saw her.

"Mama Robinson!" it said, and gave her a big hug.

Robinson gave the threep a peck on the cheek. "Hello, Tony," she said. "I brought you a prospect."

"Did you," Tony said, and looked over to me. "Chris Shane," he said. I was momentarily surprised — I didn't think my new threep was that well known already — but then remembered I had turned on my public ID earlier in the day. A second later

Tony's own ID popped up: Tony Wilton. Thirty-one. Originally from Washington, D.C.

"Hi," I said.

He waved us in. "Let's not keep you standing on the stoop," he said. "Come on, Chris, I'll show you the room. It's up on the second floor." He led us inside and up the stairs. As we walked down the second-floor hall, I glanced into one of the rooms. A body lay in a cradle, monitors nearby.

I looked over to Tony, who saw me looking. "Yup, that's me," he said.

"Sorry," I said. "Reflex."

"Don't be sorry," Tony said, opening up the door to another room. "If you live here you'll do your time checking in on all of us to make sure we're still breathing. Might as well get used to it. Here's the room." He stood aside to let Robinson and me in.

The room was large, modestly but comfortably appointed, with a window facing out to the street. "This is really nice," I said, looking around.

"Glad you like it," Tony said. He nodded to the furniture. "The room's furnished, obviously, but if you don't like what you see here we have basement storage to put it in."

"No, it's fine," I said. "And I like the size of it."

"It's actually the biggest bedroom in the house."

"None of the rest of you wanted it?" I asked.

"It's not a question of *wanting* it," Tony said. "It's a question of *affording* it."

"Got it," I said, and figured out another reason Robinson thought I might be good for this address.

"You understand what the setup here is?" Tony asked. "Mama Robinson explained it to you?"

"Briefly," I said.

"It's not really that complicated, I promise," Tony said. "We share chores and monitoring duties, make sure everyone's tubes and drains are in working order, pool funds for house improvements. Occasionally we go out as a group and do social things. We call it an intentional community, but it's more like a college dorm. Just less drinking and smoking pot. Not that we ever did that. Also less roommate drama, which we *did* do, if you remember college at all."

"Are you the doctor?" I asked. "Ms. Robinson said one of you was a doctor."

"That's Tayla," Tony said. "She's at work. Everyone's at work, except me. I'm a contract coder. Today I'm working for Genoble Systems, on their brain-interface software.

86

Tomorrow, someone else. I usually work from here, unless a client needs me on-site."

"So someone's always here."

"Usually," Tony said. "Now. Should I make like I don't know who you are, or can I admit that I was reading about you on the Agora yesterday?"

"Oh, joy," I said.

"You'll note I said everyone is at work," Tony said. "So you're not likely to get judged for that. We have a range of political opinions in the house as it is."

"So you know I'm an FBI agent," I said.

"I do," Tony said. "Deal with conspiracies and murders?"

"You'd be surprised," I said.

"I bet I would," Tony said. "Well, I just met you but I like you. You'll have to meet and get the approval of the others, though."

"How many more of you are there?"

"Four," Tony said. "There's Tayla, Sam Richards, and Justin and Justine Cho. They're twins."

"Interesting," I said.

"They're all good folks, promise," Tony said. "Can you swing 'round tonight to meet them?"

"Ah, no," I said. "I have a family thing tonight. It's my second day on the job. I'm supposed to go home for the official 'hooray, our kid is employed' dinner."

"Well, you can't miss that," Tony said. "When do you think you'll wrap up?"

"I don't know," I said. "Probably nine thirty, ten at the latest."

"Here." Tony pinged me over the common channel with an invite. "Tuesdays are our group night in the Agora. We hang out and usually frag each other's brains out in an FPS. Pop in. You can meet the crew and take a head shot or two."

"Sounds good," I said.

"Great. I'll send over the room application and we can do it up formally. We'll need first month and a deposit."

"I can do that."

"Even better," Tony said. "Presuming you get the signoff from everyone tonight, you can move in as soon as your payment arrives."

"You're not going to want a background check?" I joked.

"I think your entire life has been a background check, Chris," Tony said.

CHAPTER SIX

"Oh, fuck me," I said, the minute I saw the valet at the door to my house.

The painkillers from my oral extraction at four o'clock had started wearing off as I headed home, and that made me grumpy to begin with. But the valet meant one thing: donor dinner. Most cars could self-park but there were still people who demanded that they had to be behind the wheel, and took great pride in their dumb cars. A bunch of them were the sort of cranky old people who might support my dad's bid for senator. That made me crankier than the tooth extraction.

My mother had obviously guessed my mood as I stomped up to her, because she held out her hands placatingly. "Don't blame me, Chris," she said. "I thought it was just going to be a family dinner. I had no idea your father was going to turn it into a fund-raiser."

"I'm skeptical," I said.

"I don't blame you," she said. "But it's the truth." Behind her, catering staff laid out place settings in the formal dining room, directed by Lisle, our house supervisor. I counted out the settings.

"*Sixteen* settings, Mother," I said.

"I know," she said. "Sorry."

"Where are they all?"

"They're not all here yet," she said. "The ones that are, are down in the vet's office."

"Mom," I warned.

"I know, I'm not supposed to say that out loud," she said. "I'll amend. They're in the *trophy room.*"

"So it's not just the usual gang of idiots," I said.

"You know your father," Mom said. "Dazzle the new money with the hardware. It would be vulgar except for the fact that it works."

"Actually, it's still vulgar," I said.

"Yes, it is," Mom agreed. "And it still works."

"Dad doesn't need their money to run for senator," I pointed out.

"Your father needs them to believe he's invested in their interests," Mom said. "That's why he takes their money."

"Yeah, that's not Machiavellian at all."

"Yes, well," she said. "The things we do to get your father elected." She reached out and touched my shoulder. "And how was your day?"

"Interesting," I said. "I'm working on a murder case. And I think I may have found an apartment."

"I still don't know why you think you need an apartment," my mother said, crossly.

"Mom, you're the only person in the world who would have chosen my apartment hunting over a murder case as a topic of conversation."

"I notice you didn't address my point," Mom said.

I sighed and held up a hand to tick off points. "One, because commuting into the District from Potomac Falls every day would be a pain in the ass, and you know it. Two, because I'm twenty-seven and it's embarrassing to still live with my parents. Three, because my tolerance for being a prop for Dad's political ambitions is getting lower by the day."

"That's not fair, Chris," Mom said.

"Come on, Mom," I said. "You know he's going to do it tonight. I'm not the five-year-old he can trot out for congressional hearings and Haden fund-raisers. I'm a federal agent now, for God's sake. I don't think it's

91

even *legal* to trot me around anymore." I had a twinge as the painkillers stepped down another notch, and held up a hand to my jaw.

She caught it. "Your molar," she said.

"Lack of molar, actually." I put my hand down, fully aware of the irony of indicating jaw pain on my threep. "I'm going to go check in on myself," I said, and turned to go to my room.

"When you move, you're not going to move your body, are you?" Mom asked. There was a thread of anxiousness in her voice.

"I'm not planning to right now," I said, turning back a little to look at her. "Let's see how it works. I didn't notice any lag today, and as long as I don't there's no reason to move."

"All right," Mom said, still unhappy.

I went over and gave her a hug. "Relax, Mom," I said. "It's not a thing. I'll have the spare threep here. I'll visit. A lot. You'll start to wonder if I've actually left."

She smiled at that and patted my cheek. "Normally I'd call you on patronizing me, but this one time I'll take it," she said. "Now go check in on yourself. Don't take too long. Your father wants you to make an appearance before we all sit down to dinner."

"Of course he does," I said. I squeezed Mom's arm as I left.

Jerry Riggs, my new evening nurse, waved to me as I walked into my room. He was reading a hardcover book. "How you doing, Chris?"

"I'm in a little bit of pain, actually," I said.

Jerry nodded. "The bedsore?" he asked.

"The molar extraction," I said.

"Right." Jerry set down his book and walked over to my cradle, which had conformed to let me rest on my left side, because my current bedsore was on my right hip. He started rummaging through the bedside cabinet.

"I have some Tylenol with codeine," Jerry said. "Your dentist left it for you."

"I have to be able to function this evening," I said. "There's nothing more dangerous than a stoned threep at a political fund-raiser."

"All right," Jerry said. "Let me see what else we have here."

I nodded and went over to my body — to me. I looked as I always did, like someone sleeping. My body was neat and clean, which was not always a guarantee with a Haden. Some Hadens didn't bother with having their hair cut or trimmed because, honestly, what did it matter? My mother had quite the opposite opinion on the subject, however. As I got older I adopted her position for my own.

The cleanliness was a different and more complex issue, as it would be with a body whose various holes and systems were tubed, bagged, and catheterized. My mother was concerned about me moving out not just because she would miss me. She was also worried that, left to my own devices and schedule, I would let myself wallow in my own filth for days on end. This was an unwarranted concern on her part, I thought.

I bent over to look at my bedsore. True to advertisement, it was a nasty red welt across my hip. I touched it, and felt the dull ache of it at the same time I felt my threep hand moving across it.

I felt that sensation unique to Hadens, the vertigo that comes from perceptually being in two places at once. It's much more noticeable when your body and your threep are in the same room at the same time. The technical term for it is "polyproprioception." Humans, who generally have only one body to deal with, aren't naturally designed for it. It literally changes your brain. You can see the difference between a Haden brain and an unaffected brain on an MRI.

The vertigo happens when your brain

remembers it's not supposed to be getting input from two separate bodies. The simple solution when it happens is just to look somewhere else.

I turned and focused on the *other* other me in the room: my previous threep, which was my primary threep until I got the 660. It was a Kamen Zephyr, now sitting on an inductive charger chair. A very nice model. The body was ivory with blue and gray limb accents — I did undergrad and got my master's at Georgetown, and it seemed the thing to do at the time. My current threep was an understated matte ivory with subtle maroon pinstripe accents on the limbs. I vaguely wondered if I was letting down the alma mater.

"Here we go," Jerry said, and held up a small bottle. "Lidocaine. Should do the trick for a couple of hours. That'll get you through the dinner and then after that I'll put some extra-strength ibuprofen into your system. As long as you stay sense-forward on your threep you should be fine."

"Thanks," I said.

"Interesting that you don't always stay fully sense-forward on your threep," Jerry said, as he prepped the lidocaine.

"I don't like how it feels," I said. "If I can't feel my body it feels . . . off. Adrift. Weird."

Jerry nodded. "I can see that, I guess," he said. "Not everyone does it that way. My last client was full sense-forward on her threep all the time. Didn't like feeling what was going on with her body. Hell, didn't like acknowledging she *had* a body. She found it *inconvenient,* I think is the best way of putting it. Which was ultimately ironic."

"How so?"

"She had a heart attack and didn't even feel it," Jerry said. "She found out about it from an automated alert to her threep. We start working on her to save her and she calls in from her threep with this pissy sort of voice, telling us that we just *had* to get her up and running again, she had a three o'clock session with her shrink that she *couldn't* miss."

"Did she miss it?"

"Yup," Jerry said. He put on a pair of gloves. "She dropped dead mid-sentence, still pissy. On one hand, she really didn't feel it, which I suppose isn't a bad thing. On the other hand, well. I think it came as a surprise to her that she could die. She spent so much time in her threep I think she believed it really was her." He opened my mouth and I could feel my jaw stretch. "Okay. You might feel a poke here for a minute."

■ ■ ■ ■

Dad's trophy room is impressive, but then, that's the point. Marcus Shane isn't the kind of person to tell you he's more important than you. He's happy to let his hardware make the point for him.

The west side of the room details his early basketball career. This includes his junior high and high school jerseys, the four DCIAA trophies he won for Cardozo High, and the acceptance letter he received to Georgetown University, full scholarship. Then follows a ridiculous number of photos of him in action with the Hoyas, with whom he reached the Final Four three times, taking the championship in his junior year. The picture of him weeping as he cuts down the net is up there, with a piece of the actual net inside the same frame. It's surrounded by the Wooden, Naismith, and Robinson awards, which he won the same year, and his championship ring on a pillow. The sting of crashing out of the NCAA Finals in the semi-final round in his senior year was ameliorated by winning an Olympic gold medal. Everyone agreed that the gold medals for his Olympiad were even uglier than usual. On the other hand, it was an Olympic gold medal, so everyone could just shut up.

On to the south side of the room, and we have Dad's professional career, all of it with the Washington Wizards, into which he was drafted after a particularly abysmal sixteen-win season. A lot of people thought the team intentionally tanked their season to get a shot at Dad in the draft. Privately, Dad didn't credit the coach or the GM with that much strategic planning. That coach was gone by the end of Dad's first season, the GM by the second, and two years later, Dad drove the team into the playoffs. Two years after that, Washington won the first of three back-to-back-to-back championships.

This wall featured lots of photos of Dad suspended in air, his league and series MVP awards, some of the more iconic objects of his professional endorsement career, a display case with his four championship rings (the final one coming in his last year playing), topped off by the long thin trophy you get when you're inducted into the Naismith Hall of Fame, which he was, in his first year of eligibility.

The east side of the room begins with a magazine cover while Dad was still with the Wizards — not from *Sports Illustrated* but from a D.C. business magazine, which was the first to notice that America's hottest rookie was not buying a stupidly large house and otherwise throwing his money around like an asshole, but was instead living in a modest Alexandria town house and investing in real estate in and around the District. By the time Dad retired from basketball, he was making more money from his real estate company than he was from playing and endorsements, and he officially became a billionaire the same year he was inducted into the Hall. This side of the room is filled with various business and real estate awards and citations. There are more of these than anything else. Businesspeople sure like to give out awards.

The north side of the room was related to Dad's philanthropy work and specifically his work with Haden's syndrome — a natural cause for him after his only child (me) was stricken with the disease in its first, terrible wave, along with millions of others, including Margaret Haden, the first lady of the United States. Despite the syndrome being named after the first lady, it was Dad and Mom (the former Jacqueline Oxford, scion of one of Virginia's oldest political families) who became the public face of Haden's awareness — along with me, of course.

And so this wall was filled with pictures of

Dad testifying before Congress for the massive research and development required to deal with four and a half million U.S. citizens suddenly having their minds cut off from their bodies, being present when President Benjamin Haden signed the Haden Research Act into law, being on the board of the Haden Institute, and of Sebring-Warner Industries, which developed the first threeps, and being virtually present when the Agora, the virtual environment developed specifically for Hadens, was opened up for us to populate and to have a space of our own in the world.

Interspersed with these photos were pictures of us: me, Mom, and Dad, in various places, meeting world leaders, celebrities, and other Haden families. I was one of the first Haden children to own and use a threep, and my parents made a point of bringing me everywhere in my threep — not just so I could have a childhood filled with enviable personal experiences, although that was a nice side benefit. The point was to encourage the unaffected to see threeps as people, not freaky androids that had just popped up in their midst. Who better to do that than the child of one of the most celebrated men in the entire world?

So up until I turned eighteen, I was one

of the most famous and photographed Hadens in the world. The photo of me handing a flower to the pope in St. Peter's Basilica is regularly cited as one of the most famous photographs of the last half century — the image of a child-sized threep offering an Easter lily to the Bishop of Rome being an iconic juxtaposition of modern technology and traditional theology, one presenting a peace offering to the other, who is reaching out, smiling, to take it.

When I was in college I had a professor tell me that single image did more to advance the acceptance of Hadens as people, not victims, than a thousand congressional testimonials or scientific discoveries could have. I told him what I remembered about the pope was that he had wicked bad breath. I went to Georgetown. My professor was a priest. I don't think he was very happy with me.

My dad had taken the photo. It was dead center north wall. On the left side of it is his certificate for being a Pulitzer finalist for the Feature Photography category, which even he, to his credit, admits is kind of ridiculous. On the right side is his Presidential Medal of Freedom, given to him a couple of years back for his work with Haden's. Underneath that is the picture of him having the medal placed around his neck by President Gilchrist, and bending down, laughing, so the famously short Gilchrist could manage it.

Three months later Willard Hill was elected president. President Hill signed Abrams-Kettering into law. President Hill was not thought well of in the Shane household.

I've lived with the trophy room all my life so I never thought there was anything particularly special about it. It was just another room in the house and a boring one at that, since I wasn't allowed to play in it. And I know Dad is pretty blasé about awards at this point. Short of a Nobel Peace Prize, he's pretty much run the table. Outside of humoring visitors or hosting events, I've never seen him step foot into the trophy room. He doesn't even put things in there — he leaves that to Mom.

But then, the trophy room isn't for us. It's for everyone else. My father deals with millionaires and billionaires on a daily basis, the sort of people who have egos just this side (and sometimes way over the edge) of sociopathy. The sort of person who thinks he's the apex predator wading through a universe of sheep. Dad takes them into the trophy room and their eyes get to the size of dinner plates and they realize that whatever shit they've got going on is tiddlywinks compared to Dad. There are maybe three people in the world more interesting than Marcus Shane. They're not one of them.

Which is why Mom, when she's being indiscreet, refers to the trophy room as the "vet's office." Because that's where Dad brings people to take their balls.

Into the vet's office I walked, newly numb in the jaw, to see who tonight's set of financial and testicular donors were. I saw Dad instantly, of course. He's six foot eight. He's hard to miss.

I was not prepared for the other person I saw, standing with Dad, looking up at him, smiling, drink in hand.

It was Nicholas Bell.

CHAPTER SEVEN

"Chris!" Dad said, and then suddenly he was looming over me, as he does, to grab me in a hug. "How you doing, kiddo."

"Being crushed by you, Dad," I said, and he laughed. This was a standard call-and-response for us.

"Thanks for coming in to meet people," he said.

"We have to have a talk about that," I said. "Sometime really soon."

"I know, I know," he said, but then waved Bell over anyway. Bell walked over, drink in hand, still smiling. "This is Lucas Hubbard, CEO and chairman of Accelerant Investments."

"Hello, Chris," Hubbard/Bell said, extending his hand. "It's nice to meet you."

I shook it. "And you," I said. "I'm sorry, I'm having a bit of déjà vu at the moment."

Hubbard/Bell smiled. "I get that a lot," he said. He sipped from the glass: scotch on the rocks.

"Sorry," I said. "I was just surprised."

"So you know who Lucas is," Dad said, watching our somewhat cryptic exchange.

"No, it's not that," I said. "I mean, yes. I know who Lucas Hubbard is, of course. But I also know . . ." I trailed off. It was considered rude to acknowledge that an integrated Haden was using someone else's body.

"You know the Integrator I'm using," Hubbard said, sparing me the faux pas.

"Yes, that's it," I said. "We've met before."

"Socially?" Hubbard said.

"Professionally," I said. "Briefly."

"Interesting," Hubbard said. A rather good-looking woman walked up and stood next to him. He motioned to her. "And this is Accelerant Investments' general counsel, Samuel Schwartz."

"We've met," Schwartz said, looking directly at me.

"Have you, now," Hubbard said.

"Also professionally," I said. "Also briefly."

"Indeed," Schwartz said, and smiled. "I didn't make the connection as to who you were at first when we met, Agent Shane. I had to look you up halfway through the conversation. I do apologize."

"No apology needed," I said. "I was out of context. Speaking of which, you are looking a bit different from when I last saw you, Mr. Schwartz. It's an unexpected look."

Schwartz glanced down at his body. "I suppose it is," he said. "I know some Hadens who enjoy cross-gender integration, but I'm not usually one of them. But my usual Integrator was unavailable this evening and I was a last-minute addition to this party. So I had to work with who was available."

"You could have done worse," I assured him. He smiled again.

"I don't know how I feel about you knowing these two better than I do," Dad said, charmingly, smoothly.

"I find it a little surprising myself," I said.

"As do I," Hubbard said. "It doesn't seem possible that your father and I haven't crossed paths before, all things considered. But then, aside from our various offices, Accelerant Investments doesn't do much in the field of real estate."

"Why is that, Lucas?" Dad asked.

"As a Haden, I'm less engaged with the physical world, I suppose," Hubbard said. "It's just not front of mind for me." He motioned at Dad with his scotch. "I don't think you mind me not competing in your field."

"No," Dad said. "Although I don't mind

competition."

"That's because you're very good at beating the competition," Hubbard said.

Dad laughed. "I suppose that's true," he said.

"Of course it is," Hubbard said, and then looked at me, smiling. "It's something the two of us have in common."

As we sat down at the table for dinner I called Vann, using my inside voice so no one at the table would know my attention was elsewhere.

Vann picked up. "I'm busy," she said. I could barely hear her over the background noise.

"Where are you?" I asked.

"I'm in a bar, having a drink and trying to get laid," she said. "Which means I'm busy."

"I know that Lucas Hubbard uses Nicholas Bell as an Integrator."

"How do you know?"

"Because Hubbard is sitting across from me at the dinner table right now, using Bell."

"Well, shit," Vann said. "That was easy."

"What should I do?"

"You're off the clock, Shane," Vann said. "Do what you like."

"I thought you might be a little more excited," I said.

"When you see me tomorrow, on the job, I will be excited," Vann promised. "Right now, I'm otherwise occupied."

"Got it," I said. "Sorry to bother you."

"So am I," Vann said. "But since you did I'll tell you I've made progress on our corpse. The DNA came back."

"Who is he?"

"Don't know yet."

"I thought you said you made progress," I said.

"I did. The DNA analysis didn't come up with anything but it determined that he's probably of Navajo ancestry. Which might explain why we can't find him in the database. If he's Navajo and he lived on a reservation, then all his records would be on the reservation's databases. They're not automatically tied into the U.S. databases because the Navajo Nation is autonomous. And strangely distrustful of the United States government!" Vann fairly cackled that last line.

"How often does that happen?" I asked. "Even if you live on a reservation, if you ever leave it, you probably do something that gets you into our databases."

"Maybe this guy never left," Vann said. "Until he left."

"Do we have a request in to them?" I

asked. "The Navajo Nation, I mean."

"Our forensics team does, yeah," Vann said. "DNA, fingerprints, and facial scan. The Navajo will get to it when they get to it. They don't always put a priority on our needs."

Up at the head of the table, Dad started clanging on his wineglass, and then stood up.

"Have to go," I said. "My dad is about to make a speech."

"Good," Vann said. "I was about to hang up on you anyway." And then she did.

Dad's speech was his standard-issue "at home with donors who everyone is pretending are friends" speech, which is to say that it was light, familiar, casually intimate, yet at the same time it touched on themes important to the nation and to his not-quite-formally-announced senatorial campaign. It went over like it usually does, which is to say very well, because Dad is Dad and he's been doing the public relations thing since he was in high school. If you can't be charmed by Marcus Shane, you're probably a sociopath of some sort.

But at the end of the speech there was a switch up from the text. Dad mentioned "the challenges and opportunities that

Abrams-Kettering offers each of us," which I thought was a little out of context, since only Hubbard and Schwartz and I had Haden's. So I cheated and did a quick facial scan of the other people at the table. Five of them were CEOs and/or chairmen of companies that catered to the Haden market one way or another, with all the businesses headquartered here in Virginia.

That explained it, then. And also why Dad was especially keen to have me at the dinner.

Which meant, of course, that I was put on the spot.

"And what do you think of Abrams-Kettering, Chris?" one of the dinner guests asked me. The facial scan registered him as Rick Wisson, the husband of Jim Buchold, the CEO of Loudoun Pharma. Buchold, who was seated next to his husband, shot him a look, which Wisson either missed or ignored. I did not imagine their ride home that night would be especially pleasant.

"I don't think it will be particularly surprising to you that my opinion closely matches my father's," I said, punting the conversational ball over to Dad.

Who naturally caught it easily. "What Chris is saying is that as with most topics relating to Haden's, we talk a lot about it as a family," he said. "So what I end up saying is a result of long discussions between the three of us. Now, I think everyone knows that I was publicly opposed to Abrams-Kettering. I still think it was the wrong solution to something that wasn't a problem — we know as a group Hadens are contributing more to the national economy than they take out of it. But Abrams-Kettering *did* pass, for better or worse, and now it's time to see how we make this new environment work for us."

"That," I said, pointing down the table to my dad.

"What do you think about the walkout? And the march?" Wisson asked.

"Rick," Jim Buchold said, as pleasantly as a snarl could be offered.

"It's not out of line for dinner," Wisson said, to his husband. "Not for this dinner, anyway. And Chris here is an actual Haden."

"There's three of us at the table, actually," I said, nodding over to Hubbard and Schwartz.

"With all due respect to Lucas and Mr. Schwartz, they're not exactly going to be affected by the changes in the law," Wisson said. Hubbard and Schwartz both smiled thinly at this. "You, on the other hand, have a job and are out there on the street. You have to have some thoughts on it."

"I think everyone has the right to their own opinion and the right to peaceably assemble," I said. When in doubt, fall back on the First Amendment.

"I worry about the 'peaceable' part of it," said Carole Lamb, down the table. She was one of the people for whom the valet was hired. She was old and crankily conservative in the way only old liberals could be. "My daughter tells me the D.C. police are calling in their entire force this weekend. They're worried about rioting."

"And why is that, Ms. Lamb?" Sam Schwartz asked.

"She said they're worried that the Hadens who are marching won't be scared of the police," Lamb said. "Threeps aren't the same as human bodies."

"Your daughter is worried about a robot uprising," I said.

Lamb looked over at me and immediately blushed. "It's not that," she said, hastily. "It's just that this is the first mass Haden protest. It's different than any other protest."

"Robot uprising," I said again, and then held up a hand before Lamb got even more flustered. "Threeps aren't human bodies,

112

no. But they're not Terminators, either. The ones we use to get around on a daily basis are intentionally designed to be as much like the human body as possible, in terms of strength, agility, and other factors."

"Because it's still a human running the threep," Dad said.

"Right," I said. "And a human is going to use a machine scaled to natural human capabilities better than one that's not." I held up my hand. "This is a machine hand, attached to a machine arm. But it's rated for human power. I'm not going to be able to flip this table in a rage. The marchers aren't going to be stomping down the Mall, tossing cars."

"Threeps are still tougher than human bodies," Wisson noted. "They can take a lot of damage."

"Well," I said. "I'll tell you a story. Mom and Dad will remember this one. When I was eight, I got a new bike for my birthday —"

"Oh God, this story," Mom said.

"— and at the time I had just found out about BMX stunts," I continued. "So one morning I made a ramp out on our driveway and was jumping off of the thing, working up the courage to do a spin or something. I finally psyched myself up, pedaled as fast as

I could, zoomed up the ramp, tried a spin, and flew ass over handlebar off the bike and into the road, right into the path of a panel truck doing thirty. It hit me —"

"I really hate this story," Mom said. Dad grinned.

"— and I *disintegrated,*" I said. "The impact tore my threep apart. My head literally popped off and flew into the neighbor's bushes. I had no idea what happened. I had the feeling like I was shoved really hard, the world spun around, and then all of a sudden I was kicked back into my own body, wondering what the heck had just happened."

"If that had been your human body, you would have been dead," Dad pointed out.

"Yeah, I know," I said. "Which you or Mom mention every single time the story gets brought up. The point is" — I turned back to Wisson — "threeps might be tougher than human bodies, but they can still get damaged. And threeps aren't cheap. They cost the same as a car. Most people aren't going to want to let a cop whack on their threep with a baton any more than they'd want a cop to use a baton on their fender. So I don't think we're going to have to worry about that robot uprising. The robots cost too much money for that."

"What happened after the truck hit you?" Schwartz asked.

"Well, I was without a threep for a while," I said, and there was laughter to that. "And I think the driver of the moving truck threatened to sue Dad."

"He said I was at fault because I owned the threep and the threep came into his path, and he had the right of way," Dad said.

"He wouldn't have had a case," I said. "Personal Transports are a special class of machine under the law. Short of manslaughter, hitting a threep with a truck carries the same penalties as hitting a human body."

"Right, but I didn't want to have my name in the news over it," Dad said. "So I bought him off. Paid for the truck damage and gave him floor tickets to the Wizards."

"You've never given *me* floor tickets," Buchold said.

"Don't get any ideas," Dad said, and everyone laughed again. "Besides, Chris is an FBI agent these days. Now you'd get in trouble if you hit my kid with a truck."

"The other thing I remember is that the next threep I got was a real lemon," I said, and turned to Dad. "What model was it?"

"A Metro Junior Courier," Dad said. "A really janky model."

"Uh-oh," Hubbard said. "Accelerant owns Metro."

"Well, then," I said. "I blame you."

"Fair enough," Hubbard said. "Although this was twenty years ago, right?"

"About," I said.

"Then I didn't own it yet," Hubbard said. "We bought it eighteen years ago. No, seventeen. Seventeen?" He turned to Schwartz, who looked surprised. Hubbard looked annoyed at his counsel, but then reached out to pat his hand reassuringly. "Seventeen," he said finally. "We bought it because the stock was depressed from a bad run of models, including the Courier and the Junior Courier."

"I can believe it," I said. "It was the last Metro model we ever bought."

"They've gotten better," Hubbard said. "I can send you over one of our latest if you'd like a test drive."

"Thanks, but I just got this," I motioned to my 660XS. "I'm not in the market."

Hubbard smiled. "It's funny because we've begun discussions with Sebring-Warner about a merger."

"I read about that in the *Post* this morning," Dad said.

"That story was only about sixty percent inaccurate," Hubbard said.

"A-*ha*," I said, and then looked over at Schwartz.

"What?" he said.

"That's why you're using an Ajax 370," I said. "Market research."

Schwartz looked at me blankly. "Very perceptive," Hubbard said. "Yes, Sam's been trying out some of the models, along with some other folks on my staff. There's something to be said for hands-on experience, as it were."

"Is this related to Abrams-Kettering?" Dad asked. "The merger talks."

"Somewhat," Hubbard said. "The government subsidy for threeps dries up at the end of the year, so right now we're selling every threep we can put out there. But when January comes around everything's going to contract. Merging's a hedge against that. But I'm also interested in their R&D program, which is doing some interesting things." He turned to me. "They're doing some groundbreaking work in taste right now."

"As in esthetics, or in, like, *tasting* things?" I asked.

"Actually tasting things," Hubbard said. "It's been the one sense that's really never been well developed in threeps because there's not a practical use for it. Threeps don't have to eat. But there's no reason why they couldn't." He pointed to my place setting, which was bare of food. "Your being at the table right now would be more natural if you were eating, and not just sitting there."

"To be fair, I *am* eating," I said. "Just in the other room." *And through a tube,* which I did not say, because that might have been a little dark for dinner conversation. "And my seat cushion has an inductive charger. So my threep's eating too, so to speak."

"Even so," Hubbard said. "Chris, one of the great goals that you and your family have tried to realize is the idea of making people see threeps as human. Despite your good work, there's still a ways to go with it." He motioned over to Carole Lamb, who seemed startled by the sudden attention. "Our colleague's daughter has made that point for us just this evening. Being able to have a threep sit down to a meal and actually eat would continue that humanizing path."

"Maybe," I said. "I have to tell you I wonder where the food would go once I tasted it."

"There are better ways to humanize Hadens," Buchold said. "Like giving them back their bodies."

Hubbard turned his attention to Buchold. "Ah. Right. Jim Buchold. The one person at the table whose business *isn't* affected by Abrams-Kettering."

"I don't think you can criticize Congress of keeping Haden medical research levels at one hundred percent," Buchold said. "We're looking to solve the problem, not profit from it."

"That's noble of you," Hubbard said. "Although I saw Loudoun's last quarterly. You're profiting just fine."

Buchold turned to me. "Chris, let me ask you," he said. He pointed to my empty dinner plate. "How would you rather taste your food? Through a threep or with your own tongue?"

Now it was Wisson's turn to shoot his husband a look, and rightly so. There was no way this discussion was not going to get awkward, fast.

But before I could answer, Buchold continued on. "We've been working on research to unlock Haden's sufferers," he said. "Not to just simulate eating but to give Hadens back the basic body integrity to do things like chew and swallow. To free their bodies and bring them back —"

"Bring us back from what, exactly?" Hubbard said. "From a community of five million people in the U.S. and forty million worldwide? From an emerging culture that interacts *with* but is independent *of* the physical world, with its own concerns, interests, and economy? You're aware that a large number of Hadens have no memory of the physical world at all, aren't you?" Hubbard pointed at me. "Chris here experienced lock in at two years old. What do *you* remember from being two, Jim?"

I glanced over to Dad but he was engaged in a side discussion with Carole Lamb and my mother. He was going to be no help here.

"You're missing the point," Buchold said. "What we're trying to offer is options. The ability to break free of the physical constraints Hadens live with daily."

"Do I look *constrained* to you?" Hubbard said. "Does Chris?"

"I'm right here, guys," I said.

"Then tell me, do you feel constrained?" Hubbard asked me.

"Not really," I admitted. "But then, as you said, I don't have much basis for comparison."

"I do," Hubbard said. "I was twenty-five when I was locked in. The things I've done since then are things any person could do. That any person would *want* to do."

"You just have to borrow someone else's body to do them," Buchold said.

Hubbard smiled, showing his teeth. "I don't borrow someone else's body to pretend I don't have Haden's, Jim," he said. "I borrow someone else's body because otherwise there's a certain percentage of people who forget I'm a person."

"All the more reason for a cure," Buchold said.

"No," Hubbard said. "Making people change because you can't deal with who they are isn't how it's supposed to be done. What needs to be done is for people to pull their heads out of their asses. You say 'cure.' I hear 'you're not human enough.'"

"Oh, come on," Buchold said. "Don't get on that horse with me, Hubbard. No one's saying that and you know it."

"Do I?" Hubbard said. "Here's something to think about, Jim. Right now, neural networks and threeps and all the innovations that came out of the Haden Research Initiative Act have been kept to the benefit of Hadens. So far the FDA has only approved them for Hadens. But paraplegics and quadriplegics can benefit from threeps. So can other Americans with mobility issues. So can older Americans whose bodies are failing them in one way or another."

"The FDA has kept threeps to Haden's victims because jamming a second brain into your head is inherently dangerous," Buchold said. "You do it if you have no other choice."

"But everyone else should still *have* that choice," Hubbard said. "And now, finally, they're going to get access to these technologies. Among every other thing it does, Abrams-Kettering sets a pathway to getting these technologies out to more people. More Americans will be using these technologies in the future. Millions more. When they do, Jim, are you going to dismiss and belittle them, too?"

"I don't think you're hearing what I'm saying," Buchold said.

"I'm hearing it just fine," Hubbard said. "I want you to hear that what *I* hear sounds like bigotry."

"Jesus," Buchold said. "Now you sound like that goddamn Cassandra Bell woman."

"Oh, *man,*" I said.

"What?" Buchold said, turning to me.

"Uh," I said.

"Chris doesn't want to tell you that my Integrator for the evening is Nicholas Bell, Cassandra Bell's older brother," Hubbard said. "I on the other hand don't have a problem letting you know that."

Buchold stared at Hubbard silently for a moment. Then: "You have got to be fucking —"

"*Jim,*" Wisson said, interrupting.

"Everything all right?" Dad asked. His attention had finally returned to our end of the table.

"Everything's fine, Dad," I said. "But I think Jim has a couple of questions that might be best asked to you directly. If Carole doesn't mind swapping seats with him for a bit that would be lovely."

"Of course not," Lamb said.

"Excellent," I said, and looked over to Buchold, hoping he would take the hint, or at least be grateful to me for some face time with Dad. He nodded curtly, stood up, and swapped seats.

Hubbard leaned in. "Nice save," he said, very quietly.

I nodded, and then rubbed my jaw. The pain was coming back. I was pretty sure it wasn't because of my molar.

My internal phone went up. I answered it with my inside voice. "Yeah," I said.

"Shane," Vann said. "How far are you from Leesburg right now?"

"About ten miles," I said. "Why?"

"You've heard of Loudoun Pharma?"

"In fact I'm having dinner with its CEO

and his husband," I said. "Why?"

"It just blew up," Vann said.

"What?" I looked over at Buchold, who was speaking close in and animatedly at my dad.

"It just blew up," Vann repeated. "And it looks like a Haden was involved."

"You're joking."

"I wish I was, because then I'd be getting laid instead of heading your direction," Vann said. "Get out there now. Start mapping the place and getting data. I'll be there in about forty minutes."

"What do I tell Jim Buchold?" I asked.

"He the CEO?"

"Yeah," I said. Then I noticed Buchold reaching into his suit pocket for his phone. "Hold on, I think he may be finding out."

Buchold leaped up and ran out of the room, phone still up to his ear. Rick Wisson watched him leave, confused.

"Yup," I said. "He knows."

CHAPTER EIGHT

The Loudoun Pharma campus consisted of two main buildings. One held the offices for the C-suite, middle management and support staff, local reps and the company's lobbyists for D.C. and Richmond. The other contained the labs, which housed the scientists, the IT people, and their respective support staffs.

The office building was a wreck. Every window on the east side of the structure was shattered and had fallen out of the walls. Most of the rest of the windows were in various stages of damage. Paperwork wafted out of holes, fluttering in the air before coming to rest in the shady boulevard that separated the two buildings from each other.

The labs were mostly gone.

Fire engines from every corner of Loudoun County surrounded the rubble, and firemen looked for something to put out.

There was very little to put out. The explosion had collapsed the building on itself, smothering any incipient fire before it could catch. EMTs circled the collapsed building, using scanners to locate RFID-equipped personnel badges the Loudoun Pharma staff used.

There were six badges pinging, all for janitorial staff. The EMT deployed roach and snake bots to scurry through the wreckage toward the badges to see if they were still attached to anyone alive.

They were not.

"Here's what the security guards saw," I said, to Vann. We were in her car and I was porting the images to her dash. She was sucking like a demon on one of her cigarettes. It might have been a side effect of sexual frustration, but now was not the moment to ask. I kept the door on my side open to vent the smoke.

In the dash, we were treated to a guard-post camera view of an SUV accelerating into the parking lot and then ramming through the gate, snapping it off as it drove through.

"Back it up and pause it just before the snap," Vann said. I did. She pointed. "License plate and face," she said.

"Right," I said. "Neither of which match

126

the RFID badge that pinged when the SUV rammed through, though."

"Who does the badge belong to?"

"Karl Baer," I said. "He's a geneticist. Works in the lab. He's also a Haden, which is why we were pinged."

"That's not a threep driving the SUV," Vann said. "So whoever this is stole Baer's ID. But why would they do that and then just ram the goddamn gate?"

"They needed the ID to access the parking garage under the labs," I said. "Staff parking is in the garages. Visitor parking outside."

"And an SUV full of explosives is much more effective under the building than next to it."

"I imagine that's the thinking, yes."

"So if it's a stolen ID, do we need to be here?" Vann asked. "Still?"

I paused for a second, wondering why she would ask me that, then remembered it was still my first day with her, unbelievable as it was at this point. She was still testing me.

"Yeah, we do," I said. "One, we need to check in on Baer to make sure the ID was stolen. Two" — I pointed back to the image of the SUV about to ram the gate — "there's the fact that this SUV is registered to Jay Kearney."

"Am I supposed to know who Jay Kearney is?"

"You might," I said. "He's an Integrator. Or was."

Vann took a final suck on her cigarette and put it out on her window glass. "Show me a clean picture of Kearney," she said.

I loaded his Integrator license picture into the dash and placed it next to the image of the person driving the car. Vann leaned in and peered.

"What do you think?" I asked.

"Could be. Could be," she said. She glanced up over the dash toward the collapsed building and the flashing lights of the cops, firemen, and EMTs. "Have they found him yet?"

"I don't think they're looking for him," I said. "They're looking for the janitors. And anyway if he was in the SUV when it went up then he's a fine coat of ash all over that parking garage."

"You share this with anyone yet?"

"No one here is interested in talking to me," I said. "I'm Haden affairs, not terrorism." As I said this the distant sound of a helicopter became loud and got louder.

"That's probably terrorism right now," Vann said. "They like to make an entrance."

I motioned back at the image. "I got this

from security the same time the Leesburg cops and the Loudoun sheriffs did but I don't think they've looked at it yet."

"All right," Vann said. She wiped the images off her screen. "Where are you parked?"

"I'm not," I said. "I caught a ride with Jim Buchold, the CEO. He's over yelling at the Leesburg cops."

"Good," Vann said. She started her car.

"Where are we going?" I closed the door on my side.

"We're going to visit Karl Baer," Vann said. "Pull up his address, please."

"Do we need a warrant?" I asked, as I did it.

"I want to talk to him, not arrest him," Vann said. "But you might see if you can get a warrant for Kearney's records. I want to know who he was integrating with. See if you can pull Nicholas Bell's records too. Two Integrators possibly tied up with murder in a single day is a little much for me."

Karl Baer's apartment was in a little gray apartment complex in Leesburg, next to a supermarket and an International House of Pancakes. He was in a bottom corner apartment, tucked underneath a stairwell. There was no response when we knocked.

"He *is* a Haden," I pointed out.

"If he's living here he's got a threep," Vann said. "If he's got a damn employee badge at Loudoun Pharma then he's got a threep. He can answer the door." She knocked again.

"I'll go around back and see if I can see in a window," I said, after a minute.

"Yeah, okay," Vann said. "No, wait." She tried the doorknob. It turned all the way.

"You really going to do this?" I asked, looking at the doorknob.

"The door was open," Vann said.

"The door was closed," I said. "Just unlocked."

"Are you recording?"

"Right now? No."

Vann pushed the door open. "Look, it's open," she said.

"You're just a beacon of safe constitutional practices, Vann," I said, echoing her from earlier in the day.

She grinned. "Come on," she said.

We found Karl Baer in his bedroom, a knife shoved into his brain. A threep was standing beside his cradle, knife handle in hand, flush with Baer's temple.

"Holy shit," I said.

"Go open the window blinds," Vann said.

I did what she told me. "If anyone asks, you came around the back, looked in and saw this, and that's when we entered the apartment."

"I don't have a good feeling about this," I said.

"What's to feel good about?" Vann asked. "Are you recording yet?"

"No," I said.

"Start," she said.

"I'm on."

Vann went over to the light switch and flipped it on with her elbow. "Start mapping," she said. She put on a pair of gloves as I did so. After I was done mapping, she went over and picked up a tablet on the side table next to Baer's cradle and turned on the screen.

"Shane," she said. She turned the tablet around so I could see the screen. Jay Kearney was on it.

"Is it a video?" I asked.

"Yeah," Vann said, turning the screen back to her. I walked over to her and she pressed "play."

On the screen Jay Kearney came to life. He was holding the tablet so that he and Karl Baer were both caught by the camera.

"This is Karl Baer," Kearney said. "I am speaking for myself and for my good friend

Jay Kearney, with whom I am now integrated. For the past eight years I have worked at Loudoun Pharma as a geneticist, as part of a team working to reverse the effects of Haden's syndrome.

"When I joined Loudoun, I believed that what I was doing was right for Haden's. None of us asked to be trapped within our bodies. I know I didn't. I was a teenager when I got sick and all the things I loved to do were taken from me. Working to reverse the changes that Haden's had brought into my life made sense to me. I looked forward to the chance to have that new life.

"But as I went on I began to realize that Haden's wasn't some life sentence. It was just another way to live. I began to see the beauty of the world we Hadens were creating, the millions of us, in our own spaces and in our own way. And I began listening to the words of Cassandra Bell, who said that people like me, people who were working to quote-unquote cure Haden's, were in fact killing the first new nation of humanity to come along in centuries.

"She's right. We are. *I* am. And it's time to put a stop to it now.

"It's not something I could have done by myself. Fortunately my friend Jay believes as I do and believes it enough to help me.

Others, who will remain nameless, helped along the way to provide us with materials and planning. And now all that needs to be done is to set it all into motion. Jay and I will do it together. And when his part is over, then I will come back here in order to join him on the next part of our journey together. I guess if you're seeing this you know how I did this.

"For my family and friends, I know that my actions — *our* actions — may not seem comprehensible. I know that there's a chance that a few innocent people will be harmed or even killed. I regret this and apologize to those who will lose loved ones tonight. But I ask them to understand that if I don't take these actions now, then what Loudoun Pharma is doing will lead to the extinction of an entire people. A genocide committed through quote-unquote kindness.

"To my colleagues at Loudoun Pharma, I know many of you will be angry with me, now that my actions have set back your work and research by years. But what I ask of you now is to spend that time you have to think about the consequences of what you are doing. Read and listen to the words of Cassandra Bell as I have. I believe in what she has to say. I believe in her. I follow her philosophy in the things I do today. I believe that you might do the same in time.

"Good-bye and all the best to Hadens everywhere. I am with you, always."

"None of this makes any goddamned *sense,*" Jim Buchold said.

We were in the family room of Buchold and Wisson's home outside Leesburg. The Leesburg police, Loudoun County sheriffs, and FBI apparently had to just about forcibly remove Buchold from the Loudoun Pharma campus in order to get him out of the way so they could do their work. As a result Buchold was pacing around his family room, feeling useless. Wisson had fixed his husband a drink to calm him down. It sat undrunk on the table. Eventually Wisson helped himself to it.

"Why doesn't it make any goddamned sense?" Vann asked.

"Because Karl was a principal investigator for Neuroulease."

"Which is," Vann prompted.

"It's the drug we were developing to stimulate the voluntary nervous system in Haden's victims," Buchold said. In spite of myself I felt vaguely annoyed at the use of the word "victim" in that sentence. "Haden's suppresses the ability of the brain to speak to the voluntary nervous system. Neurolease encourages the brain to develop new pathways to the system. We've done tests on chips that worked and have been working on genetically modified mice. Progress was slow but encouraging."

"Is 'neuroulease' the actual chemical?" I asked.

"It's the brand name we're planning to use for it," Buchold said. "The actual name of the chemical compound is about a hundred and twenty letters long. The most recent iteration of the compound — the one Karl was working on — was called LPNX-211 for internal recordkeeping."

"And Dr. Baer never showed any indication of developing a moral opposition to what he was researching," Vann asked.

"Of course not," Buchold said. "I didn't spend that much time with him, but as far as I know the only things that Karl actually cared about were his work and Notre Dame football. He went there for undergrad. When he had a presentation he always managed to put in a slide with the team in it. I tolerated it because his work was that good."

"What about his relationship with Jay Kearney?" I asked.

"Who?"

"The Integrator whose body we think

135

Baer used to drive the vehicle into the parking garage," Vann said.

"Never heard of him," Buchold said. "Karl always used his threep at work."

"Did you see Kearney integrating with Baer outside of work?" I asked.

Buchold glanced over at his husband. "We didn't exactly run in the same social circles," Wisson said. "I don't encourage Jim to be overly friendly with his staff. It's better if they see him as a boss rather than a friend."

"So that would be a no," Vann said.

"It's not because he's a Haden — was a Haden," Buchold said. He turned to me. "I treat all my employees equally. We have a compliance officer in HR to make sure of it."

"I believe you," I said.

"Yes, but you also heard that son of a bitch Hubbard running me down tonight," Buchold said. "I have fifteen Haden researchers on my staff. None of them would be there if they thought I was treating them as subhuman, or what we were doing was bad for Hadens."

"Mr. Buchold," I said, and held up a hand. "I'm not here to judge you. And I'm not here to run back to my father and whisper into his ear about you. Right now I am here investigating the bombing of your facilities. Our primary suspect at the moment is one of your employees. Our only interest is finding out if he's really the bomber, and why he did it." Buchold seemed to relax a bit at that.

And then Vann tensed him all up again. "Did Dr. Baer ever talk about Cassandra Bell?" she asked.

"Why the hell would he do that?"

"Jim," Wisson said.

"No," Buchold said, shooting a look at his husband. "I never heard him speak about Cassandra Bell."

"What about the researchers around him?" Vann continued.

"There would be casual talk about her because she's on record opposing our line of research," Buchold said. "We always wondered if protesters would show up like they do because of the animal testing we have to do. But none ever did and I don't think anyone really gave her a whole lot of thought. Why?"

I looked over to Vann to see what she thought. She nodded at me. "Dr. Baer left behind a suicide note," I said. "He mentioned Cassandra Bell in it."

"How? Is she behind this in some way?" Buchold asked.

"We don't have any reason to believe so,"

137

Vann said. "But we also have to follow up all the leads."

"I knew this was going to happen," Buchold said.

"What was going to happen?" I asked.

"Violence," Buchold said. "Rick will tell you. Those dipshits passed Abrams-Kettering and I said to him that sooner or later there was going to be a mess. You don't just take five million people sucking on the government teat and punt them into the street and expect them to go without a fight." He looked over at me. "No offense."

"None taken," I said, which wasn't entirely true, but I let it go. "How far does this set you back?"

"You mean our research?"

"Yes."

"It sets us back by years," Buchold said. "There's data in the lab that wasn't anywhere else."

"You don't have multiple copies of your data?" Vann asked.

"Of course we do," Buchold said.

"And you can't pull it down off your networks?"

"You don't understand," Buchold said. "We don't ever put anything genuinely sensitive online. The moment we do that the hacking begins. We'll put up dummy

138

servers with nothing on them but encrypted pictures of *cats,* for fuck's sake, and we won't tell anyone we've put them out there. Within four hours we've got hackers from China and Syria cracking them open. We'd be idiots to put actual confidential data into an outside-accessible server."

"So all your data was stored locally," I said.

"Stored locally," Buchold said. "Stored multiply on internal servers."

"What about archives?" Vann asked. "Data stored off-network."

"We did that, of course. And stored it in a secure room on campus."

"So all of it — local *and* archived data — went up with the lab building." Vann glanced over to me with an expression that I suspect meant *these people were sloppy.*

"Right," Buchold said. "It's possible we can piece together some recent data from e-mails and the computers in the office building. If they weren't destroyed by either the blast or by the fire-suppression system. But realistically speaking — years of research. Gone. Dead. Destroyed."

"Oh, look, it's midnight," I said, to Vann, as she drove me home. "My first real day on the job is over."

Vann smiled at this, the cigarette in her mouth bouncing as she did so. "I'm not going to lie to you," she said. "It's been a little more hectic than most first days."

"I can hardly wait for tomorrow," I said.

"I doubt that." Vann drooled smoke out of her lips.

"You know that shit's going to kill you, right?" I asked. "The smoking. There's a reason why no one does it anymore."

"There's a reason why I do it," she said.

"Yeah? What is it?"

"Let's say we keep some mystery in our relationship," Vann said.

"Whatever," I said, with what I hoped was just the right amount of casual flip. Vann smiled again. Score one for me.

My phone went off. It was Tony. "Shit," I said.

"What?"

"I was supposed to meet with my maybe new roommates tonight," I said.

"Do you want me to write you a note?" Vann asked.

"Cute," I said. "Hold on." I opened the channel and spoke with my inside voice. "Hey, Tony."

"So we were all hoping that you might pop by tonight," Tony said.

"Yeah, about that," I began.

"But then I saw that Loudoun Pharma exploded and they think it might be a terrorist plot or something, and I thought to myself, I'm guessing Chris might be a little busy this evening."

"Thank you for understanding," I said.

"Looks like you had an exciting day."

"You have no idea."

"Well, then, let me end it with a bit of good news," Tony said. "The group tried you in absentia and found you guilty of being a probably worthy flatmate. You are hereby sentenced to the nicest room in the brownstone. May God have mercy on your soul."

"That's great, Tony," I said. "No, really. I appreciate it."

"That's good to hear. And the rest of us appreciate you paying rent so that we're not thrown out in the street, so we're even. I'm sending your house code now. Once you're here change it so no one but you knows it. I got your first and last and security deposit, so you're good to go. Show up anytime."

"Probably tomorrow," I said. "I'm already close to my parents' place. I'm going to crash here for the night."

"Sounds good," Tony said. "Now get some rest. You sound beat. Good night."

"Night," I said, and then switched back to

my outside voice. "I got the apartment."

"That's nice," Vann said.

"It's actually a room in an intentional community," I said.

"Funny, you don't look like a hippie."

"I'll work on it," I promised.

"Please don't," she said.

Chapter Nine

The next morning every road in D.C. was jammed from 5:30 A.M. onward. More than a hundred Haden long-range truckers got onto the interstate loop around the city and arranged their trucks in geometrical patterns designed to induce maximum disruption to automatic driving systems, and drove at twenty-five miles an hour. Commuters, frustrated with the loop being more locked up than usual, switched over to manual and tried to get around the blockages, which of course only made things worse. By seven o'clock the loop was at a complete standstill.

And then, for extra added fun, Haden truckers locked up Interstate 66 and the toll road into Virginia.

"Late on the third day of your job," Vann said to me, from her desk, as I got into the office. She pointed to the desk next to hers as she did it, indicating that it was my desk now.

"Everyone's late today," I said. "I should be graded on that curve."

"How did you manage to get in from Potomac Falls, anyway?" Vann asked. "Tell me you borrowed your dad's helicopter. That would be kind of amazing."

"As it happens, Dad *does* have a helicopter," I said. "Or his company does. But it's not allowed to land in our neighborhood. So, no. I got dropped off at the Sterling stop of the Metro and took the train in."

"And how was that?"

"Unpleasant," I said. "It was super crowded and I got a lot of nasty looks. Like it was my fault the roads were crushed. I almost said, look, people, if it were my fault, I wouldn't be on the goddamn train with the rest of you, now would I."

"It's going to be a long week with this shit," Vann said.

"It's not an effective protest if it's not pissing people off."

"I didn't say it wasn't effective," Vann said. "I didn't even say I wasn't sympathetic. It just means it's going to be a long week. Now, come on. Forensics has got news for us."

"What news?" I asked.

"On our dead guy," Vann said. "We know who he is. And apparently there's something

144

else, too."

"First off," Ramon Diaz said, "meet John Sani, your no-longer-mystery man."

We were back in the imaging suite, looking at a highly detailed, larger-than-life image of Sani on the morgue slab. It was cleaner and less annoying to the medical examiners to have field agents look at their handiwork this way. The model Diaz was projecting could be manipulated to examine any part of the body that the examiners scanned or opened. At this point the body did not look as if it had been cut into any more than it already had been at the neck. This was the "cover" scan.

"So the Navajo came through for us," Vann said.

"They did," Diaz said. "Looks like they sent his information to us around midnight their time last night."

"Who is he?" I asked.

"As far as the information we have tells us, he's not anyone," Diaz said. "The Navajo Nation have him on file for a single drunk and disorderly when he was nineteen. No time, community service. Other than that what we've got is his birth certificate and Social Security, a few medical records, and his high school transcripts, which run

145

through tenth grade."

"How'd he do?" Vann asked.

"The fact it stops at the tenth grade might tell you something."

"No driver's license or other sort of ID?" I asked.

"No," Diaz said.

"What else?" Vann asked.

"He's thirty-one and was in less than great health," Diaz said. "Some liver damage and heart disease, and signs of incipient diabetes, which is not too surprising in someone with a Native American background. Missing a few teeth in the back. Also, that slash in his neck is consistent with a self-inflicted wound. He did it to himself and he did it with that broken glass you found."

"Is this everything?" I asked.

Diaz smiled. "No, it's not. I have something for you that I think you're going to find really interesting."

"Cut the suspense, Diaz," Vann said. "Get to it."

"They did an X-ray of his skull before they took out his brain," Diaz said. He popped up the three-dimensional scan on Sani's head. "Tell me what you see."

"Holy shit," I said, immediately.

"Huh," Vann said, after a second.

The X-ray of Sani's head showed a net-

146

work of thin tendrils and coils in and around the brain, converging on five junctions distributed radially around the interior surface of the skull, the junctions themselves linked to one another in a mesh of connections.

It was an artificial neural network, designed to send and receive information from the brain, displayed in almost perfect detail.

Two groups of people had structures like these. I belonged to one of those groups. Vann belonged to the other.

"This dude's an Integrator," I said.

"What's his brain structure?" Vann asked Diaz.

"The report says it's consistent with someone who contracted Haden's," Diaz said. "And that's consistent with his medical records, which show he had meningitis as a kid, which could mean the Haden's variety. He's got the brain structure to be an Integrator."

"Shane," Vann said, still looking at the X-ray.

"Yeah," I said.

"Problems with this scenario," Vann said.

I thought about it for a minute. "This guy didn't get through high school," I said, finally.

"So?" Vann said.

"So Integrator training is a post-graduate thing," I said. "You undertake it after getting a suitable undergraduate degree, like psychology. What's yours?"

"Biology," Vann said. "American University."

"Right," I said. "Plus there's supposed to be a raft of psychological and aptitude tests you have to clear before they let you into the program. It's one of the reasons there's so few Integrators."

"Yes," Vann said.

"It's expensive, too. The training process."

"Not for the student," Vann said. "The NIH covers the costs."

"They must have been pissed at you when you left," I said.

"They got their money's worth from me," Vann said. "Bring it back around."

"Okay, so the question here is, here is a guy who didn't finish high school and who we have no record of anywhere outside of the Navajo Nation, which means he didn't have Integrator training." I pointed to the X-ray. "So how does this guy get all that wiring in his head?"

"That's a good question," Vann said. "It's not the only question. What else is wrong about this picture?"

"What *isn't* wrong about this picture?" I asked.

"I meant specifically."

"Why would an Integrator want to integrate with another Integrator?" I asked.

"More specific than that."

"I don't know how to get more specific than that," I said.

"Why would an Integrator want to integrate with another Integrator, and bring a headset?" Vann asked.

I looked at her blankly for a couple of seconds. Then, "Oh, shit, the *headset.*"

"Right," Vann said.

"That reminds me," Diaz said, to me. "I got inside that headset like you asked, to see if there was any useful information on those processor chips."

"Was there?" I asked.

"No," Diaz said. "There were no chips inside the headset."

"If there are no chips inside, then it wouldn't work. It's a dummy headset," I said.

"That would be my thinking, yes," Diaz said.

I turned to Vann. "Seriously, what the hell is going on here?" I said.

"What do you mean?" Vann asked.

"I mean, what the hell is going on here.

We've got two Integrators, one of whom shouldn't be an Integrator, and a dummy headset. It doesn't make any sense."

Vann turned to Diaz. "Fingerprints on the headset?"

"Yes," he said. "They match Sani, not Bell."

"So Sani brought the headset to the party, not Bell," Vann said, then looked back at me. "What does that suggest to you?"

"Maybe that Bell didn't know Sani was an Integrator," I said. "And that Sani didn't want him to know he was one, either."

"Right," Vann said.

"Okay, but again, why?" I asked. "What possible use is there for Sani to convince Bell that he's just a tourist? Without the headset he can't even be that. Unless there's some Integrator-to-Integrator ability I don't know about."

"No," Vann said. "There's a sort of neural feedback loop that happens when you try to put one Integrator into the head of another. You can fry people's brains that way."

"Like *Scanners*?" I asked.

"Like what?"

"An old movie. About psychics. They could make your head blow up."

Vann smiled. "Nothing that outwardly dramatic. But inwardly it's not supposed to

150

be pleasant. It's blocked at the network level in any event."

"So it couldn't have been that," I said. "Plus the whole suicide thing again."

Vann was quiet again.

Then: "What time is it in Arizona?"

"It's two hours behind here, so about eight thirty," I said. "Maybe. Arizona is weird about time zones."

"You need to go out there today and talk to some people," Vann said.

"Me?"

"Yes, you," Vann said. "You can get there in ten seconds for nothing."

"There's the small fact I will have no body," I said.

"You're not the only Haden on the FBI staff," Vann said. "The Bureau keeps spare threeps at the major field offices. Phoenix will have one for you. It won't be *fancy*" — she motioned to my threep — "but it will get the job done."

"Are the Navajo going to cooperate with us?" I asked.

"If we let them know we're trying to figure out the death of one of their own, they might come around," Vann said. "I have a friend in the Phoenix office. I'll see if he can make things easier. Let's get you out there by ten their time."

"I can't just call?" I asked.

"You need to tell some family their son or dad is dead and then ask them a bunch of personal questions," Vann said. "Yeah, no, you can't just call."

"It'll be my first trip to Arizona," I said.

"Hope you like hot," Vann said.

At 10:05 I found myself in the Phoenix FBI field office, looking at a bald man.

"Agent Beresford?" I asked.

"Damn, that's creepy," the man said. "This threep's been in the corner for three years without moving, and suddenly it gets up. It's like a statue coming to life."

"Surprise," I said.

"I mean, we've been using it as a hat rack."

"Sorry to deprive you of your office furniture."

"It's only for the day. You Shane?"

"That's right."

"Tom Beresford." He held out his hand. I took it. "I don't mind telling you I've never forgiven your dad for crushing the Suns in four."

"Oh, that," I said. He was talking about Dad's second NBA title. "If it means anything, he always said that series was closer than it looked."

"It's nice of him to lie like that," Beres-

152

ford said. "Come on, I'll take you down to meet Klah."

I started walking and stopped. "Jesus," I said, and started jerking my leg.

"Something wrong?" Beresford stopped and waited on me.

"You weren't kidding when you said this thing didn't move," I said. "I think something's rusted up in this thing."

"I can get you a can of WD-40 if you want."

"Nice," I said. "Just give me a second." I fired up the threep's diagnostic system to find out what was going on. "Great, it's a Metro Courier."

"Is that a problem?" Beresford asked.

"The Metro Courier is like the Ford Pinto of threeps."

"We could try to find you a rental threep if you want," Beresford said. "I think Enterprise might have some at the airport. It'll just take forever and you'll spend your day filling out requisition forms."

"It'll be fine," I said. The diagnostic said there was nothing wrong with the threep, which may have meant there was something wrong with the diagnostic. "I'll walk it out."

"Come on, then." Beresford started off again. I followed, limping.

"Agent Chris Shane, Officer Klah Redhouse," Beresford said, after we reached the lobby, introducing me to a young man in a uniform. "Klah went to Northern Arizona with my son. As it happens he was in Phoenix on tribal business, so you got lucky. It would be a two-hundred-eighty-five-mile walk to Window Rock otherwise."

"Officer Redhouse," I said, and held out my hand.

He took it and smiled. "Don't meet a lot of Hadens," he said. "Never met one who was an FBI agent before."

"A first time for everything," I said.

"You're limping," he said.

"Childhood injury," I said. And then, after a second, "That was a joke."

"I got that," he said. "Come on. I'm parked right outside."

"Be right there," I said, and then turned to Beresford. "There's a possibility that I might need this threep for a while."

"It's just collecting dust with us," Beresford said.

"So it won't be a problem if I keep it in Window Rock for a while," I asked.

"That's going to be up to the folks up there," Beresford said. "Our official policy is to defer to their sovereignty, so if they want you away when you're done, head to our office in Flagstaff. I'll let them know you might be on the way. Or get a hotel room. Maybe someone will rent you a broom closet and a plug."

"Is this a problem?" I asked. "I'm not really versed in the relations between the FBI and the Navajo."

"We don't have any problems at the moment," Beresford said. "We've cooperated with them just fine recently, and they have Klah taking you up, which says they don't have a problem with you. But other than that, who knows. The U.S. government gave the Navajo and a lot of the other Native American nations a whole lot more autonomy a couple of decades back, when it downsized the Bureau of Indian Affairs and the Indian Health Service. But that's also given us an excuse to ignore them and their problems."

"Ah," I said.

"Hell, Shane, you might be able to sympathize," Beresford said. "The U.S. government just pulled the plug on the Hadens, didn't it? It's something you folks might say you have in common with the Navajo."

"I'm not entirely sure I want to be going around making that comparison," I said.

"That's probably wise," Beresford said. "The Navajo have a two-hundred-year head start in the 'getting screwed by the U.S.

government' category. They might not appreciate you jumping on the train. But now you might understand why some of them might decide to be touchy about you showing up and asking questions. So be polite, be respectful, and go if they tell you to go."

"Got it."

"Good," Beresford said. "Now go on. Klah's good people. Don't keep him waiting."

CHAPTER TEN

The ride up to Window Rock took four and a half hours, with Redhouse and me passing the time in innocuous conversation followed by long lapses of silence. Redhouse seemed to enjoy my stories about getting to travel the world with my father and noted that his own travels had been far less extensive.

"I've been in the four states the Navajo Nation sits in," he said. "And the most time that I spent away from it was when I went to Flagstaff for college. Other than that, been nowhere but here."

"Have you wanted to go anywhere else?" I asked.

"Sure," he said. "When you're a kid all you want to do is be somewhere else."

"Pretty sure that's a universal thing," I said.

"I know," Redhouse said, and smiled. "And now I don't mind it so much. I like my family better now that I'm older. Have a fiancée. Have a job."

"Did you always want to be a police officer?" I asked.

"No," he said, and smiled again. "I went to college for computer science."

"That's kind of a left turn," I said.

"Just before I went to college the Council decided to invest in a huge server facility outside Window Rock," Redhouse said. "It would serve the needs of the Navajo and other nations, and then also be used by the surrounding state governments and even the federal government for nonconfidential processing and storage. Solar powered and zero emission. It was going to employ hundreds of Navajo and bring millions of dollars into Window Rock. So when I went to college I studied computing so that I could have a job. The Flagstaff news site even did a story about me and some of my classmates at Northern Arizona. They called us 'The Silicon Navajos,' which I didn't like very much."

"So what happened?"

"We built the facility and then none of the promised state or federal contracts came in," Redhouse said. "We were told about budget cuts and reorganizations and changes in agendas and new governors and presidents coming in. We have this state-of-the-art facility now and it's operating at three percent of capacity. Not so many people got hired to staff it at three percent. So I went to the police academy and became a police officer."

"Sorry about the switch," I said.

"It's not so bad," Redhouse said. "I had family who were officers before me, so you could say it was a tradition. And I'm doing some good, so that helps. But if I'd known my degree was going to be useless I might have not scheduled so many eight A.M. classes. Did you always want to be an FBI agent?"

"I wanted to be one of those CSI agents," I said. "Problem for that was my degree is in English."

"Oof," Redhouse said. "We'll see the computer facility as we drive in. You can get a look at what wasted potential looks like."

An hour later, just south of Window Rock, we rolled by a large, featureless building surrounded on three sides by solar panels.

"I'm guessing that's it," I said.

"That's it," Redhouse said. "The one positive thing about it is that since we don't need all the solar capacity we installed, we sell energy to Arizona and New Mexico."

"At least you'll make a profit somehow."

"I wouldn't call it a profit," Redhouse

159

said. "It just means running the computer facility bleeds us more slowly than it would otherwise. My mother works for the Council. She says that they're going to give it a couple more years, tops."

"What will they do with the building?" I asked.

"That is the question, isn't it, Agent Shane?" Redhouse said. He sat up, pressed a button on his dash, and took over manual control of the police car. "Now, let's get you checked in at the station and then we can take you to go see Johnny Sani's family. My captain is probably going to want to have an officer accompany you. Is that going to be a problem?"

"I don't think so."

"Okay, good," Redhouse said.

"Is it going to be you?" I asked.

Redhouse smiled once more. "Probably."

Sani's family lived in a well-kept double-wide in an otherwise less-than-spiff trailer park outside of Sawmill. The family consisted of a grandmother and a sister. Both sat on a couch looking at me, numbly.

"Why would he kill himself?" his sister, Janis, asked me.

"I don't know," I said. "I was hoping you might be able to tell me."

"How did he do it?" asked the grandmother, May.

"*Shimasani,* you don't want to know that," Janis said.

"Yes I *do,*" May said, forcefully.

I looked over to Redhouse, who was standing next to the chair I was sitting in, holding the glass of tea they had offered him. They offered me one as well. It sat on the table in front of me, between me and Sani's relatives.

Redhouse nodded at me. "He cut his throat," I said.

May looked at me balefully but said nothing else. Janis held her grandmother and looked at me, expressionless. I waited for a couple of minutes and then began again.

"Our records show —" I said, and then stopped. "Well, actually, we don't have any records for John."

"Johnny," Janis said.

"Excuse me," I said. "Johnny. All the records we have for Johnny are from here. From the Navajo Nation. So our first question is why that's the case."

"Until last year Johnny never left here," Janis said.

"All right," I said. "But why is that?"

"Johnny was slow," Janis said. "We had a doctor test him when he was thirteen. He said his IQ was seventy-nine or eighty. Johnny could figure things out if he worked at it, but it took him a long time. We kept him in school as long as we could so he could have friends, but he couldn't keep up. He stopped going and we stopped making him go."

"He wasn't always that way," May said. "He was a smart baby. A smart little boy. When he was five he got sick. He wasn't the same after that."

"Was it Haden's?" I asked.

"No!" May said. "He wasn't crippled." She stopped and considered what she had said. "Sorry."

I held a hand up. "It's perfectly all right," I said. "Sometimes people get sick with Haden's but they don't get locked in. But it can still do damage. When you say he got sick, did he have a fever? And then meningitis?"

"His brain swelled up," May said.

"That's meningitis," I said. "We scanned his brain after he died and we saw the brain structure there that was consistent with Haden's. But we found something else, too. We found that he had something we call a neural network in there too."

Janis looked up at Redhouse for this. "It's like a machine in his head, Janis," he said.

"It let him send and receive information."

"I have one in my head back home," I said, and tapped my head. "It lets me control this machine here so I can be here in the room with you."

Janis and May both looked confused. "Johnny didn't have anything in his head," May said, finally.

"I apologize for asking, but are you completely sure?" I asked. "A neural network isn't something that's accidentally put into someone's head. It's there to either send brain signals or to receive them."

"He lived with me his entire life," May said. "He lived here with his mother and Janis, and then when his mother died I looked after him. No way this could happen to him here."

"So it would have to have been put in after he left," Redhouse said.

"About that," I said. "Why would Johnny decide to leave here if he'd never gone anywhere in his life?"

"He got a job," Janis said.

"What kind of job?" I asked.

"He said he was an executive assistant," Janis said.

"For whom?"

"I don't know," Janis said.

"Johnny got a friend to take him down to

that computer building in Window Rock," May said. "He'd heard they had an opening for a janitor, and that was something he could do. He wanted to be able to help me out. He went down and asked about the job and then the next day they asked him to come down again. And then when he came back that night, he gave me a thousand dollars and told me it was half of his first paycheck from his new job."

"The janitorial position," Redhouse said.

"No, the other one," May said. "He said when he got there they asked him if he would like a different job that would pay better and let him travel. All he'd have to do is help his boss do things. He said it was like being a butler."

"So he left," I said. "What then?"

"Every week I'd get a money order from Johnny, and he would call sometimes," May said. "He told me to move someplace nice and get new things, so I moved here. Then a few months ago he stopped calling but the money orders still arrived, so I didn't worry too much."

"When did the last money order arrive?"

"It came two days ago," Janis said. "I picked up my grandmother's mail for her."

"Do you mind if I look at it?" I asked.

They both looked dubious at this.

"Agent Shane isn't going to take it as evidence," Redhouse said. "But it might have something on it that's important."

Janis got up to get the money order.

"Johnny never said anything about who he worked for?" I asked May.

"He said that his boss liked to be private," May said. "I didn't want Johnny to lose his job, so I never asked more than that."

"Did he like his job?" I asked. By this time Janis had walked over to me with the money order. I scanned it quickly on one side, flipped it over, and did the same to the other side, then handed it back to her. "Thank you," I said.

"He seemed to like it," May said. "He never said anything bad about it."

"He was excited to travel," Janis said, sitting down again. "The first couple of times he called he mentioned that he was in California and in Washington."

"The state or the District?" Redhouse asked.

"The District," Janis said. "I think."

"But then he said his boss didn't like him talking about where he'd been, so he didn't say anymore."

"The last time he called, did he say anything unusual or tell you anything unusual?" I asked.

"No," May said. "He said he hadn't been feeling well . . . no. He said he was worried about something."

"Worried about what?" I asked.

"A test?" May ventured. "Something that he had to do that he was nervous about. I don't remember."

"Okay," I said.

"When do we get him back?" Janis asked. "I mean, when does he get to come home?"

"I don't know," I said. "I can check."

"He needs to be buried here," May said.

"I'll see what I can do," I said. "That's a promise."

May and Janis looked at me expressionlessly.

"They handled it well," I said, after Redhouse and I left the trailer and headed to the car.

"Some of us try not to show too much emotion about death," Redhouse said. "The thinking is if you go on about it, you can keep a spirit from moving on."

"Do you believe that?" I asked.

"It doesn't matter whether I believe it or not," Redhouse said.

"Fair point," I said.

"Anything on the money order?"

"Serial number and routing information," I said. "You want it?"

"I wouldn't mind," Redhouse said. "I don't know if the FBI would be happy with you for sharing information."

"I think my partner would tell me that sharing with the local police is the polite thing to do, unless you hate that cop in particular."

"You have an interesting partner."

"That I do," I said, and got into the car. "Let's go down to the server farm."

"Johnny Sani," Loren Begay said. He was the head of HR for the Window Rock Computational Facility, as well as the head of several other departments, including sales and janitorial. The staff at WRCF was as bare bones as Redhouse had advertised. "I went to school with him. For a while."

"I'm asking about something a little closer in time than that," I said. "His family said he applied for a job here last year. Is that right?"

"He did," Begay said. "I had to fire a janitor for sleeping on the job. Needed someone who could take the overnight shift. He applied. So did sixty other people. I gave it to one of the other janitors' sister."

"Johnny Sani's family says that you called him back for a follow-up and that's when he got offered a different job," Redhouse said.

"I never called him back," Begay said.

"You didn't?" I asked.

"Why would I call him back?" Begay asked. "The man's slow as they come. He could barely fill out the application."

"You don't need much of an education to push a broom," Redhouse said.

"No, but I want someone with enough sense not to touch any buttons he's not supposed to," Begay said. "This place isn't to capacity, but we still have clients."

"Who are your clients, Mr. Begay?" I asked.

Begay looked over to Redhouse.

"It's okay," Redhouse said.

Begay looked unconvinced about the okayness but spoke anyway. "All of the Nation's governmental departments are in here, plus a few others from nations around the country. Then we've got a few private clients, mostly businesses from around here or that do business around here. The biggest of those would be Medichord."

"What's Medichord?" I asked.

"Medical services company," Begay said. "They contract to run the Nation's medical services. Been doing that for six, seven years."

"I remember when they came in," Redhouse said. "Promised to train and promote Navajo medical personnel in return for an exclusive contract."

"Have they?" I asked. Redhouse shrugged.

"It's quasi-governmental and confidential medical information, so Medichord keeps all the Navajo data here instead of linking it up with the rest of their network," Begay said.

"No one else would use this facility to do a job search?" I asked.

"I wish they would," Begay said. "We've got the office space and we could use the business. But no."

"Do any of the private companies send reps or IT guys here?"

"The companies we got, if they had an IT department, they probably wouldn't need us so much," Begay said. "But they don't need to come here anyway. They can access their servers and data remotely with standard software. What we do is host and act as backup if for some reason what IT people they have do something stupid. Which does happen."

"Can someone hack into this place?" I asked.

"I should tell you no, but you're a Haden, so I'm guessing you're not stupid about

169

these things," Begay said. "So I'll tell you that if anything is connected to the outside world, it's hackable. That said, all the Nation data is on servers that are accessible only from Nation computers that are either GPS-tagged or require two-factor authentication or both."

"And that includes this Medichord company," I said.

"It does," said Begay. "Why are you asking about Johnny Sani?"

"He died," I said.

"That's too bad," Begay said. "He was a nice guy."

"I thought you said he was slow."

"He was slow," Begay said. "Doesn't mean he wasn't nice."

"This keeps getting more fucked up as we go along, doesn't it?" Vann asked me. It was seven thirty in D.C. and from the ambient sound around her I could tell she was in a bar again, possibly picking up from last night on her quest to get laid. I was in the Window Rock Police Department, at a spare desk, using my inside voice.

"We have two choices at this point," I said. "We have to believe that either a guy who couldn't get a job pushing a mop is also a savant Integrator who somehow lured Nicholas Bell into that hotel room on the pretense that he was a tourist looking for a thrill, or we have to believe that someone tricked this poor son of a bitch away from his home, implanted a neural network in his head, and then convinced him to play along with their plan, whatever that was, which somehow involved Bell."

"And then commit suicide," Vann said. "Don't forget that."

"How can I forget?" I said. "I talked to this guy's family today."

"On a brighter note, I got a judge to okay our record pull for Bell and Kearney," Vann said.

"And?"

"Bell's don't tell us anything we didn't already know," Vann said. "Bell just signed a long-term contract with Lucas Hubbard, as in, just *today.* He is also first call with a bunch of well-off Hadens when he's not tied up with Hubbard. And then he does piecework for the NIH, just like every other Integrator. Well, until next Monday, when Abrams-Kettering kills *that* little program."

"What about Kearney?" I asked.

"He's got a long-term contract, too," Vann said. "And as it happens, his is with one Samuel Schwartz, lead counsel for Accelerant."

"That explains last night," I said.

"You lost me," Vann said.

"Hubbard and Schwartz were at my dad's little soirée last night," I said. "Hubbard was riding Bell, but Schwartz was riding a woman Integrator. Said that his usual Integrator had a previous engagement."

"Yeah, blowing up Loudoun Pharma," Vann said. "Who was the woman Integrator?"

"I don't know," I said. "You know it's not polite to ask."

"Go through the D.C. Integrator listings," Vann said. "You'll find her."

"So, Bell with Hubbard and Kearney with Schwartz," I said.

"What about it?"

"Doesn't that seem a little coincidental?" I asked.

"That two Integrators involved in weird shit on the same day work for the two most powerful people at the same corporation?"

"Yeah," I said.

"Honestly?" Vann said. "Yeah. But here's the thing about that. There's ten thousand working Integrators in the whole world. Maybe two thousand of them are in the U.S. So there aren't that many of them to go around. D.C.'s got maybe twenty in the area. Meanwhile there are probably a hundred thousand Hadens in the area, because Hadens flock to urbanized areas that can support them. One Integrator for five thousand Hadens. You're going to see a lot of overlap."

"Maybe," I said.

"Definitely," Vann said. "If you want to start making connections, we're going to need more to go on."

"All right, one more data point to throw at you," I said. "Medichord."

"What about it?"

"Medical care and services company," I said. "Has the contracts here in the Navajo Nation."

"Okay," Vann said. "So?"

"Medichord is part of Four Corners Blue Cross," I said. "Guess who Four Corners Blue Cross is owned by."

"If you say Accelerant, you're going to make me unhappy," Vann said.

"Have another drink," I suggested.

"I'm pacing myself," Vann said. "I want to be able to feel later tonight."

"A lot comes back to Hubbard and Schwartz and Accelerant," I said. "We have too much piling up for it to be coincidence. I mean, hell, Schwartz is even Bell's lawyer."

"All right," Vann said. "But let me say it again: If you're going to suggest Schwartz was somehow complicit with the Loudoun Pharma bombing you're going to need more than an Integrator contract. And you're forgetting that when the bombing was going down, Schwartz was at a party with one of the most famous men on the face of the Earth and an FBI agent who, if hauled up in front of a court, would have to admit to seeing him there. *You* are his alibi, Shane."

"There is that," I said.

"Plus Baer was actually Kearney's client," Vann said. "He contracted with him three times in the last two years. It's evidence of a prior relationship."

"Not all of my ideas are going to be gold," I said.

"Stop thinking for the evening," Vann said. "You've done enough for the day. When are you coming back?"

"I'm about to finish up here," I said. "The Window Rock police are letting me park my loaner threep here for a couple of days in case I need to come back. Once that's squared away I thought I might try visiting that place I'm renting a room in."

"Crazy idea," Vann said. "Get to it. Good night, Shane."

"Wait," I said.

"Talking to you is cramping my evening's planned festivities," Vann said.

"Johnny Sani," I said.

"What about him?"

"The family wants the body back."

"When we're done with him they're welcome to him. The FBI will work with them so they can have someone pick up the body."

"I don't think his grandmother and sister have that sort of money," I said.

"I don't know what to tell you about that, Shane," Vann said.

"All right," I said. "I'll let them know." I hung up and switched back over to my outside voice. "I'm about done here," I said, to Redhouse.

"No one's using that desk," he said, pointing to where I was sitting. "If you want to just plug in there, there's a socket on the floor. Captain told me to ask you to let us know before you're going to drop by, but otherwise you're fine for a few days."

"I appreciate it," I said.

"Did you talk to them about Sani's body?" Redhouse asked.

"I did," I said. "When we're done with it I'll give you a contact in D.C. to have the body shipped."

"That's not going to be cheap."

"When they find out how much it is, let me know," I said. "I'll have it dealt with."

"Who do I tell them is dealing with it?"

Redhouse asked.

"Tell them it's an anonymous friend," I said.

CHAPTER ELEVEN

I was on the corner of Pennsylvania and Sixth Avenue, walking away from the Eastern Market Metro, when I heard them in Seward Square: a bunch of young, probably drunk, and almost certainly stupid dudes braying at each other about something.

That in itself didn't interest me. Stupid, drunk young men are a fixture of any urban setting, especially in the evening hours. What got my attention was the next voice I heard, which was a woman's, and which didn't sound particularly happy. The calculus for that many drunk young men and a single woman didn't strike me as especially good. So I continued on Pennsylvania into Seward Square.

I caught up with the group where the little walkway cut across the grass from Pennsylvania and Fifth. There were four dudes who had taken it on themselves to surround someone, who I assumed was the woman in question. As I got closer, I saw that the woman was also a Haden.

That changed the dynamic of what was going on a bit. It also meant these guys were drunker or more stupid than I had previously guessed. Or some combination of the two.

The woman in the center of the dude pocket was trying to shoulder her way through the group. When she did, the four would move and re-form their pocket around her. It wasn't entirely clear what they were planning to do but it was also clear that they weren't interested in letting her get away.

The woman moved again and the four men moved again, and that was the first time I saw the aluminum bat one of them was carrying.

Well, that was no good.

So I walked up, making as much noise as threepily possible as I did so.

One of the men caught the movement and got the attention of the others. In a minute, all four of them were looking at me, the woman still in the center of their pocket. The one with the bat was bobbing it lightly in his hand.

"Hi there," I said. "Softball practice get out late?"

"What you want to do is just keep walk-ing," one of them said to me. It was clear to me that this was meant to be threatening, but he was pretty drunk, so it just came out as the drunk version of threatening, which isn't very threatening at all.

"What I want to do is check on your friend here," I said, and pointed to the Ha-den in the middle of the group. "Are you okay?" I asked her.

"Not really," she said.

"All right," I said, and then looked at each of the men in turn, using the second I held each one's gaze to scan their faces and send the scans to the FBI database for identifica-tion. "Here's my idea, then. Why don't you let her walk away, and then you all and I can talk about whatever it is you wanted to have a conversation with her about. It'll be fun. I'll even buy a round for you all." *Because what you need is another drink,* I thought, but did not say. I was trying to make this all nice and pretend friendly. I was pretty sure it wasn't going to work, but it was worth it to make the attempt.

It didn't work. "How about you fuck off, you fucking clank," said another one of them. He was just as drunk as the first, so this was as ineffectively blustery as the first threat.

So I decided on a course of lateral motivation. "Terry Olson," I said.

"What?" said the dude.

"Your name is Terry Olson," I said, and then pointed to the next one. "Bernie Clay. Wayne Glover. And Daniel Lynch." I pointed to the one holding the bat. "Although I'd bet twenty bucks that you go by Danny. And your last name is full of irony at the moment."

"How do you know who we —" Olson began.

"Shut the fuck up, Terry," said Lynch, thereby inadvertently confirming the identity of at least one of the four. These guys were geniuses, all right.

"He's right, Terry," I said. "You *do* have the right to remain silent. And you probably should. But to answer your question, I know who you are because I just did a facial scan of the four of you, and your information popped right up from the database I'm plugged into. It's the FBI database. I'm plugged into that database because I'm an FBI agent. My name is Agent Chris Shane."

"Bullshit," Lynch said.

I ignored him. "I tried to be nice to you, but that's not how you wanted to do this," I said. "So why don't we try it this way. While we've been standing here having our little conversation, I've already put in an alert to the Metro police. Their station house is just two blocks away, which is something I have to believe you didn't know, because otherwise you wouldn't have been stupid enough to try to bash someone here.

"So. You are going to let her" — I pointed to the woman — "come over and stand by me, and then you four are going to go home. Because if you're still here when the cops show up, at least one of you is in trouble for underage drinking, *Bernie,* and at least one of you already has an assault charge on his sheet, *Danny.* The cops take a dim view of each."

Three of the four looked at me uncertainly. The fourth, Lynch, I could tell was calculating his odds.

"I figure at least one of you is thinking he's not going to get into *that* much trouble for taking a shot at a threep," I said. "So this is where I remind you that D.C. law treats crimes against threeps the same as it does against human bodies. So *all* of you are going to be on the hook for assault. And, since it's pretty clear to me you're targeting this person because she's a Haden, you've got a hate crime charge to go with it.

"So you just want to think about that," I said. "While you're thinking about that, I should mention that I've been recording this entire event from the minute I walked up, and that footage is already in the FBI's servers. So far, all I have is four guys being drunk and stupid. Don't let's change that."

Terry Olson and Bernie Clay stepped aside. The woman began walking toward me. As she cleared the men, Lynch let out a grunt and pulled back the bat to take a swing at her head.

Which is when I zapped him, because I had my service stunner behind my back the entire time and had him already zeroed in as the target. All I really had to do was fire when my interior reticle went red. I had him pegged as one of the "not quite clear on long-term consequences" types as soon as I had walked up, on account of there was only one idiot in attendance with a bat. He'd come out to dance. The others were just drunken wingmen.

Lynch stiffened and then fell to the ground, convulsing and vomiting. The other three men bolted. The woman knelt next to Lynch, checking him.

"What are you doing?" I asked, coming up to the two of them.

"I'm making sure he's not aspirating his own vomit," she said.

"What are you, a doctor?"

"As a matter of fact, yeah," she said.

"Can you do that while I'm cuffing him?" I asked. She nodded. I cuffed him.

"Great," I said, and stood back up. "Now I really *do* have to call the police."

She looked up at me. "You hadn't already?"

"I was pulling their data from the database and targeting this asshole," I said. "I was a little bit busy. Why didn't you, if you don't mind me asking?"

"They just seemed like harmless drunks," she said. "They came up from behind me and I didn't think about it until they started talking to me. And I didn't realize they were a problem until *this* asshole started asking me how far I thought my head would fly if he took a bat to it."

"Tell me you have that part recorded, at least."

"I do," she said. "And I told him that I did. He just laughed."

"I don't credit Mr. Lynch here with too many brains," I said. "Either that or he figured that after he was done playing Babe Ruth with your head, there wouldn't be a recording left. Now. Are you done examining him, Doctor?"

"I am," she said. "He'll live. And thank you, by the way."

"You're welcome," I said. I held out a hand. "Chris Shane," I said.

"I know who you are," she said, taking it.

"I get that a lot," I said.

The doctor shook her head. "It's not that," she said. "I'm Tayla Givens. I'm your new housemate."

Tayla and I had just finished up our statements to the arresting officers when I noticed someone walking up on us. It was Detective Trinh.

"Detective Trinh," I said, to her. "This is unexpected."

"Agent Shane," she said. "You've had an exciting evening."

"Just wrapping up," I said.

"You planning to make a federal case out of this one, too?"

"Not really," I said. "The Haden in this case lives in D.C. So this is going to be handled by Metro."

"That's probably wise," Trinh said.

"Are you planning to be involved?" I asked. "We're in the first police district right now. I was under the impression you worked out of the second."

"I work out of the second," Trinh said. "I live here. I was having a drink at Henry's when the report came in over the radio.

Thought I'd come over and see how you were doing."

"I'm fine now," I said.

"And maybe to have a chat with you."

"All right," I said.

"Privately," Trinh said, nodding to Tayla.

I looked over to Tayla. "You want me to get them to take you home?"

"We're less than a hundred yards from where we live," Tayla said. "I think I can make it on my own."

"All right," I said.

"See you there soon," she said, and headed home.

"You live with her?" Trinh asked, as Tayla walked off.

"New housemate," I said. "This is actually the first time I've met her."

"Interesting way to meet your new housemate," Trinh said. "She's lucky you were around. We've been having a spike of Haden bashings today."

"Why is that?" I asked.

"The walkout and the stunt with the trucks on the loop, but I'm sure you knew that," Trinh said. "When you spend days making it difficult for other people to do their thing, they get pissy about it. And because so many of you are flooding into town for the march, there are lots of targets of opportunity, as it were. It's open season on threeps. We had five attacks in the second district today."

"And how do you feel about it?" I asked.

"I'll be happy when the march is over and I can get back to busting college kids for peeing on the sidewalk."

"Huh," I said. "What can I help you with, Detective Trinh?"

"I was curious about what you think of your new partner," Trinh said.

"We get along so far," I said.

"You heard about her last partner."

"What about her?"

"Did Vann tell you what happened with her?"

"I understand there was a mishap with a firearm," I said.

"That's one way of putting it," Trinh said. "There are other interpretations."

"Like what?"

"Like Vann's partner decided putting a bullet in her gut was a better option than dealing with Vann anymore."

"Seems drastic," I said.

"Desperate times," Trinh said. "Desperate measures."

"I don't know anything about that," I said.

"No, I guess you wouldn't," Trinh said.

"You also know Vann used to be an Integrator."

"I'd heard that," I said.

"Ever wonder why she quit?"

"I've known her for two days," I said. "One of which I mostly spent in the mountain time zone. So we haven't had time to exchange life stories."

"Pretty sure she knows yours," Trinh said.

"Everyone knows mine," I said. "It's not a big trick."

"Let me catch you up on hers, then," Trinh said. "She left because she couldn't hack it. The government spent all that money making her an Integrator and she ended up being phobic about people using her body. You might want to get her to tell you about her last couple of integration sessions. The rumors about them are pretty dramatic."

"I wouldn't know about that either," I said.

"It explains all the self-medicating," Trinh said. "Unless you've missed the smoking and drinking and barhopping, looking for people to bang."

"I've noticed it," I said.

"She's not hugely picky on that score."

"Really," I said. "Does that explain you, then?"

Trinh smiled at me. "I never fucked Vann, if that's what you're asking. I'm not entirely sure about her and her old partner, though. I don't suppose it will be an issue with you."

"Do you have a problem with Hadens, Trinh?" I asked. "Because you don't just punt in a crack like that last one right out of the blue."

"I don't think you understood me," Trinh said. "I think it's a *good* thing she won't have an opportunity to fuck with you that way. But I won't be surprised if she finds another way to do it."

"Right," I said. "Look, Trinh. It's late and I've had a really long day. So if you could get to the point of this little conversation, I'd appreciate it. I mean, aside from you taking a dump all over my new partner."

"The point is that you should be thinking about your partner, Agent Shane," Trinh said. "She's smart but not as smart as she thinks she is. She's good, but not as good as she thinks she is, either. She talks a good game about what other people should be doing but when it comes to her own shit, she gets sloppy. Maybe you've noticed that already and maybe you haven't. But speaking as a voice of some experience on that matter, if you haven't noticed it yet, it's something you'll notice soon."

"So she's a ticking time bomb ready to explode, and I don't want to be anywhere near her when she goes off," I said. "Straight from the cliché checklist. Got it."

Trinh held her hands in a way that expressed bored equanimity. "Maybe I'm wrong, Shane," she said. "Maybe I'm just an asshole who had a bad experience with her when I had to deal with her. And maybe the two of you will get along just fine and you won't feel like putting a bullet into your gut, or whatever. In which case, great. I hope the two of you are happy together. But then, maybe I'm not wrong. In which case, watch your partner, Shane."

"I'll do that," I said.

"There's some weird shit going on with Hadens," Trinh said. "That thing at the Watergate. And I know you're involved with whatever's happening with Loudoun Pharma. If the two of you are working on something big, then the last thing you're going to need is her falling apart. When she goes down you don't want her to take you with her."

"More clichés," I said.

Trinh nodded. "It's a cliché. Fine. On the other hand, you're one of the most famous Hadens out there, aren't you. Or used to be, anyway. Still famous enough that people

189

called you a scab for showing up to work the other day. How will it look when you fuck up because of Vann, Shane? How will it look for your dad, the next senator from Virginia?"

I didn't have anything to say to that.

"Just a little something for you to think about," Trinh said. "Take it however you want. Have a good night, Shane. Hopefully you don't have to save anyone else before you get home." She walked off.

There was a welcoming committee of threeps waiting for me when I got to the town house. They tossed confetti at me when I walked through the door.

"Whoa," I said, fending off the tiny bits of paper.

"We wanted to make you feel at home on your first night," Tony said.

"I don't usually have confetti thrown at me when I come home," I said.

"Maybe you should," Tony said.

"Why do you have confetti anyway?" I asked.

"Left over from New Year's," he said. "Never mind that now. We also wanted to thank you for stepping in with Tayla's little problem out there. She told us about it when she came home."

"It's not the usual way to meet your new housemate," Tayla said.

"Let's not make it a regular thing," I said.

"I would be okay with that," Tayla said.

"And these are your other new flatmates," Tony said, pointing at the two remaining threeps. "That's Sam over there —"

"Hey," Sam said, raising a hand.

"Hello," I said.

"— and this is the twins, Justin and Justine," Tony said, pointing to the remaining threep. I was about to ask for clarification when a text popped into my field of vision, from Tony. *Go with it, I'll explain later,* it said.

"Hello," I said, to the twins' threep.

"Hello," at least one of the twins said back.

"Can we do anything for you to make you comfortable?" Tony asked. "I know you've had a fun-filled couple of days."

"Actually, all I want to do right now is get some sleep," I said. "I know that's not very exciting, but it's been a really long day."

"Not a problem," Tony said. "Your room is like you saw it the last time you were here. The desk chair has an induction pad in it. It should work for you until you get something better in there."

"Perfect," I said. "In that case, good night, everyone."

"Wait," said the twins, and then handed

me a balloon. "We forgot to throw this at you when you came in."

"Thanks," I said, taking it.

"We blew it up ourselves," the twins said.

I thought about the implications of that statement. "How?" I finally asked.

"Don't ask," they said.

CHAPTER TWELVE

And of course I couldn't sleep. After three hours of trying I finally gave up and went to my cave.

For a Haden, personal space is a touchy subject. In the physical world there has always been a debate on how much space a Haden actually needs. Our bodies don't move and most of them are in specialized medical cradles of greater or lesser complexity. A Haden needs space for their cradle and the medical equipment that attaches to it, and strictly speaking that's all we need.

Likewise, for our threeps, space shouldn't be an issue. Threeps are machines, and machines shouldn't need personal space. A car doesn't care how many other cars are in the garage. It just needs space to get in and get out. Put both of those together, and when people first started designing spaces for Hadens and their threeps, they were all like the efficiency apartments LaTasha

Robinson showed me: small, clinical, no-nonsense.

Then people started noticing that Hadens had developed a spike of major depression, independent of the usual causes. The reason was obvious if anyone took any time to think about it. Haden bodies might be limited to their cradles, and threeps might be machines, but when a Haden was driving a threep, they were still a human being — and most human beings aren't happy feeling like they live in a closet. Maybe Hadens don't need as much physical space as naturally mobile people, but they still need *some.* Which is why those efficiency apartments were the Haden residence of last resort.

In the nonphysical world (not the *virtual* world, because for a Haden the nonphysical world is as real as the physical one) there is the Agora, the great global meeting place of the Hadens. Dodgers — the people who aren't Hadens — tend to think of it as something like a three-dimensional social network, a massively multiplayer online game in which there are no quests, other than simply standing around, talking to each other. One reason they think this is because the public areas open to Dodgers (and yes, we call them Dodger Stadiums) work very much like that.

Explaining how the Agora works to some-one who is not a Haden is like explaining the color green to someone who is color-blind. They get a sense of it, but have no way to appreciate the richness and complex-ity of it because their brains literally don't work that way. There's no way to describe our great meeting places, our debates and games, or how we are intimate with each other, sexually or otherwise, that doesn't sound strange or even off-putting. It's the ultimate in "you have to be there."

For all of that, in the Agora proper, there is no substantial sense of privacy. You can close off the Agora for periods of time, or temporarily create structures and rooms for exclusivity — people are still people, with their cliques and groups. But the Agora by design was built to create a community for people who were always and inevitably isolated in their heads. It was built open on purpose, and in the two decades since its creation it had evolved into something with no direct analogue to the physical world. It's an openness that leaks into how Hadens deal with each other in the physical world as well. They leave their IDs visible, have common channels, and swap information in a way that would strike Dodgers as promis-cuous and possibly insane.

Not all Hadens, mind you. Hadens who were older when they contracted the disease were tied more deeply into the physical world, where they had already spent almost all of their lives. So after contracting the disease, they lived mostly in their threeps and used the Agora — to the extent they used it at all — as a glorified e-mail system.

The flip side of this were the Hadens who contracted the disease young and were less attached to the physical world, preferring the Agora and its system of living to forcing their consciousness into a threep and clanking through the physical world. Most Hadens existed between the two spaces, both in the Agora and in the physical world, depending on circumstance.

But at the end of the day, neither the physical world nor the Agora could provide what most Hadens really needed: a place where they could be alone. Not *isolated* — not the lock in that Haden's syndrome forced on them — but by *themselves,* in a place of their own choosing, to relax and to think calmly. A liminal space between worlds, for themselves and the select few that they chose to let in.

What that liminal space is depends on who you are, and also the computing infra-structure you have to support it. It can be as simple as a house from a template, stored on a shared server — free "tract housing" supported by ads that presented themselves in picture frames, which computationally collapsed once the Haden went out the door — to immense, persistent worlds that grew and evolved while the very rich Hadens who were the worlds' owners resided in floating palaces that hovered over their creations.

My liminal space was something in between those two. It was a cave, large and dark, with a ceiling from which glow worms hung, imitating a nighttime sky. It was, in fact, a re-creation of the Waitomo Caves in New Zealand, if the caves were about ten times larger and had no traces of being a tourist attraction.

In this cave, cantilevered out over a dark, rushing subterranean river, was a platform on which I would stand, or sit in the single, simple chair I put there.

I almost never let people into my cave. One of the few times I did was when I was dating another Haden in college, who looked around, exclaimed, "It's the Batcave!" and started to laugh. The relationship, already a bit rocky, blew up not long after that.

These days I think the comment was more on point than I would like to admit. Up to that point I had spent a lot of my time being a public person whose movements were followed no matter where I was. My own space was dark and silent, a place where I could be an alter ego — one who could methodically hack away at homework, or muse on whatever notions of mine were posing as deep thoughts at the time.

Or in this particular case, attempt to fight crime.

Over the last two days, too much had been happening to allow me to spin out all the connections among events, to process the data and maybe get something useful out of it. Now was the time. I was up and awake anyway.

I started pulling images out of memory and throwing them up into the darkness. First, the image of Johnny Sani, dead on the carpet of the Watergate Hotel. This image was followed by the image of Nicholas Bell, hands up, on the hotel room bed. Samuel Schwartz and Lucas Hubbard followed, represented here not by threeps or Integrators but by file photos of their approved media icons — images based on their physical body's facial features but altered in such a way to give them the appearance of mobility and vitality. The icons were artificial, but I couldn't fault them for it. They weren't the only Hadens with approved media icons. I had one. Or used to, in any event.

Next up, Karl Baer, from an image taken from his Loudoun Pharma ID, and Jay Kearney, from his Integrator license. I paused for a moment to access the Integrator database, to find the woman Schwartz had integrated with the night before.

Her name was Brenda Rees. Up went her image.

After a moment of consideration, up went images of Jim Buchold and my father, the latter mostly for my own internal sense of navigation. Finally I put up a placeholder image for Cassandra Bell, who had no approved media icon.

Now to add connections. Sani connected to Nicholas Bell. Nicholas Bell to Hubbard, Schwartz, and his sister, Cassandra. Hubbard to Schwartz and to my father. Schwartz connected to Hubbard, my father, Brenda Rees, and Jay Kearney. Kearney to Schwartz and Baer. Baer to Kearney and Buchold. Buchold back to Dad. It was a cozy little sewing circle.

Background now. Off of Sani I placed his last money order to his grandmother, paused for a moment to access the FBI server to make a request to search the serial and routing numbers to get its location of origin. That done, I popped up the Window Rock Computing Facility, and drew a line off of it for Medichord, and connected that back to Lucas Hubbard.

From Buchold I connected a line to Loudoun Pharma. I did a search on the news stories of the day about the bombing. Baer's confessional video had been first leaked and then officially released, so intense speculation was now falling on Cassandra Bell for being either explicitly or implicitly connected to the bombing. I put a line from her to Loudoun Pharma.

Off of Cassandra Bell I ran a search of stories on the Haden work stoppage and the upcoming march on the Mall. Trinh hadn't been lying — in the last day there were twenty attacks on Hadens in Washington, D.C., alone. Most of those came in the form of attacks on threeps. There were some bashings like the one I had broken up, but also a couple where people took manual control of their cars and ran them into threeps. One person pushed a threep into the path of a bus, damaging both the threep and the bus.

I wondered what the thinking was there. "Killing" a threep didn't do anything but wreck the hardware, which was replaceable, while the person attacking the threep was still on the hook for physically assaulting a person. Then I recalled Danny Lynch to memory and remembered that logical thinking was not the strong suit in many of these encounters.

In at least a couple of these attacks, it was the Haden who ended up on the winning side of the encounter, which had its own set of problems. Videos of android-like machines thumping on human bodies called up something atavistic in the dumber, usually male, usually young, quarters of humankind. I didn't envy the Metro police the next several days.

A ping from the FBI server. The money order had come from the post office in Duarte, California. I popped up an encyclopedia article on the city and learned that its civic motto was "City of Health," which seemed pretty random until I saw that it was the home of the City of Hope National Medical Center. The City of Hope helped develop synthetic insulin, and was deemed a "Comprehensive Cancer Center" by the National Cancer Institute. Also, and more relevant for my purposes, it was one of the top five medical institutions in the country for Haden's syndrome research and treatment.

If Johnny Sani was going to get a neural

network installed, that would have been a good place for it.

But then, if he had gotten a neural network installed there, he would have popped up in our databases.

I went back to Cassandra Bell and opened up a search on her, plucking out an encyclopedia biography and recent news articles not attached to Loudoun Pharma.

Cassandra Bell was one of the very few Hadens who had never not been locked in. Her mother contracted Haden's while she was pregnant with Cassandra and passed it on to her in the womb.

Normally that would have been fatal. In the large majority of cases where a pregnant woman contracted Haden's, the virus slipped past the placental barrier like it wasn't there and ravaged the unborn child.

Only about 5 percent of the unborn who contracted Haden's survived to birth. Almost all of them were locked in. Half of those who survived childbirth died before the first year, due to the virus suppressing the infant's immunological system, or other complications brought on by the disease. Nearly all those who survived after that experienced severe issues brought on by the damage the virus did to the early brain development of the child, and by the isolation Haden's created, stunting their early emotional and social development.

That Cassandra Bell was alive, intelligent, and sane qualified her as some sort of minor miracle.

But to call her "normal" might have been stretching. She had been raised almost entirely inside the Agora, first by her mother, who ended up being locked in. When she died from unrelated factors when Cassandra was ten, the girl's upbringing was shepherded by Haden foster parents and her older brother, Nicholas, who had been infected at the same time as his mother and who developed his Integrator abilities then.

In her way, Cassandra was as famous as I had been, another public curiosity among the Hadens. Far from being intellectually stunted, Cassandra showed remarkable mental acuity, passing a high school equivalency test at age ten and then rejecting admission to MIT and CalTech because they would have required her to use a threep, which she refused to do.

Instead she became an activist for Haden separatism, arguing that Hadens should let go of the limitations of the physical world, imposed on them by use of threeps, and embrace and extend the metaphor of living that the Agora afforded. She didn't suggest

Hadens not interact with Dodgers — just interact with them on their own terms, rather than on the Dodgers'.

One's receptiveness to Cassandra Bell's arguments correlated significantly to how much time one spent in the physical world versus the Agora. But the number of Hadens willing to listen to her had increased significantly once Abrams-Kettering picked up traction and was then signed into law. It was she who suggested and instigated the walkout. It was also rumored that she was finally going to breach the physical world to speak at the march on the Mall this upcoming weekend.

Basically, at the tender age of twenty, Cassandra Bell was compared to Gandhi and Martin Luther King by her admirers, and to various terrorists and cult leaders by her detractors.

Baer's and Kearney's actions at Loudoun Pharma would not be helping her image at the moment, and people were already beginning to thump on Hadens, including her, for the walkout. I scrolled through her recent comments and proclamations to see what she had to say about the bombing.

On that, she was, for the moment, silent. This was not helping her in the media. Still, possibly better to be silent than to say something stupid.

On reflection, it seemed strange that I had never met Cassandra Bell. We were two of the most notable young Hadens in existence. But then the majority of her notoriety began to accrue around the same time I was trying to step away from the limelight and to have something like a private life.

Also, be honest, I said to myself. *You're the establishment. She's the radical.*

And that was true enough. Through my father and his activities, I was in the physical world more than most young Hadens. Cassandra Bell, on the other hand, was never in it, other than by reputation.

I set aside Cassandra Bell for a moment and went back to Jay Kearney, who had blown himself up on Karl Baer's behalf. A scroll through his client list confirmed, as Vann had said, that Baer was indeed a client of Kearney's, with three appointments in twenty-one months. The last of these was eleven months ago. According to Kearney's appointment notes, they went parasailing.

But aside from brief notes on the nature of their appointments, there was nothing apparently connecting the two that I could see. Three appointments in two years was evidence of a prior relationship, but it wasn't much of a relationship.

The FBI had gotten warrants for every scrap of Baer's and Kearney's lives the instant it was clear they had done the bombing. I reached into that data trove to pull out messages and payment records. I wanted to see how much cross talk there was between them, either in personal correspondence or in a financial trail of crumbs that suggested that the two of them interacted in any significant way.

There was very little. The messages clustered around integration appointments and discussed things like potential activities, how much Kearney would charge for his time, and other pedestrian affairs. Likewise, their financial records coincided at integration appointments only, when Baer would pay Kearney for the appointment.

This lack of a trail didn't mean that the two of them didn't meet or plan the bombing. It only suggested that if they did, they weren't idiots about it. But it didn't seem a lot to go on.

I stopped and looked up, and stepped back from the wall of images and searches I had constructed, looking for the structure in it, and in the connections. I imagine to a lot of people it would look like complete chaos, a mess of pictures and scraps of news.

I found it calming. Here was everything I

knew so far. It was all connected in one way or another. I could see the connections out here in a way I couldn't see them when they were jumbled in my brain.

Next steps, I heard Vann say in my head. I smiled at it.

One. There were two nexuses of interaction that I saw. One was Lucas Hubbard, to whom Nicholas Bell, Sam Schwartz, and my father connected, and with whom Jim Buchold argued on a matter related to their mutual business.

The other was Cassandra Bell, to whom Nicolas Bell, Baer, and Kearney were connected, whom Buchold was antagonistic toward, and Hubbard, possibly, based on his argument with Buchold, was sympathetic toward.

So: Dive into both, particularly Cassandra Bell. She was the only person in all of this whom I had not physically met. Arrange an interview if at all possible.

Two. Baer and Kearney: Still unconvinced about the connection here. Dig deeper.

Three. Johnny Sani. Find out what he was doing in Duarte and if anyone knew him there. Learn if there was a connection between him and the City of Hope.

Four. Two outliers in this tangle: My dad and Brenda Rees. I was pretty certain my dad was *not* up to no good, running for senator notwithstanding. In any event I had a massive conflict of interest if I wanted to investigate him.

As for Brenda Rees, might as well get an interview with her and see if she had anything useful to say.

Five. Nicholas Bell. Who said he was working when he met with Sani, but also appeared to have been there to integrate with Sani, even though it was impossible, because they were both Integrators and because the headset was fake.

So what the hell was really going on in there?

And why did Johnny Sani commit suicide?

Those were the two things that taking all these data points out of my brain and spreading them out into space didn't make any clearer.

CHAPTER THIRTEEN

A light ping echoed through my cave. I recognized the tone as a noninvasive hail, a call that would be delivered if the recipient was conscious, but not if not. Hadens, like anyone else, hated to be woken up by random calls in the middle of the night. I pulled up a window to see who it was. It was Tony.

I cleared the call, audio only. "You're up late," I said.

"Deadline on a gig," Tony replied. "I had a hunch you might have been lying when you said you wanted to sleep."

"I wasn't lying," I said. "I just couldn't sleep."

"What are you doing instead?"

"Trying to figure out a whole bunch of shit that unfortunately I can't tell you much about. And you?"

"At the moment, compiling code. Which I *can* tell you about but which I don't imagine you care about," Tony said.

"Nonsense," I said. "I am endlessly fascinated."

"I'll take that as a challenge," Tony said, and then the data panel popped up a button. "That's a door code. Come on over."

Tony was offering me an invite to his liminal space, or at very least a public area of it.

I hesitated for a second. Most Hadens were protective of their personal spaces. Tony was offering me an intimacy of sorts. I hadn't known him that long.

But then I decided I was overthinking it and touched the button. It expanded into a doorframe and I stepped through.

Tony's workspace looked like a high-walled retro video game cube, all black space with the walls defined by neon blue lines, off of which branched geometric patterns.

"Don't tell me, let me guess," I said. "You're a *Tron* fan."

"Got it in one," Tony said. He was at a standing desk, above which a neon-lined keyboard hovered. Beside that was a floating screen with code, with a toolbar slowly pulsing, marking the amount of time until Tony's code compiled. Above him, rotating slowly, was a swirl of lines, apparently haphazardly connected.

I recognized them immediately.

"A neural network," I said.

"Also got that in one," Tony said. His self-image was, like most people's, a version of his physical self, fitter, more toned, and stylishly clothed. "If you really want to impress me, you'll tell me the make and model."

"I haven't the slightest idea," I admitted.

"Amateur," Tony said, lightly. "It's a Santa Ana Systems DaVinci, Model Seven. It's their latest-released iteration. I'm coding a software patch to it."

"Should I be seeing any of this?" I asked, pointing at the code in the display. "I would guess this is all supposed to be confidential."

"It is," Tony said. "But you don't look like much of a coder to me — no offense — and I'm willing to guess that the DaVinci up there looks mostly like artfully arranged spaghetti to you."

"That it does."

"Then we're fine," Tony said. "And anyway it's not like you can record anything in here." Which was true. In personal liminal spaces, visitor recording was turned off by default.

I looked up at the model of the neural network hovering over Tony's head. "It's strange, isn't it?" I said.

"Neural networks in general, or the Da-

Vinci Seven in particular?" Tony asked. "Because confidentially speaking the D7s are a pain in the ass. Their architecture is kind of screwy."

"I meant in general," I said, and looked up again. "The fact we've got one of these sitting in our skulls."

"Not just in our skulls," Tony said. "In our brains. Actually *in* them, sampling neural activity a couple thousand times a second. Once they're in, you can't get them out. Your brain ends up adapting to them, you know. If you tried to remove it, you'd end up crippling yourself. More than we already are."

"That's a cheerful thought."

"If you want really cheerful thoughts, you should worry about the software," Tony said. "It governs how the networks run, and it's all really just one kludge after another." He pointed at his code. "The last software update Santa Ana put out accidentally caused the gallbladder to get overstimulated in about a half a percent of the operators."

"How does that happen?"

"Unexpected interference between the D7 and the brain's neural signals," Tony said. "Which happens more often than it should. They run all the software through brain simulators before they upload it into customers, but real brains are unique, and Haden brains are even more so because of how the disease messes with the structure. So there's always something unexpected going on. This patch should fix the problem before it causes gallstones. Or at least if gallstones happen, they won't be traced back to the neural network."

"Wonderful," I said. "You're making me glad it's not a Santa Ana network in my head."

"Well, to be fair, it's not just Santa Ana," Tony said. He nodded at me. "What do you have in there?"

"It's a Raytheon," I said.

"Wow," Tony said. "Old school. They got out of the neural network business a decade ago."

"I didn't need to hear that," I said.

Tony waved it off. "Their maintenance is handled by Hubbard," he said.

"Excuse me?" I said. I was momentarily shocked.

"Hubbard Technologies," Tony said. "Lucas Hubbard's first company, before he formed Accelerant. Hubbard doesn't build networks — another Accelerant company does that — but Hubbard makes a lot of money off of maintaining the systems of companies who left the field after the first gold rush. He did a lot of the early coding and patching himself, if you believe his corporate PR."

"Okay," I said. The sudden intrusion of Hubbard into my head, literally as well as figuratively, had thrown me off.

"I've done work for Hubbard, too," Tony said. "Just a couple of months ago, as a matter of fact. Trust me, they have their issues."

"Do I want to know?" I asked.

"Suffered any colon spasms recently?"

"Uh," I said. "No."

"Then nothing you need to worry about."

"Lovely."

"I've worked with them all," Tony said. "All the networks. The biggest issue isn't neural interference, actually. It's basic security."

"Like people hacking into the neural networks," I said.

"Yeah."

"I've never heard of that happening."

"There's a reason for that," Tony said. "First, the architecture of the neural networks is designed to be complex to make them hard to program on, and hard to access from outside. The D7 being a pain in the ass to deal with is a feature, not a bug. Every other network since the first iteration is designed that way too.

"Second, they hire people like me to make sure it doesn't happen. Half my contracts are for white-hat incursions, trying to get into the networks."

"And what do you do when you get in?" I asked.

"Me? I file a report," Tony said. "With the first iteration of networks the hackers would run blackmail schemes. Fire up a series of gory pictures or put 'It's a Small World' on a repeating loop until the victim paid to make it stop."

"That sucks," I said.

Tony shrugged. "They were dumb," he said. "Honestly. A computer inside your brain? What the hell did they *think* was going to happen with that? They got serious about patching when some hacker from Ukraine started giving people arrhythmia just for kicks. That shit's actual attempted first-degree murder."

"I'm glad they fixed that," I said.

"Well, for now," Tony said. His code had compiled and he waved his hand to execute it. From above, the network pulsed. It wasn't just a pretty image. It was an actual simulation of the network.

"What do you mean 'for now'?" I asked.

"Think about it, Chris," Tony said. He pointed at my head. "You've got what's effectively a legacy system in your head. Its upkeep is currently being paid for out of the budget of the National Institutes of Health. When Abrams-Kettering goes into effect next Monday, the NIH will stop paying for upkeep once its current batch of contracts expires. Santa Ana and Hubbard aren't updating and patching out of the goodness of their corporate hearts, you know. They get paid to do it. When that stops, either someone else is going to have to pay for it, or the updates stop coming."

"And then we're all screwed," I said.

"*Some* people will be screwed," Tony said. "I'll be fine because this shit is my job and I can hack my own network. You'll be fine because you can afford to hire someone like me to maintain your network. Our roommates will be fine because I like them and don't want them to have spam piped into their brains against their will. And the middle-class Hadens will probably be able to pay for a monthly subscription of updates, which is something I know Santa Ana, at least, is already planning for.

"Poor Hadens, on the other hand, are kind of fucked. They'll either get no updates, which will leave them vulnerable to software rot or hacking, or they'll have to deal with some sort of update model that features, I don't know, ads. So every morning, before they can do anything else with their day, they'll have to sit through six goddamn advertisements for new threeps or nutritional powder or bags for their crap."

"So, spam," I said.

"It's not spam if you agree to it," Tony said. "They just won't have much of a choice."

"Swell."

"It's not just updates," Tony said. "Think about the Agora. Most of us think of it as a magical free-floating space somewhere out there." He gestured with his hands. "In fact it's run out of an NIH server farm outside of Gaithersburg."

"But it's not on the chopping block," I said. "There'd be a panic if it was."

"It's not being cut, no," Tony said. "But I know the NIH is talking to potential buyers." He pointed up at the neural network. "Santa Ana's putting in a bid, Accelerant's making one, GM's in, and so is just about every Silicon Valley holding company."

He shrugged. "Whoever eventually buys the farm will probably have to promise to leave the character of the Agora unchanged for a decade or so, but we'll see how much that'll be worth. It's going to be monthly access fees from there for sure. I don't know how you'd do billboards in the Agora, but I'm pretty sure they'll figure it out sooner than later."

"You've thought about this a lot," I said, after a minute.

Tony smiled, looked away, and made a dismissive wave. "Sorry. It's a hobbyhorse of mine, I know. I'm not this humorless about most things."

"It's fine," I said. "And it's fine that you're thinking about it."

"Well, there's also the side effect that once all these government contracts go kerplooey, my line of work is going to get tougher," Tony said. "So this is not me being socially active out of the goodness of my own heart. I like to eat. Well, be fed nutritionally balanced liquids, anyway. The Hadens who are walking out this week are making the point that our world is about to be wildly disrupted, and the rest of America doesn't really seem to give a shit."

"You're not part of the walkout, though," I said.

"I'm inconsistent," Tony said. "Or maybe I'm a coward. Or just someone who wants to bank as much money as he can now because he expects things to dry up. I see the wisdom of the walkout. I don't see it as something I can do right now."

"What about the march on the Mall?" I asked.

"Oh, I'll definitely be going to that," Tony said, and grinned. "I think we'll all be going. Are you planning on it?"

"I'm pretty sure I'll be working it," I said.

"Right," Tony said. "I guess this is a busy week for you."

"Just a little."

"Got thrown into the deep end, it looks like," Tony said, looking back to his code. "You picked a hell of a week to start your gig."

I smiled at that and looked up again at the pulsing neural network, thinking. "Hey, Tony," I said.

"Yes?"

"You said a hacker gave people heart attacks."

"Well, arrhythmia, actually, but close enough for government work," Tony said. "Why?"

"Is it possible for a hacker to implant suicidal thoughts?" I asked.

Tony frowned at this for a minute, considering. "Are we talking general feelings of depression, leading to suicidal thoughts, or specific thoughts, like 'Today I should eat a bullet'?"

"Either," I said. "Both."

"You could probably cause depression through a neural network, yeah," Tony said. "That's a matter of manipulating brain chemistry, which is something networks do already" — he pointed up at his network simulator — "although usually accidentally. The patch I'm doing now is designed to stop just that sort of chemistry manipulation."

"What about specific thoughts?"

"Probably not," Tony said. "If we're talking about thoughts that feel like they're originating from a person's own brain. Generating images and noises that come from the outside is trivial — we're both doing it right now. This room is a mutually agreed-upon illusion. But directly manipulating consciousness so that you make someone think they're thinking a thought you give them — and then making them act on it — is difficult."

"Difficult or impossible?" I asked.

"I never say 'impossible,' " Tony said. "But when I say 'difficult' here I mean that as far as I've heard no one's ever done it. And I don't know how to do it, even if I wanted to, which I wouldn't."

"Because it's unethical," I prompted.

"Hell *yes*," Tony said. "And also because I know if I've figured it out, someone else has too, because there's always someone else smarter out there, who may not have ethics. And that would really mess with shit. It's hard enough to believe in free will as it is."

"So," I said. "Really difficult but not actually impossible."

"Really really really difficult," Tony allowed. "But theoretically possible because, hey, it's a quantum physics universe. Why do you ask, Chris? I sense this is not an entirely idle question."

"What's your work schedule look like?" I asked.

Tony nodded upward. "It looks like my patch is doing what it's supposed to. Once I clean it up a bit, which should take less than an hour, I'll send it off and then I'm free."

"Have you ever done work for the federal government?"

"I live in Washington, D.C., Chris," Tony said. "Of course I've done work for the government. I have a vendor ID and everything."

"Do you have a security clearance?"

"I've done confidential work before, yes," Tony said. "Whether on the level you seem to be thinking about is something I guess we'd have to find out."

"I may have a job for you, then," I said.

"Involving neural networks?"

"Yes," I said. "Hardware and software."

"When would you want me to start?"

"Probably tomorrow," I said. "Probably, like, nine A.M."

Tony smiled. "Well, then," he said. "I should probably finish up what I'm doing so I can at least attempt to get some sleep."

"Thanks," I said.

"No," Tony said. "Thank you. It's not every day that a new housemate comes bearing work. That makes you officially my favorite housemate."

"I won't tell," I said.

"No, go ahead and tell," Tony said. "Maybe it will inspire a competition. That'll work out for me. I could use the work."

CHAPTER FOURTEEN

"Don't tell Trinh I said this to you," Captain Davidson said, pointing to the five Hadens he had in his holding cell, "but I would be *delighted* if the FBI took these idiots off our hands."

The five Hadens, or more accurately their threeps, glared at me, Vann, and Davidson from the other side of the holding cell. We could tell they were glaring because their threep models came with customized heads that displayed faces and expressions. The faces these threeps carried were not their owners' actual faces, unless their owners were the spitting images of George Washington, Thomas Jefferson, Patrick Henry, Thomas Paine, and Alexander Hamilton. The threeps were also wearing colonial-era uniforms, which may or may not have been historically accurate. It was like an elementary school diorama of the Continental Congress come to life.

The threeps were just threeps, of course. The Hadens driving them were somewhere else in the country. But when you're a Haden and you're arrested in your threep, if you disconnect, that's considered resisting arrest and fleeing the scene. This fact was courtesy of a young, rich Haden who in the early years of threeps carelessly knocked down an old lady, disconnected from her threep in a panic, and then spent three years and a couple hundred thousand dollars of Mommy's money trying to get out of what would have been a standard-issue moving violation. She eventually also ended up adding perjury and bribery to her docket. She should have just done the community service.

Thus our colonials, cooling their heels and glaring through their pixels.

"What you in for, George?" I asked Washington. Davidson had called us in to deal with several different Hadens in his holding cells. This was the first bunch.

"For exercising our constitutional Second Amendment rights," Washington said. His real name was Wade Swope, from Milltown, Montana. His information was popped up in my view. "Here in the dictatorship of the District of Columbia, a man is apparently stripped of his right to bear arms."

Vann turned to Davidson. "Shocked, shocked I am to find men with guns somehow landing in jail."

"Yes, well," Davidson said. "Our founding father here is correct that he has the right to bear arms, which in this case were long rifles for each of them. The part he's skipping over is where his little group of colonial fighters went into a coffee shop — private property — and started to make a scene, and when they were told to take a hike, commenced to wave their rifles around. We have it on the store video, not to mention the phone of every single person in the store."

"We're here to be the security detail for the march," said Thomas Jefferson, aka Gary Height, of Arlington, Virginia. "We're a militia, consistent with the Constitution. We're here to defend our people."

"You might be a militia," I said. "But I don't think waving your firearms around in a coffee shop accurately describes 'well-regulated.'"

"Who cares what you think?" said Patrick Henry, aka Albert Box of Ukiah, California. "You're standing with them. Those who oppress us." He pointed to me. "*You* are a traitor and a sellout."

It occurred to me that Henry/Box actually

had no idea who I was, although I don't know if that would have changed his opinion any. I glanced over at Vann and Davidson. "Oppressing *us,* as in we Hadens, or oppressing *you,* dudes waving around firearms in a coffee shop?" I asked. "I want to be clear on the depth of my traitorness."

"You know what confuses me, Shane," Davidson said, before any of them could answer.

"Tell me," I said.

Davidson motioned at the colonial Hadens. "On one hand these guys seem like your basic crazy conservative types, with the Second Amendment and their Yankee Doodle hats. But on the other hand they're saying they're security for a march protesting reductions in government benefits. Which seems pretty *liberal* to me."

"It's a puzzler," I agreed.

"I don't know," Davidson said. "Maybe it's not about politics. Maybe these guys are just assholes."

"Seems the simplest explanation," I said.

"We have a right to assemble —" Washington/Swope began, clearly winding himself up.

"Oh, Jesus, don't," Vann said. "It's too early in the fucking A.M. for your brand of pathetic patriotic bullshit."

Washington/Swope clammed up, surprised.

"Better," Vann said, and leaned in toward the lot. "Now. Your threeps are here, but each of your physical bodies are in a different state. That makes you the FBI's problem. Which means you are *my* problem. And *I* say five jackasses dressed up like the back of a two-dollar bill, claiming to be a militia and waving around rifles in a goddamn Georgetown coffee shop violates Title Eighteen of the U.S. Criminal Code, chapters twenty-six, forty-three, and one hundred two."

I quickly pulled up the relevant chapters of Title Eighteen and noted that chapter 43 was for "False Personation." I didn't suspect that anyone would confuse Swope with the real George Washington. I also knew to stay quiet.

"So, here's the deal," Vann continued. "You have two options. The first is I decide not to make a federal case of it, and you idiots walk your threeps over to the precinct storage room, where you power them down and then we yank out the batteries. You'll have three days to arrange to have your threeps and your precious rifles shipped back to you, or we'll assume you're donating them to the Metro police.

"The second option is I *do* make a federal case out of it. In which case we confiscate your threeps and rifles, and a law enforcement official comes to all of your houses to wheel you off to the nearest Haden-capable federal detention center, which is probably not actually anywhere close to you. Then you get the joy of spending all the money every single member of your entire family will *ever* earn on lawyers, because in addition to those three chapters of Title Eighteen I covered with you, I'm going to throw every other single thing I can think of into the indictment."

"That's bullshit," said Thomas Paine, aka Norm Montgomery of York, Pennsylvania.

"Maybe it is and maybe it isn't," Vann said. "But whatever it is, I will *absolutely fucking bury you* in it. And I will *enjoy* it, because you chose to waste my time making me deal with you. So, decision time. Door number one or door number two. Choose wisely. And if you don't choose in ten seconds, we're going with door number two. Choose."

Seven seconds later our founding fathers chose door number one and Davidson was yelling for an escort to walk them down, one at a time, to evidence and storage.

Then we moved on to the next Haden in

the pen, this one in for punching some woman who had called her a "clank."

"Welcome to the next four days," Vann said to me as we exited the second district headquarters. "We've got a bunch of incarcerated threeps in the first, third, and sixth district to get at, too. Then when we're done with those we can come back here to the second and start all over. And then over and over again until the march is done and all the Hadens go home. You should probably tell your caregiver to put you on a caffeine drip."

"What about Johnny Sani and Loudoun Pharma?" I asked.

"Terrorism's got Loudoun Pharma," Vann said. "We're only on the edges of that one. Sani's in our morgue and not going anywhere. Both of them can probably wait until Monday. Unless you think you've got something."

"I think I have something," I said. "Maybe."

"Maybe?" Vann said. "We don't have time for 'maybe' at the moment. We've got a whole line of threeps that we have to decide what to do with."

"I want someone to look at Sani's neural network."

229

"We've already got our forensics people looking at it."

"I want someone looking at it who knows their way around one," I said. "Someone who works on them every day."

"You have someone in mind?" Vann asked.

"My new housemate," I said.

Vann reached into her jacket pocket for her e-cigarette. "You're getting an early start on your cronyism," she said.

"It's not that," I said, annoyed. "Johnny Sani had an IQ of eighty. He had no business having an Integrator's neural network in his head. Someone installed it in him and someone used him, and then when they were done with him, they made him slit his own throat somehow. I think there's something going on in the software of that network."

"Something that forced him to slit his own throat?" Vann said.

"Maybe," I said.

"There's that 'maybe' again," Vann said. She sucked on her cigarette.

"Tony does neural network software all the time," I said. "And he contracts with the companies who make them to test their security and troubleshoot issues. He would know what to look for. Or at the very least, he would be able to see if something was wildly off."

"And 'Tony' in this case is your new housemate."

"Yes," I said. "He's done confidential work for the government before. Has a vendor ID and everything."

"Is he expensive?" Vann asked.

"Does it matter?" I asked.

"Of course it matters," Vann said, and it was her turn to look annoyed with me. "One of us is going to have to make the case for any expenditures we make outside ourselves. And if they don't like it, they're going to yell at me to yell at you."

"I think it's going to be worth it," I said.

Vann took another suck on her cigarette. Then: "Fine, let's get him in. I'll tell them it's related to the Loudoun Pharma thing if they bitch about it."

"And they'll buy that," I said.

"Maybe," Vann said.

"Because I really do think there's something going on there," I said. I recounted to Vann my brainstorming session of the night before.

"Do you do that a lot?" Vann asked, after I finished. "That tossing things into space and drawing lines between them thing."

"When I can't sleep? Yes."

"You need to find some other evening

activities," Vann said.

"I'm not even going to touch that one," I said.

Vann smiled wryly at that, took one more suck on her cigarette, and then started to put it away. "Well, I don't want to take a run at Lucas Hubbard if we don't have anything to take a run at him with. If we come after him I want him off guard. We can ask after Cassandra Bell, but I guarantee you the terrorism people already have a microscope shoved up her colon after the Loudoun Pharma thing, so she may not want to speak to us, and terrorism might not want us stepping on their dicks even if she does. What was the name of that woman Integrator that Schwartz was using?"

"Brenda Rees."

"I'll knock on her door today," Vann said. "See if anything shakes loose there."

"Am I not going with you?" I asked.

"No," Vann said. "Since you seem to think all this is on some sort of timetable, you need to go out to California to follow up on that money order and then head over to that City of Hope place to see if anything comes of that. That should keep you busy."

"What about Tony?" I asked.

"Give me his information and I'll get him set up and over to the morgue today," Vann said. "If he's a flake, I'm going to take it out on you."

"He's not a flake, I promise."

"He better not be. I'd hate to have to kill him and frame you for it."

"That reminds me," I said.

"Me threatening to kill someone reminds you of something?" Vann asked, surprised. "We haven't known each other that long, Shane."

"I had a run-in with Detective Trinh last night," I said.

"Really."

"Yeah. Among other things, she implied that you drove your former partner to attempt suicide."

"Huh," Vann said. "What else did she tell you?"

"That you have high work standards for other people but not yourself, that you're sloppy, a little bit dangerous when it comes to procedure, and that you have various addictions that are either the result of, or the contributing factor to you, washing out of the Integrator corps."

"Did she tell you I set puppies on fire, too?" Vann asked.

"She did not," I said. "It may have been implied."

"What do you think?"

"I don't think you set puppies on fire," I said.

Vann smiled at that. "I mean the things Trinh actually said."

"This is my third day with you," I said. "You ride me hard — which I don't mind, by the way — but then you do stuff like you did in there, where you let a bunch of assholes with firearms slip away rather than charge them with assault. If they did lawyer up, the fact you threatened them with 'false personage' wouldn't have helped your case any."

"You caught that," Vann said.

"I did," I said. "So maybe that qualifies as sloppy. I do notice that you smoke a lot, and when we talk after six P.M. you always seem to be in a bar, looking for someone to screw. As far as I can see it doesn't affect your work, and your free time is your own. So I don't actually care, aside from thinking that basting your lungs with insect poison is a bad idea in general."

"Do you think it has to do with my time as an Integrator?"

"I haven't the slightest idea," I said. "I don't get the feeling you're in a rush to tell me about those days, which tells me something really fucked up probably happened way back when. But either you'll tell me when you want to, or you won't. The same with whatever the hell is going on between you and Trinh, because clearly she's got a bug up her ass about you."

"That's an interesting way to put it," Vann said.

"Here's the only thing Trinh said that I worry about," I said. "She thinks you're going to fall apart on me, and that when you fall apart, you're going to end up taking me with you."

"And what do you think about that?"

"Ask me after the march is done," I said. "Maybe I'll have an answer for you then."

Vann smiled again.

"Look, Vann," I said. "If you promise me that you're not going to fall apart on me, I'm going to believe you. But don't promise me that if you're not going to be able to follow through. If you can't promise, that's fine. But it's something I want to know up front."

Vann paused for a moment, looking at me. "Tell you what," Vann said, finally. "When this weekend is done you and I will sit down somewhere, and I'll have a beer and you'll do whatever, and I'll tell you why I stopped being an Integrator, and why my last partner shot herself in the gut, and why that asshole Trinh has it in for me."

"Can't wait," I said.

"In the meantime: I'm not going to fall apart on you, Shane. I promise."

"I believe you," I said.

"Well, good," Vann said, and took out her phone to look at the time. "That's settled, then. Now come on. We have two more district houses to hit."

"I thought I was going to California," I said.

"No one's going to be around until nine A.M. out there," Vann said. "That's still a couple hours away. Let's see if we can punt a bunch more troublemakers back home before then. One of the threeps in the first district holding cell is there on a drunk and disorderly. I want to hear how *that* happened."

CHAPTER FIFTEEN

I looked around and I was in an evidence room in the FBI offices in Los Angeles. An FBI agent was looking at me. "Agent Shane?" she asked.

"That's me," I said, and started to get up. Which is when I encountered a small problem. "I can't move," I said, after a minute.

"Yeah, about that," the agent said. "Our actual spare threep is being used by one of our local agents. Her regular one is in for some maintenance. The only threep we had available for you was this one. It's been in storage for a while."

"How long is a while?" I asked. I found the diagnostic settings and started running them.

"I think maybe four years," the agent said. "Maybe five? Could be five."

"You're letting me use a threep that's evidence for a crime?" I asked. "Isn't that, I

don't know, tainting the chain of possession?"

"Oh, that case is over," the agent said.
"The owner of that threep died in our
detention center."

"How did that happen?"

"He got shivved."

"Someone shivved a Haden?" I said.
"That's pretty cold."

"He was a bad man," said the agent.

"Look, uh —" I realized I had not gotten
the agent's name.

"Agent Isabel Ibanez," she said.

"Look, Agent Ibanez," I said. "I don't
want to appear ungrateful, but I just ran a
diagnostic on this threep, and its legs don't
work at all. There appears to be significant
damage to them."

"It's probably because the threep got hit
with a shotgun blast," Ibanez said.

"A shotgun blast," I repeated.

"During a firefight with FBI agents, yes,"
Ibanez said.

"The owner *really* must have been a bad
man."

"Pretty much, yes."

"You understand that having a threep that
can't move its legs is going to be a hindrance
to the work I need to do today," I said.

Ibanez stepped to the side and then motioned to the wheelchair she had previously been standing in front of.

"A wheelchair," I said.

"Yes," Ibanez said.

"A threep in a wheelchair."

"Yes," Ibanez repeated.

"You understand the irony, right?"

"This office is ADA compliant," Ibanez said. "And as I understand it you are going to a post office, which are also required by law to be ADA compliant. This should be sufficient."

"You're actually serious about this," I said.

"It's what we have available at the moment," Ibanez said. "We could rent you a threep, but that would require approvals and paperwork. You'd be here all day."

"Right," I said. "Would you excuse me a moment, Agent Ibanez?" I disconnected from the wounded threep before she had a chance to say anything else.

Twenty minutes later I stepped out of an Avis office in Pasadena with a shiny new maroon Kamen Zephyr threep I had rented out of my own pocket, got into the equally maroon Ford I had also rented, and headed toward the Duarte post office. Take that, paperwork.

The Duarte post office was an unassuming box of beige bricks, with arches at the

239

windows to give it a vaguely Spanish air. I went in, stood in line politely while three separate old ladies got stamps and mailed packages, and when I got to the front of the line displayed my badge on my threep's chest monitor to the postal clerk and asked to see the postmaster.

A small, older man came to the front. "I'm Roberto Juarez," he said. "I'm the postmaster here."

"Hi," I said. "Agent Chris Shane."

"That's funny," Juarez said. "You have the same name as that famous kid."

"Huh," I said. "I suppose I do."

"Was one of you, too," he said. "A Haden, I mean."

"I remember that."

"Must be annoying for you sometimes," Juarez said.

"It can be," I said. "Mr. Juarez, about a week ago a man came into your post office to get a money order. I was hoping to talk to you about him."

"Well, we get a lot of people asking for money orders," Juarez said. "We have a lot of immigrants in the area, and they send remittances back home. Was this an international or domestic money order?"

"Domestic," I said.

"Well, that will narrow it down a little,"

Juarez said. "We do less of those. Do you have a picture?"

"Do you have a tablet I could borrow for a second?" I asked. I could display the picture on my chest screen but it turns out people feel uncomfortable staring into your chest. The postal clerk, whose name tag listed her as Maria Willis, gave me hers to use. I signed in and accessed the picture of Sani — cleaned up, eyes closed — and showed it to them. "It's not the best picture," I said.

Juarez looked at the picture blankly. Willis, on the other hand, put her hand up to her mouth in surprise.

"Oh my God," she said. "That's Ollie Green."

"Ollie Green?" I repeated the name. "As in Oliver Green, and like the color."

Willis nodded and looked at the picture again. "He's dead, isn't he," she asked.

"Yes," I said. "Sorry. You knew him?"

"He would come in every week or so to get a money order, an envelope, and a stamp," Willis said. "He was nice. You could tell he was a little *slow*" — she looked at me to see if I understood the implication — "but a nice man. Would make small talk if you let him and there wasn't a line."

"What would he talk about?" I asked.

"The usual things," Willis said. "The weather. Whatever movie or TV show he'd seen recently. Sometimes he'd talk about the squirrels he saw on the walk here. He really enjoyed them. He once said he'd like to get a little dog who could chase them. I told him that if he did that, the squirrel and the dog would end up getting run over."

"He lived nearby, then," I said. "If he was walking over to the post office."

"I think he said he lived at the Bradbury Park apartments," Willis said. "Bradbury Park, Bradbury Villa. Something like that."

I immediately did a search and found Bradbury Park Apartment Homes about half a mile away. Next stop, then. "Did he ever talk about his work?" I asked.

"Not really," Willis said. "He mentioned it once but then said what he was doing was confidential, so he couldn't talk about it. I didn't think about it much at the time. I thought he was trying to make a joke."

"Okay."

"I don't think he liked his job, though," Willis said.

"What makes you think that?" I asked.

"The last few times he was in he didn't seem really happy," Willis said. "He was quiet, which was unusual for him. So I asked him if everything was all right. He said the job was getting him down. He didn't say anything else other than that."

"All right," I said.

"And now he's dead," Willis said. "Did that have to do with his job?"

"I couldn't really say at this point," I said. "We're still looking at things."

Juarez cleared his throat. I looked behind me and saw two new little old ladies, waiting. I nodded to him in acknowledgment.

"Looks like I need to wrap up," I said. "Anything else about Oliver Green that sticks out in your memory?"

"He asked about a post office box one of the last times he was here," Willis said. "Wanted to know how much one was and what he'd need to get one. I told him the price and that he'd need two forms of ID. He seemed to lose interest after that. I told him he'd probably be better off with a security deposit box anyway."

"Why?"

"Because he said he had something he wanted to put somewhere safe."

"Oliver Green," said Rachel Stern, the Bradbury Park Apartments manager. "Nice man. Rents a one-bedroom ground floor, near the orchard and laundry room. Well, he doesn't rent it directly. His company does."

I looked up at that. "His company."

"Yes," Stern said. "Filament Digital."

"I don't know that I've heard of it," I said.

"They do something with computers and medical services, I think?" Stern said. "I'm not really sure. I know they do a lot of work with City of Hope, which is why they rent the apartment from us. So the people they have working there will have a place to stay."

"So Mr. Green isn't its first tenant," I said.

"No, there have been a few before him," Stern said. "Most of them have been fine. One a couple of tenants back we had to tell to keep quiet after ten P.M. He liked to play his music loudly."

"But not Green."

"No," Stern said. "Model tenant. Traveled a lot, especially recently. Hardly knew he was there." She looked puzzled for a moment. "Is Mr. Green in trouble with the FBI for something?"

"Not exactly," I said. "He's dead."

"Oh my God," Stern said. "How?"

"Ms. Stern, would it be okay if I looked at Green's apartment?" I asked, changing the subject.

"Sure," Stern said. "I mean, if he was alive I suppose you would need a warrant, but now that he's dead . . ." She trailed off for a moment, apparently trying to decide how to proceed. Then she nodded to herself and turned to me. "Of course, Agent Shane. Come with me." She motioned me out of the door of her office.

"This is a nice complex," I said to her as we walked, mostly to make chitchat, and to keep her from thinking about whether she really should ask for a warrant.

"It's all right," she said. "We have nicer complexes elsewhere. This one is in the middle of our portfolio. But Duarte's a nice little town, I have to say. Agent Shane, do you mind if I ask you a question?"

"Go right ahead," I said.

"Are you related in any way to Sienna Shane?"

"I don't think so," I said. "Is she somebody famous?"

"What? Oh, no," Stern said. "I went to high school with her in Glendora, and when I went back to our ten-year reunion she said a cousin of hers got Haden's. I thought maybe it might be you."

"Nope," I said. "I'm not even from here. I was born in Virginia."

"Why did you ask me if she was famous?"

"When people ask you if you know some-one, they're often someone famous," I said.

"That's all."

"I can't think of anyone famous named Shane," Stern said, and then pointed at an apartment. "Here we are."

I looked up and then grabbed her arm. "Hold up a second," I said.

"What is it?" Stern asked.

I pointed at the apartment's patio. Most of it was hidden by a privacy wall, but the top of the sliding glass patio door was visible. It was open, just a crack.

"Does Green have roommates?" I asked, quietly.

"Not on the lease," Stern said.

"Was the patio door like that before?"

"I don't think it was," Stern said.

I reached for my stunner to flick the clasp on my holster and then realized I was wearing a rental threep. "Shit," I said, looking down at where my stunner wasn't.

"What is it?" Stern said.

"You have your phone on you?"

"Yes."

"Stay here," I said, and then pointed to the apartment door. "If I don't come out of that door in exactly one minute, call the police. Then get back to your office and stay there. Got it?"

Stern looked at me like I had just turned into an octopus or something. I left her, went to the patio wall, and heaved myself over it, landing as quietly as possible on the bare patio. I crouchwalked over to the patio door, turned on my recording mode, slid the door open enough to slip through, and entered the apartment. I stood up.

A matte-black threep was there, standing in the dining nook, twenty feet away, an envelope in its hand.

We both stared at each other for a good five seconds. Then I closed the patio door behind me and locked it. I turned back to the threep.

"FBI," I said. "Freeze."

The other threep bolted for the front door.

I went after it, leaping over a couch to do it, and collided with the threep about three feet short of the entrance, ramming it into the wall. The drywall cracked but held.

The threep tried to hit me in the head but had no leverage. I grabbed it and heaved it, sending it stumbling back between the living room and dining nook. The envelope it had in its hand fell to the ground.

"You're under arrest for breaking and entering," I said, walking toward the threep in an arc to keep it from thinking about trying for the patio door. "You're also under arrest for assaulting a federal officer. Give up now. Don't make this more awkward than it already is."

The threep feinted toward the door and then headed into the kitchen, which was dumb, because it was walled in on three sides. I came around to the open side. The threep looked around, saw a set of knives in a butcher-block holder, grabbed one, and held it at me.

I looked at it and then looked at the threep. "Are you *kidding* me?" I said. My threep's body was carbon fiber and graphene. A knife was gonna do dick to it.

The threep flung the knife at me, and I flinched involuntarily. It pinged off my head and back onto the kitchen floor. When I came back up, the threep had pulled a large pot out of the pile of dirty dishes in the sink and aimed it directly for my head. There was a gonging sound as it connected, twisting my head aside and caving in a portion of it.

It was then I realized that my rental threep's pain receptors were dialed up really high. Some part of my brain recognized this made sense, since the rental place wanted to keep its customers from doing anything stupid with the threep, and dialing up the sensation of pain would certainly do that.

The rest of my brain was going *ow jesus fuck ow ow.*

The threep raised its arm back for another swing and brought it down again. I made a fist and punched the pot as it came down and then shoved myself into the threep, driving my elbow into the threep's neck as I did so.

That's what I wanted to do, anyway. What I ended up doing was a lot less kung fu and a lot more drunken scuffle. But on the other hand I managed to push the threep backward and make it stumble. Which was the point.

On the stove was a skillet with the remains of some scrambled eggs in it. I grabbed it and looked back at the threep, who was back up, pot in hand.

"Come on," I said. "Are we really going to do this?"

The other threep spun the handle of the pot in its hand, waiting.

"Look," I said. "The police have already been called. They're on their way. You might as well —"

The threep went high with its pot and swung down heavy. I backed up and stepped to the side, avoiding the pot. The threep's arms came down, leaving its head exposed. I smacked my skillet into it like I was a tennis player returning a volley. The threep fell back flat on its ass.

I took advantage and kicked it in the side as it tried to scramble back up, sliding it farther back and to the right, into the kitchen. Its right arm, the one holding the pot, was splayed out. I drove my legs into it, immobilizing it, pushed the body into the stove, driving the other arm under the threep body. I raised my skillet.

The threep looked at it, and then at me.

"Yeah, I know, a goddamn skillet," I said.

Then I drove it into the threep's neck, edgewise, seven or eight times, until the carbon fiber casing cracked. Then I reached over and picked up the knife from the floor and slid it under the cracked casing, until I could feel the tip resting against the bundle of control fibers that went from the threep's processor to its body systems.

"See, *this* is how you use a knife in a threep fight," I said, and then hammered the knife on its handle with the skillet.

The knife severed the bundle fibers. The threep stopped fighting me.

I wedged the knife in and cracked open the neck a little more, looking in until I could see the cord that carried power from the battery back to the processor in the head. I reached into the neck and wrapped a finger around it. Then I looked at the threep.

"I know you're still there and I know you can hear me," I said. "And I know this threep can still talk. So why don't we do this the easy way." I looked around at the mess. "Well, the *easier* way, anyway. Tell me who you are and why you were here. I have your threep. I have its onboard memory. I'm going to find out all of it sooner or later."

The threep said nothing. But whoever had been controlling it was still there, still looking at me.

"Have it your way," I said, and yanked at the power cord, feeling it rip away at one of its terminals. The threep was now officially dead.

I stood up and looked around the apartment. It looked like a couple of idiots had trashed the place. I went to the door and opened it and saw Rachel Stern, on the phone, gawking at me.

"I heard noises," she said. "I called the police."

"Excellent idea," I said. "Call the FBI's L.A. office while you're at it. Tell them I need an entire crime scene team and whoever they've got handling technology forensics. Tell them the sooner they're here, the better."

"Are you okay?" Stern asked, looking at my threep's head.

"Well, let me put it this way," I said. "I don't think I'm getting the deposit back on this threep." I turned away from her and wandered back into the apartment.

On the floor was the envelope the threep had dropped.

I picked it up. It was a plain white envelope on which the words "For grandma and Janis" had been written in very large, not-terribly-adult writing. The envelope was sealed. I debated for a moment and then opened it. On the inside was a data card.

"Hello," I said.

A call pinged into my field of view. It was Klah Redhouse.

"Agent Shane," I said.

"So, uh, Chris, this is Officer Redhouse," Redhouse said.

"I know," I said.

"You know that thing you're investigating."

"I do," I said.

"Well, I have some people here who want to talk to you about it."

"Important people, I would guess."

"That would be a good guess," Redhouse said.

"They wouldn't happen to be at your desk with you at the moment, would they?" I asked.

"Actually, yeah," Redhouse said. "How could you tell?"

"The nervous stammer, mostly," I said.

There was a little laugh on the other end. "You got me," he said. "Anyway, these people were hoping they might get to talk to you today."

I held up the data card to get a closer look at it. "I think that can be arranged," I said. "I have people there I want to talk to, too."

Chapter Sixteen

"Tell me you have video of your fight," Vann said to me, when I got back into the office.

"I'm fine," I said, coming around to her desk. "Thanks for asking."

"I didn't ask because I knew you were fine," Vann said. "You were in a threep. The worst that could happen is you get a dent."

"That's not the worst that could happen," I said. My last moments in the Los Angeles area consisted of handing my insurance information over to a very annoyed manager at the Pasadena Avis, so they'd deal with the threep I had brought back with a cracked and dented head.

"You survived," Vann said.

"The other threep got it worse," I allowed.

"And do we know who the other threep was yet?" Vann asked.

"No," I said. "The L.A. forensics team is looking at it now. But when I was looking at it I didn't find any make or model information on it."

"Which is weird," Vann said.

"It's *very* weird," I said. "Every commercial threep carries that information by law, along with a vehicle identification number." I raised my arm to show where my threep's number was etched, just below the armpit. "There was none of that."

"Theories?" Vann asked.

"One, it's a prototype model," I said. "Something that's not on the market yet. Two, it's a market model with aftermarket modifications, including stripping off make and model numbers and the VIN. Three, it's a ninja."

"Ninja threep," Vann said. "That's funny."

"It wasn't so funny when it was trying to bash my head in with a pot," I said. "The L.A. team said they will let me know when they find something. I told them to pay special attention to the processor and memory. They looked at me like I was an asshole."

"No one likes to be told how to do their job, Shane," Vann said.

"I'm not hugely impressed with the L.A. office, I have to tell you," I said. "But maybe their trying to put me in a threep in a wheelchair set me off a bit." A fleeting memory of a very annoyed call from Agent

Ibanez, who waited ten minutes for me to return before figuring out I was gone for good, surfaced in my memory. I won the argument when I pointed out that if I had showed up at the Bradbury Park Apartments in a wheelchair, our mystery threep would be long gone, and with important evidence.

Which reminded me about the evidence. "I need to go back to Arizona this afternoon," I said.

"Random shift in conversation, but okay," Vann said.

"It's not random," I said. "Johnny Sani left a data card for his sister and grandmother. It's what the ninja threep was there for. It's got data on it but it's password protected."

"Whatever password Johnny Sani is going to think up is not going to be that difficult to figure out," Vann said.

"Probably not, but it will still be easier to ask his family first," I said. "Pretty sure it was meant for them. I made a copy of data. I need to take the copy to them and see if they know what to do with it."

"Are you going to ask them if they know why Johnny was living under an assumed name, too?"

"I will, but I don't expect they're going to

know," I said, and thought about it a bit. "What's weird is that Oliver Green doesn't seem to have any ID, either."

"What do you mean?" Vann asked.

"When I was talking to the lady at the post office, she said that Sani wanted to rent a P.O. box, but when she said he'd need two forms of identification, he lost interest," I said. "And the apartment wasn't rented by him, it was rented by Filament Digital. He didn't need any ID there, either."

"What is Filament Digital?"

"It's a component manufacturer for neural networks," I said. "It's a Chinese company. I called and no one answered. It's the middle of the night over there right now."

"They don't have a U.S. office?" Vann asked.

"As far as I can tell that apartment *was* the U.S. office," I said. "I have the L.A. office looking into that, too."

"The L.A. office must love you right about now," Vann said.

"I don't think I'm their favorite person, no," I said. "What have you been up to?"

"I cleared out some more of the Hadens from Metro's holding pens," Vann said. "Most of them took the 'get the hell out of D.C.' option, but there were a couple who didn't and a couple who really needed to be prosecuted, so they're all now guests of the federal government for the next few days. We'll deal with them after the march. The Metro people tell me things are getting a little tense out there. Oh, and I shook up that Integrator."

"Which one?" I asked. "Brenda Rees?"

"Yeah, her," Vann said. "I called her up and identified myself and said that I would like her to come meet with me to answer a couple of questions. She asked why and I said we were following up on the Loudoun Pharma explosion. Then she asked why I'd want to talk to her about that, and I told her we were just following up on an anonymous tip."

"We didn't get any anonymous tip about her," I said.

"No, but it made her nervous when I said it, which I thought was interesting."

"Anyone would be nervous if you told them you were following up an anonymous tip about a bombing by talking to them," I pointed out.

"What's important is *how* they get nervous," Vann said. "Rees got all quiet and then asked to meet this evening."

"We bringing her here?" I asked.

"I gave her the address of a coffee shop I like in Georgetown," Vann said. "Feels less formal, and will get her to relax and open up."

"So first you make her paranoid and then you want her to feel comfortable," I said. "You don't need me to help you play 'good cop, bad cop.' You can do it all on your own."

"This is the sort of thing your pal Trinh calls 'sloppy,' " Vann said.

"I'm not sure she's wrong," I said.

"If it works she's wrong."

"That's a dangerous philosophy," I said. Vann shrugged.

A call popped up in my field of view. It was Tony. "You didn't tell me I would be working in an *actual* morgue with an *actual* brain when I took this gig," he said, after we got our greetings out of the way.

"I had to be circumspect until you were vetted," I said. "Sorry."

"It's all right," Tony said. "I've just never seen a real live brain before. Also I had to dial back my sense of smell pretty much down to zero."

"Have you found anything?" I asked.

"I've found a lot of things," Tony said. "I think maybe I should talk to you about them. And your partner too, probably."

"Let's meet," I said.

"Not in the morgue," Tony said. "I think I

need to get away from all this meat."

"Okay, here's the first thing," Tony said, and he popped up the image of Johnny Sani's brain, still in its skull, peeking through the veil of tinsel that was the neural net. We were in the imaging lab: me, Vann, Tony, and Ramon Diaz, who seemed amused at Tony taking over his imaging console.

"It's a brain," Vann said. "And?"

"It's not the brain I want you to look at," Tony said. "It's the neural network."

"Okay," Vann said. "What about it?"

"It's totally unique," Tony said.

"I thought every neural network was unique," I said. "They adapt to the brain they're in."

"Right, but every model is the same before it's installed," Tony said. He pointed at my head. "The Raytheon in your head is the same as every other version of that model. Once it's in your head the tendrils and receptors are placed in ways that will be unique to your brain. But it's still the same hardware and the same initial software."

Vann pointed at the network on the screen. "And you're saying this one isn't any of the current commercial models out there."

"I'll go further than that," Tony said. "This

doesn't match any model ever created. All neural networks have to be submitted to the FDA for approval, or to the matching agency in other countries. All submitted designs are pooled into a single database for those agencies to use, and for people like me to use for reference. This design isn't in the database."

"So it's a prototype," Vann said.

"We don't put prototypes into people's brains," Tony said. "Because they're prototypes and they might kill you if they screw up. We model them extensively on computers and animals and specially cultivated brain tissue before they're approved. By definition if it's in someone's brain, it's a final design." He pointed at the network. "This is a final design. But it's not in the database."

"Can we see the network without the blood and gore?" I asked.

Tony nodded. The image of Sani's head was wiped away, replaced by a wire-frame representation of the network. "I didn't have time to pretty up the model," Tony said.

"That's fine, it all looks like spaghetti to me," I said.

"Then why did you want to see it?"

"So I didn't have to look at someone's head all opened up," I said.

"Right," Tony said. "Sorry."

"You said this isn't any version you've seen before," Vann said.

"That's right," Tony said.

"Well, then, does it look *similar* to any you've seen before?" Vann asked. "Every car maker I know of has a 'house look.' The same thing might apply for neural networks."

"I thought of that," Tony said. "And what I see is that whoever made this took a lot of design choices from existing models. The default filament spread looks very much like a Santa Ana model, for example. But then the juncture architecture is pretty much a straight rip-off from Lucturn, which is the Accelerant company I was telling you about this morning, Chris." He looked at me for acknowledgement. I gave it. "And there are lots of other little touches that come from other manufacturers past and present. Which maybe tells us something."

"What is that?" Vann asked.

"I don't think this is meant to be a commercial model network," Tony said. "It's a really *good* neural network. It's really efficient and elegant, and just from the design I'm guessing that the brain-network interface is really clean."

"But," I said.

"*But,* that's because this brain is a lot of best-of-breed architecture from other existing designs, designs which are patented to hell and gone," Tony said. He waved at the image of the network. "If someone tried to put this design on the market, they'd get their asses sued by every other neural network manufacturer out there. This thing would be in litigation for years. There's no possible way this would ever get to market. None. Whatsoever."

"Does it matter if it's a network for an Integrator?" I asked. "It's such a tiny market, relative to the Haden market. You could argue that it doesn't represent a commercial threat."

"Not really," Tony said. "There's no real difference in the architecture of a Haden network and an Integrator network. The major difference is how they array in the brain, because Haden and Integrator brain structures are different, and in the software that runs the network."

"So why make it?" Vann asked. "Why make a network you can't sell?"

"That's a good question," Tony said. "Because the other thing about creating a neural network is that it's not something you're going to do in your spare time at home. The first functional neural network

263

ever made cost a hundred billion dollars to research and develop. The costs have come way down since then, but it's a relative thing. You have to pay for simulations and testing and modeling and manufacturing and everything else." He waved at the network again. "So this will still have set someone back somewhere in the neighborhood of a billion dollars."

"A billion dollars right down the hole," Diaz said.

"Right," Tony said. He seemed a little surprised that Diaz was still there. "And that's the thing. You don't spend a billion dollars on a neural network you can't sell. You especially don't spend a billion dollars *now,* because up to now Haden research costs were heavily subsidized by the government. Abrams-Kettering ends that. The Haden population in the U.S. is less than four and a half million, almost all of whom already have networks in their heads. Even if this architecture were legally viable, it *still* doesn't make sense to spend that much money because the market's already saturated and the number of new Haden's cases that pop up every year in the U.S. won't get you into the black. Even worldwide you'd have a hard time with it."

"It's a boondoggle," I said.

"It really is," Tony said. "As far as I can see, anyway. Maybe I'm missing something."

"Let's look at it from the other side," Vann said.

"What do you mean?" I asked.

"Let's stop asking *why* someone would do this for now," Vann said. "Let's ask *who* could do it. If we have some idea of who could do it then maybe we can come back around to why they would do it. So. Who could do it?"

"Lucas Hubbard could do it," I said. "A billion isn't nothing to him, but he'd have to lose several billion before he would seriously feel it."

"Yeah, but you're describing *every* owner of a Haden-related company, aren't you," Tony said. "We threw a shitload of money at Haden's because the first lady had it. Hell, Chris, that old picture of you with the pope probably kept Haden funding rolling for a year or two. I'm no big fan of Abrams-Kettering, but one thing they weren't wrong about was that Haden's funding's become a long trough a bunch of piggies are feeding from. Hubbard's one. So is Kai Lee, who runs Santa Ana. So are about twenty other people in the C-suites of these companies. Any of them could have funded something like this without it hurting them."

"Yeah, but Hubbard's got a connection to Sani," I said.

"The dead guy," Tony said. I nodded. "What's the connection?"

"Accelerant owns the company that's licensed to provide health care to the Navajo Nation," Vann said. "And Sani's Navajo."

"It's not a really great connection, is it," Tony said, after a moment.

"Working on it," I said.

"Hubbard wouldn't want to toss a billion dollars away at the moment anyway," Tony said. "Accelerant is trying to merge Metro with Sebring-Warner, and might just try to buy it outright. If he does that, a cash payout is going to be part of that deal."

"You're strangely well versed on the business dealings of Accelerant," Vann noted.

"I keep up with all the companies I do work for," Tony said, looking over to her. "It's part of how I know which clients are going to have work for me. And what I know right now is that all the companies in Haden-related industries are getting ready for the crash. They're either merging or buying each other outright, or trying to diversify as fast as they can. Abrams-Kettering's knocked over the trough. It's done."

"So we're saying that even if Hubbard or Lee or anyone else *could* fund something like this, they wouldn't," I said.

"Not right now," Tony said. "That's my guess. I mean, I'm not an FBI agent or anything."

"Who else is there, then?" Vann said, looking at me. It was apparently time for a test again.

I thought about it for a minute. "Well, there's *us,* isn't there," I said.

"The FBI?" Diaz said, incredulously.

"Not the FBI, but the U.S. government," I said. "A billion dollars wouldn't matter to Uncle Sam and it's possible we'd build something we wouldn't commercially exploit, either for pure research or just because it's pork for some congressperson's district."

"So we have this developed in some NIH institute as busy work," Vann said.

"The U.S. government has been known to pay farmers not to plant crops," I said. "No reason that principle couldn't go high tech." I turned to Tony. "Any maybe that's why it's not in the registry, since it was never intended to be commercial."

"That's great," Tony said. "But it still doesn't explain how this" — he gestured at the network — "got into someone's head."

"Working on it," I said again.

"Work harder," Tony suggested.

"What about the software?" I asked.

"I've only glanced at it," Tony said. "I was going to get to that next, but I thought you might not want to wait for a hardware report. From what I can see it's pro-grammed in Chomsky, which makes sense because that's the language designed specifi-cally for neural networks. The software's got substantially fewer lines of code than most Integrator software I've seen. Which means it's either really efficient, or that whoever programmed it only wanted it to do specific things."

"When will you be able to tell us which it is?" Vann asked.

"I should be able to give you a general report this evening," Tony said. "If you want more specifics, you'll need to let me take the code home with me tonight."

"That would be fine," Vann said.

"Uh, I should tell you that when I work in the evening I get time and a half."

"Of course you do," Vann said. "Just as long as you have an early report ready for us by seven."

"Can do," Tony said.

"And you," Vann said, looking at me. "You think you'll be back from Arizona by then?"

"I should be," I said.

"Then fly, Shane. Fly." Vann walked off, reaching into her jacket for her e-cigarette.

CHAPTER SEVENTEEN

In the offices of the Window Rock Police Department is a conference room. In the conference room today was a display, with a password-protected video file waiting to be opened.

I was also in the room. So were May and Janis Sani. Klah Redhouse and his boss, Alex Laughing, sat across from the two women. Standing the back of the room were Gloria Roanhorse, speaker of the Navajo Nation, and Raymond Becenti, its president.

It was the last two who had been making Redhouse jittery when he spoke to me earlier in the day. It's one thing to have your boss breathing down your neck about a case. It's another thing to have the two most powerful people in the Navajo Nation doing the same thing.

I glanced over to Redhouse. He still didn't look entirely thrilled to be in the room.

"I don't know any password," May Sani

was telling Redhouse. "Janis doesn't either. Johnny never told us any passwords."

"We don't think he did," Redhouse said. "We think maybe he wanted to give it to you but then he died before he could do it. But we do know he wanted the two of you to see this. So maybe the password would be something that meant something to you, or something only the two of you would know."

Janis looked over to me. "You couldn't just break the password?" she asked.

"We didn't want to do that," I said. "It would be disrespectful to Johnny, and to the two of you. If you want, we can try. But it might take a long time. I agree with Officer Redhouse here that before we try doing that, you should take a few guesses."

"When people make passwords, they sometimes use the names of family members or pets," Redhouse said, and went over to the keyboard that was wirelessly connected to the display. "For example, 'May.'" He typed in the word. It came up wrong. "Or 'Janis,'" Redhouse said. That one also came up blank. "Any pets?"

"We had a dog when Johnny was a boy," Janis said. "His name was Bentley. Our mom named him." Redhouse tried it. It came up blank. Several combinations of the three names likewise came up uselessly.

"We'll be here all day," Roanhorse whispered to Becenti, who nodded.

"Did Johnny know any Navajo?" I asked. "Did he speak or write the language?"

"A little," Janis said. "We were taught it at school, but he didn't do very well in school."

"He loved the stories about the Code Talkers," May said. "The ones from World War Two. There is that old movie about them that he used to watch when he was a boy."

"*Windtalkers?*" Redhouse asked.

"I think so," May said. "I didn't like watching it. Too much blood. One year for his birthday I got him a Code Talkers dictionary. He would read that a lot."

I pulled up a Navajo Code Talkers dictionary online. It had several hundred words in it, a number of categories, including names of airplanes, ships, military units, and months.

"*Tah Tsosie,*" I said.

Everyone in the room looked at me strangely. "What did you just say?" Redhouse asked me.

"*Tah Tsosie,*" I repeated. "I just looked up the Code Talkers dictionary. The month of May is *Tah Tsosie.* I am aware I'm pronouncing it terribly."

"You really are," Redhouse said, smiling.

"Johnny called me that for a little while after I gave him the book," May said.

"It's worth a shot," I said, to Redhouse. He typed it in.

The file opened.

"May, Janice," President Becenti said. "Do you want to see it alone first?"

"No," May said. She reached over to her granddaughter, who took her hand. "Stay."

Redhouse hit the keyboard again to play the file.

And there was Johnny Sani, alive to me for the first time.

"Hello, Grandma. Hello, Janis," he said, staring into the lens, which he held close to his head so that it obscured most of the background. "I think maybe they can hear what I do on my phone so I went and bought a camera. I'm going to hide this for now, so if something happens to me you'll find it.

"I think there's something wrong with me. I think maybe something they did to me is making me sick.

"You remember I went in to look at a job for a janitor. After I did that I got a call from someone who said he was a recruiter for another job. Said that it would pay really well. He said to go back to the computing

272

facility and that there would be a driverless car waiting for me. All I would have to do is tell it my name and it would take me to my job interview. So I did and the car was there and I told it my name.

"The car drove me to Gallup, to a building where a threep was waiting for me. He said his name was Bob Gray and that the job would be acting as a personal assistant for an important man. I asked them what that meant, and he said it mostly meant running errands and taking him to places he wanted to go. He said I would get to travel and see the world and it would pay well, and all that sounded good to me.

"I asked Bob, why me? And he said it's because I was special in ways I didn't even know about. Then he gave me two thousand dollars in cash and said that was the first week's salary right up front and I could keep it even if I said no. He said the job paid cash so I wouldn't even have to pay taxes on it or nothing.

"Well, I took the job right then. Bob said that the CEO liked his privacy so I shouldn't tell people anything but that I got a job. So I did.

"And then after I said good-bye to you, the car drove me to California. Bob met me and showed me my apartment and said it was mine now. Then he gave me some more money.

"The next day Bob took me to meet my boss, who was named Ted Brown and who was also a threep. He said that as his assistant I would become an Integrator, which is someone who took people places in his head. They would need to put a computer into my brain for that to happen. I was scared at first but they told me it wouldn't hurt and that Ted would only need me to do it every once in a while and the rest of the time I could do what I wanted. But because my job was secret they would have me use a code name, named Oliver Green.

"They took me to a doctor's office and I went to sleep and when I woke up they had cut all my hair off my head and said that they had put a computer into my brain. I had headaches for the next few days. They said it was the computer getting used to my brain. They said it would take a couple of weeks for it to get used to me.

"When that was done Ted and Bob came over and said it was time to try integrating. Ted said that he would come over into my brain and move my body around. I said okay, and then I felt a little sick, and then my arm moved by itself. That scared me but Bob told me to relax and not to worry.

Then Ted walked my body around my apartment for a while.

"After that Ted would use my body a little bit every day. We would go to the store or the library and once he even mailed a money order for you at the post office. And I thought, this isn't so bad, I just had to remember to relax.

"We did this for three months. I asked him when we would travel and he said soon.

"And then it started to happen.

"One day I was watching a show and I blinked and the show was over and another show was on. And I thought I must have fallen asleep and not even known. Then the next day I put a burrito in the microwave and pressed a button to start it and I blinked again and it was dark outside and the burrito was cold. I could tell I cooked it because stuff leaked out of it. But it was done cooking for so long that it got cold again.

"It started to get worse. I would be doing something and then I would be somewhere else, doing something else. I would put on one shirt and then another shirt would be on me. I once went to put on a show that is on TV on Monday and it was Tuesday, and it was morning, not night.

"I didn't tell Ted about it because I was

worried I would get fired if he knew I was sick. But I finally got so scared that I had to tell him. He sent me to the doctor and the doctor said I was fine and that sometimes people who were Integrators had what he said were 'dropouts.' He said they would stop and that when they did I would get my memory back. I tried not to worry but it kept happening.

"Then one day I looked up and I was in a group of men I didn't know and one of them was talking to me and I had no idea what he was saying. Then he said something about killing someone. I don't remember the name. He asked me a question and I didn't know what he was talking about so I stayed quiet and didn't do anything. And then one of them said, 'He lost the connection,' and another one said, 'shit,' and then another one asked if that meant the other guy was in the room. I was pretty sure he meant me. I just stayed quiet and did nothing and then it was the next day. Bob came by to ask me how I was doing. I lied to him and I said I was fine.

"I think I figured it out. I thought I was having dropouts because they put the computer in my head. But I think it's really that Bob and Ted are using the computer in my head to give me dropouts.

"The thing is, the dropouts are getting longer now. The last one I lost three whole days. I don't know if I can do anything about it. I thought about trying to run away but I have a computer in my head now. I know they will find me. And they can make me drop out any time they want. And I think when they drop me out they use me to do bad things. Or they are going to make me do bad things.

"I don't know what to do now. I'm making this so that if you find out that I've done something bad, you'll know it wasn't really me. You know I wouldn't do that. I don't know if I can stop them from using me to do something bad. But I promise you if I can I will.

"All I wanted was a job. I wanted to give you someplace nice to live, Grandma. And you too, Janis. I'm sorry. I love you."

The picture wheeled from Johnny Sani's face, showing the interior of his bedroom in Duarte. Then it went blank.

"Who in goddamned hell does something like that?" Becenti said. It was fair to say he was fuming.

By this time May and Janis Sani had left the conference room, distraught. Captain Laughing had escorted them out, motion-

277

ing to Redhouse that the conversation should continue in his absence. President Becenti did not need any prompting.

"Is that actually even possible?" Redhouse asked me.

"To black someone out and then control their body?" I asked. Redhouse nodded. "I've never heard of it ever happening."

"That's not the same thing as it not being possible," said Speaker Roanhorse.

"No, ma'am, it's not," I said. "But if it was something that was possible, it's surprising that it hasn't been done before. Neural nets are built to be resistant to hijacking," I said, and paused.

"What?" Redhouse asked.

I briefly debated what to tell them, but then thought, screw it, this is the Navajo Nation's leadership. I wasn't blabbing to just anyone. "The neural network in Johnny Sani's head is one of a kind," I said. "It's entirely possible it's fine-tuned for something like this. It would make him a unique case."

"Why him?" Becenti asked. "Why do this to Johnny Sani?"

"Anyone else leaves a trail," I said. "Johnny Sani never left the Navajo Nation. All his medical records are here. He has no outside identification except for his Social Security number, and he's never used that for any-thing. He doesn't appear to have ever had a job that wasn't paid in cash, under the table, including this one. He doesn't have a whole lot of friends, and very few family mem-bers."

"In other words, if you want to use some-one for a medical experiment, he's perfect," Redhouse said.

"That's about right," I said.

Becenti fumed some more. "I knew Johnny Sani," he said, to me.

"Yes, sir," I said. "I had heard that." What I had actually heard, from Klah Redhouse, was that in his earlier days Becenti had car-ried a torch for Johnny and Janis's mother, June. It was never reciprocated, as far as anyone could tell, but that didn't make it any less real to the current Navajo Nation president. Old flames die hard.

Becenti pointed to the display, which had reset to the beginning of the video, with Johnny Sani's head in the frame. "I want you to find out who did this," he said. "And then I want you to snap their head off."

"I will do what I can, Mr. President," I said. I was not entirely sure if protocol called for "Mr. President," but I didn't think it would hurt.

"Anything we can do to help, you let us

know," he said.

"Officer Redhouse has already been an immense help," I said. "I'll let him know if there's anything else I need."

Becenti nodded and left the room.

"When are you going to release the body to the family?" Roanhorse asked, after Becenti had gone.

"Soon," I said, to her. "Our specialist is finishing up his examination of the network in Sani's head. As soon as that's done I think we can release the body."

"I understand you're helping the Sanis get Johnny back here," she said.

I glanced over at Redhouse at this comment. His expression was blank. "Arrangements will be taken care of, yes," I said. "The person helping has asked to remain anonymous to avoid any possibility of spectacle."

"I'm wondering why this anonymous person decided to help," Roanhorse said.

"Because somebody should help, and this somebody could," I said.

"You do understand what 'anonymous' means," I said to Redhouse, after Roanhorse had left the room.

Redhouse pointed after her. "That's the speaker of the Navajo Nation and also a good friend of my mom," he said. "You try to keep a secret from her."

"Don't let it get back to the Sanis," I said.

"It won't," Redhouse said. "And now you better give me something to do to help you, because you put a target on my head with the president."

"I was trying to make you look good!" I protested.

"I appreciate the gesture," Redhouse said. "But you're not the one he's going to be calling, asking for updates."

"There *is* something you can do for me," I said. "Go through the Nation's medical records. See if there's anyone else like Johnny Sani. Someone who got sick with Haden's, got meningitis, but then recovered."

"What do I do when I find them?"

"Tell them not to take any jobs from strangers, for one," I said.

Redhouse smiled at that and departed. I called Tony.

"Trying to get a report ready," he said, as soon as he connected.

"I won't try to stop you," I said. "But I do want you to check something specific for me."

"Can I charge extra?" Tony asked.

"As far as I'm concerned, sure."

"Then tell me what it is."

"Check the code for anything that could knock out the Integrator," I said.

"Like, make them unconscious?"

"Yes," I said. "The Integrator unconscious but the body still functional."

"Can't be done," Tony said. "Integrators aren't just passive receptacles for their clients. They need to be aware to assist."

"I believe you," I said. "Check anyway."

"And I suppose you want this for the seven o'clock."

"That would be nice," I said.

"I'm charging you holiday rates," Tony said.

"Works for me," I said. "Get to it."

"Already gone," he said, and disconnected.

I looked up and saw Johnny Sani looking at me. I looked back him, silently.

CHAPTER EIGHTEEN

"All right, you are not going to believe *this* shit," Tony said, walking up to our standing table at Alexander's Café, in Cady's Alley, Georgetown. Vann had designated it as her place to interrogate Brenda Rees in a relaxed atmosphere. We were at a standing table because cafés disliked threeps hogging chairs, a small piece of technological bigotry that I didn't really give a crap about one way or another.

"Who are you?" Vann asked the other threep, walking up with Tony.

"Tayla Givens," she said, before I could answer for her. "Tony and Chris's roommate. Tony told me we were stopping here on the way to a movie."

Vann looked at me to see if I cared if Tayla heard what we were about to talk about. I gave her a small body movement that effectively communicated the thought *meh*. Vann turned back to Tayla. "This is a confidential discussion, so don't talk about it."

"If you want I can turn off my hearing," Tayla said. "I do it often enough around Tony anyway."

"Hey now," Tony said.

Vann smiled. "It's fine. Just don't repeat anything."

"Tony's technically a patient of mine," Tayla said. "I'll file it under physician's confidentiality."

Vann turned back to Tony. "What shit are we not going to believe?"

"Chris, you asked me to look for code in the software that knocks the Integrator unconscious," Tony said.

"Yeah," I said. "And you found it?"

"No," Tony said. "I told you that you needed the Integrator to be conscious to assist their client, and that still stands. What the software actually does — or can do — is *much* weirder. It robs the Integrator of their free will. And then it wipes their memory."

"Explain this," Vann said. She was suddenly very attentive.

"Integrators stay conscious for two reasons," Tony said. "One, it's their body and they have to have veto control over any dumbass thing a client wants to do, like pick a fight or jump out of a plane without a parachute. Two, because integration isn't totally clean, right? The neural network transmits the client's desires to the Integrator's brain. The brain picks it up and moves the body and makes it do what the client wants. But sometimes the signal isn't strong enough and the Integrator needs to step in and make it happen."

"The Integrator has to read intent and assist," Vann said. I suddenly realized that Tony didn't know Vann had history as an Integrator.

"Exactly," Tony said. "So knocking out an Integrator isn't just morally wrong, it also defeats the purpose of integrating in the first place, which is giving the client the illusion of a functioning human body. A body with a knocked-out Integrator is going to have a hard time walking, or doing anything with anything approaching standard dexterity."

"But someone found a way around this," Vann said.

"I think so."

"How."

"The code I'm looking at plays with the Integrator's proprioceptive sense," Tony said. "It gives the Integrator the sense they can't perceive their own body."

"It paralyzes them," Tayla said. She had clearly not turned off her hearing.

"No," Tony said. "See, that's the sneaky part. You don't want to paralyze the Integrator, because then the client can't use the body. What you want to do is rob the Integrator of *any sense of their body* while at the same time leaving the body receptive to input. The Integrator has lost control of the body, but the body is ready to be used."

"The Integrator experiences lock in," I said.

"Exactly," Tony said. "They go Haden. But unlike us" — Tony motioned to the three of us, excluding Vann — "the body is good to go."

"But if the Integrator is locked in, then the body *isn't* good to go," I said. "You said it yourself. They need to be there to assist."

"That's the other sneaky part," Tony said. "In addition to locking in the Integrator, the code fools the brain into thinking the signal from the client is also the signal from the Integrator. So when the client says 'Raise the arm,' what the body hears is both the client and the Integrator saying it. And it raises the arm. Or moves the leg. Or chews the food."

"Or jumps out of the airplane without a parachute," Vann said.

"Or that," Tony agreed.

"You said it also wipes out the memory,"

Vann said.

"Yeah," Tony said. "Although maybe it's not accurate to say it wipes it out. What it does is inhibit the Integrator brain from forming long-term memories of what the client is doing. Everything exists in short-term memory only. As soon as the client disengages, everything the client was doing with the Integrator body is flushed from the brain."

"It feels like lost time," I said.

"But not for the client," Vann said.

"Probably not," Tony said. "Assuming the client's brain is working normally, memories will be recorded normally as well."

"So the client can do whatever they want and the Integrator won't remember it," Tayla said.

"Right," Tony said. "But here's the *really* fucked-up thing. The Integrator won't remember any of it — but while it's happening? The Integrator *feels* it. The code isn't suppressing the Integrator consciousness. It doesn't have to because it's cut off proprioception and is dumping the consciousness into the short-term memory buffer. Writing code to suppress Integrator consciousness would just be a waste of time. So for every second the client has the Integrator locked in —"

"The Integrator feels like she's drowning," Vann said.

"Yeah," Tony said. "Or that feeling you get when you're dreaming and you can't move. Or, well, being a Haden."

"How does this relate to the hardware?" Vann asked.

"It relates very well," Tony said. "The hardware is optimized to the software, not the other way around. The network has a dense concentration of filaments accessing the dorsal spinocerebellar tract, for example. That's the part of the brain that handles conscious proprioception. Once you know the software, the hardware design makes perfect sense. This is a purpose-built network."

"Designed to take over someone's brain," Vann said.

"Pretty much," Tony said.

At the end of the alley I saw a familiar face. "I think I see Brenda Rees," I said. I waved until she saw me. She smiled, waved back, and started walking toward us.

"And we have to get going if we want to catch our movie," Tayla said, to Tony.

"Last question," Vann said. "Any way this software can work on a network that's *not* this one?"

"You mean on a different Integrator,"

Tony said.

"That's right," Vann said.

"Long answer or short answer?" Tony said. Tayla groaned.

"Short answer."

"Seems unlikely," Tony said.

Brenda Rees reached into her handbag, pulled out a gun, and aimed it at Vann.

I yelled "Gun!" and pulled Vann down at the same time, covering her body with my threep. One bullet cracked my back panel and another pinged off my arm. I felt an excruciating pain with both and immediately turned off my pain perception. The patio of Alexander's erupted in screams and panic. I grabbed my stunner and wheeled up to return fire. Rees was taking off down the alley with the panicked crowd.

"Oh, *fuck,*" Vann said. I looked down to see her bleeding from the shoulder. Tayla was already there, applying pressure.

Vann looked up at me. "The fuck you doing, Shane?" she said. "Get her."

"Tayla," I said.

"I got this," she said, not looking up from Vann's shoulder.

I ran after Rees.

Rees had run left onto Thirty-third Street. As I got onto Thirty-third I saw her go left again onto M. There was the sound of another gunshot, followed by screams. I turned the corner and was nearly knocked over by people running. I went into the street to avoid them and saw Rees halfway down the block, scanning for me.

I didn't have a shot. There were still too many people around. I ran straight to her instead.

She saw me when I was about twenty feet from her, managed to raise her gun and take a shot at me. It either missed or nicked me in a way that I didn't feel at the time. I barreled into her and knocked her into a wall, taking a chunk of her leg out as it jammed into a fire hose coupling. Her gun flew away.

My momentum smashed me into the wall a fraction of a second later. I let go of Rees. She scrambled away, limping out into the street, reaching for something else in her handbag. I trained my stunner on her and prepared to fire.

And then held fire when she turned and I saw the grenade in her hand, pin pulled.

"You've *got* to be fucking kidding me," I said.

Rees smiled, limped farther out into the street, and released the lever.

Then her face changed.

She looked confused for a second, and then saw what she had in her hands.

She screamed, dropped the grenade, and turned to run away from it. I ducked my head in against the wall and waited for the detonation.

It punched me into the wall.

Fragments from the grenade embedded into the wall above me and jammed into the glass storefronts all around me.

I looked up and around to see if there were any casualties. The only people I saw were running away too quickly to have been wounded.

I looked over to Rees.

The grenade had taken off her legs.

I went over to her and was amazed she was still alive, looking down at her body. Her left arm was a mangle. Her right arm pawed at her leg.

She saw me. "I can't hear anything," she said to me, shakily. "I can't hear. Help me."

"I'm right here," I said, even though she couldn't hear me. I took her right hand and held it.

She started to cry. "I didn't want this to happen," she said. "I didn't choose this."

"It's all right," I said. On my inside voice I was calling 911.

She stopped looking at the mess of her legs and looked at me. "You," she said. "I remember you. Dinner. I remember."

I nodded, to let her know I remembered her too.

"He wasn't there the whole time," she said. "I was there the whole time. I was. I was. But not him. He wasn't. He wasn't. He."

She stopped talking. I held her until she died.

Five minutes later I looked up to see Detective Trinh looking down at me, gun drawn, two other cops behind her, both aiming at my head.

"Don't you start," I said.

"You want to explain this to me, Agent Shane?" Trinh said.

"It's complicated," I said.

"I have time."

"I'm not sure I do."

She motioned to Rees with her gun. "Who is that?" she said.

"For your purposes, her name is 'Property of the FBI,' " I said.

I got back to Alexander's and found Vann on a stretcher, oxygen mask on her face, EMTs prepping her for travel. "I'm fine," she said.

I glanced over to Tayla, who was wiping blood from her threep with a towel the EMTs had given her. "She's not fine," Tayla said. "She's got a bullet in her shoulder. It looks like it missed anything major but she's still on the way to the hospital. I would take her to Howard so I could look after her myself, but Georgetown is closer. I'll go with her there. I know some people. She'll get looked after."

"Thank you, Tayla," I said.

"I didn't want to see that movie anyway," she said.

"What should I do?" Tony asked.

"I need you to go back and look at that software some more," I said.

"Why?"

"Remember when you said that you didn't think that software could work on a different neural network?"

"Yeah," Tony said.

"I have a pretty good idea you were wrong about that," I said. "Get back to the morgue. I'm sending you something."

"You're kidding," Tony said, when he realized what I was saying.

"I wish I were," I said.

"Shane," Vann said.

I turned to my partner.

She pointed. "Your back is cracked."

"It stopped a bullet," I said. "I'm fine. I'll get the panel replaced tomorrow."

"Thank you."

"You owe me."

Vann smiled at that. "Rees," she said.

"Dead."

"How."

"Grenade."

"The *fuck*," Vann said.

"I don't think she was herself," I said.

"You think she was like Sani."

"Yeah," I said. "I do. And there's another thing. Before she died, I think she was telling me that the night Loudoun Pharma went up she wasn't integrated with Samuel Schwartz the whole time she was at my dad's dinner party. She was his cover while he went off and did something else."

"Loudoun Pharma," Vann said.

"Maybe," I said.

"You're going up against a corporate lawyer on that one," Vann said. "Good luck with that."

"I'm on it."

"Your housemates," Vann said.

"What about them," I asked.

"If Rees was integrated . . ."

"Then whoever was riding her saw them."

"I'll call in your address," Vann said. "We'll get agents over there."

"Add some for yourself," I said. "You were the one she took a shot at."

"I was the only one *she* took a shot at,"

Vann said.

It took me a second to get what she was saying. "Oh, shit," I said, and disconnected.

"Whoa," Jerry Riggs said, startled, as I sat up in the Kamen Zephyr. "Jesus, kid. You have to warn me when you do that. That threep hasn't moved the whole time I've been here."

"Jerry," I said. "You have to go. Now."

"What's wrong?"

"I'm pretty sure someone's coming to kill me," I said.

Jerry laughed at this, and then stopped. "You're actually serious," he said.

"Jerry," I said. "Please. Get the fuck out, already."

Jerry gawked at me, set down the book he was reading, and walked quickly to the door.

I looked at myself in my cradle, peaceful. Then I headed out the door myself.

Mom and Dad were in the kitchen, having a private dinner with the help gone for the day. They both looked up at me as I came in.

"Chris," Dad said.

"What happened to your 660?" Mom asked, looking at my threep.

The lights went out.

"Get out of the house," I whispered to

them. "Do it now." The Zephyr had a night-vision option. I switched it on and looked around. I reached out and picked a knife out of the butcher block. After a moment I reached out and took a heavy iron skillet off the hook it was hanging from. Prepared either way.

I reached my room as someone was opening the sliding glass door that led to my room's front patio. The man was stocky, short, and stepped through with his handgun pointed down and in front of him. He spotted the constellation of lights that surrounded my cradle, powered by backup batteries that would last for twelve hours. The lights would give him more than enough illumination to put a bullet into my brain. He stepped through, back mostly to me, and raised his handgun. He looked thoroughly professional.

Except that he didn't check his six.

Or his seven, more accurately, which is where I came in at him from, swinging the skillet directly into his head.

He went down, gun firing two shots. The first bullet punched a hole in my cradle. There was a searing pain in my side as small chunks of the cradle drove themselves into my flesh. The second shot went wide, up and over the cradle to connect with the sliding door that led to my room's back patio. It shattered.

I got the shooter with the pan but not as solidly as I could have. He kicked out a leg and jammed it into my knee. If I were in a human body, I would have gone down screaming. As it was I lost my balance and fell, dropping the skillet.

I fell and he rose, lining up another shot. I took the knife I still had in my hand and jammed it hard into the top of his boot. He screamed and leaped back, grabbing at the knife to remove it.

I jumped up to push him further off balance and he wheeled the gun up at me, firing.

I felt the bullet enter my threep on my left waist, tearing down through the leg. A maintenance alert immediately popped into my field of view, telling me that I had entirely lost control of my left leg. I knew that because I fell face-first onto the room tiles, cracking the faceplate of the Zephyr as I did so.

I rolled and looked up to see the man leaning up against the doorframe of my room, keeping his weight off his injured foot, lining up his shot. The knife was still in his foot and the skillet was behind me.

There was no way I was going to stop him in time.

"Hey!" my father said, and the man turned just in time to take a shotgun blast in the side.

The shotgun blast took me by surprise, but probably less than it surprised my assassin. He flew straight out of the doorframe, spinning, landing facedown less than a foot from me. He didn't groan or breathe.

He was dead.

"Chris!" Dad's voice.

"I'm all right," I called back. "Both of me. One more than the other." I gathered my useless leg up behind me and sat up.

Mom ran up, flashlight in hand, flashing it in my eyes, blinding me. I dialed my eyes back to normal mode. "Throw me the flashlight," I said.

She did. I ran it up and down the assassin. There was a gaping hole where a few of his ribs used to be. Dad got him at pretty close range.

"Is he dead?" Mom asked.

"He's dead," I said.

"You sure?"

"Pretty sure," I said.

"Jesus," Dad said. "I just killed a man."

"Yeah, you did," I said. I aimed my flashlight over at Dad. "Don't take this the wrong way, but I think you just ended your Senate run."

Dad didn't have anything to say to that. I think he might have been a little bit in shock.

I took the body and rolled it over. Whoever it was, he was young, dark-haired, and dark-eyed.

"Who is he?" Dad asked.

"I don't know," I said.

"Why would someone want to kill you?" Mom asked.

"I'm an FBI agent," I said.

"It's your third day on the job!"

"Fourth," I said. I was feeling a little punchy myself. I'd had a long day. "Mom. Dad. I need you to do something for me. When the police come, the story needs to be that this was a house robbery gone wrong. Tell Jerry that's the story too."

"He's in your room," Dad said. "Your threep has been shot."

"I came home for dinner with you two," I said. "We heard noises. I insisted on taking point because I'm the FBI agent."

Dad looked dubious. "Come on, Dad," I said. "You're one of the most famous men on the damn planet. I think you can sell that story."

"Why do you need us to tell this story?"

Mom asked.

I looked over at the dead man in the room. "Because I need the person who did this to believe I don't know what he's up to."

"Chris," Mom said. "The man who did this is dead."

"That's exactly what I want him to think," I said.

Mom looked at me like I was nuts.

My field of vision lit up with something other than a maintenance alert. It was Klah Redhouse. I told my parents to hold on and I took the phone call.

"You okay?" Klah asked. My punchiness was apparently evident by voice alone.

"Ask me that tomorrow," I said.

"I did what you asked and looked through the Nation's medical records," Redhouse said. "I got clearance from President Becenti."

"What did you find?"

"There were two people who matched what you were looking for," Redhouse said. "One of them was a woman, Annie Brigmann. She died three years ago. The man she was driving with fell asleep with her in the car and drove off the road. She wasn't wearing a seat belt. The car rolled over her."

"The other one?"

"His name is Bruce Skow," Redhouse said. "I tried to look him up. He went missing from his home about three months ago."

"Hold on a second," I said. I looked over to my assassin, took a picture of his face, and sent it off to Redhouse. "Tell me if that's him," I said.

"That looks like him," Redhouse said. "You know him?"

"He's in my parents' house right now," I said. "Dead."

"That can't be coincidence," Redhouse said.

"No," I said. "No, it can't."

"What do you want me to do with this?" Redhouse asked.

"I need you to wait for me," I said. "It won't be long. I just need a little time."

"You have earned credit," Redhouse said. "You've got time."

"Thanks," I said, and disconnected. I could hear the sirens coming up the driveway.

CHAPTER NINETEEN

An hour with the Loudoun County sheriffs, who seemed delighted to buy into the "home robbery gone wrong" story. I left just as the media, and Dad's media people, started to arrive. That was something they could handle. At some point I would need the FBI to take possession of Skow's body, because I needed to confirm what was in his head. I would worry about that later.

My threep in D.C. was where I had left it, and had a police guard, although whether it was a guard or a cop waiting to arrest me wasn't clear for the first couple of minutes. A diagnostic showed that the damage to the threep from the bullet into the back was worse than I originally thought, and I had a couple of hours before it locked up entirely. I reflected on the fact that in a single day I had managed to seriously damage three separate threeps.

An hour arguing with Trinh and the Metro

police about having Rees's body released to the FBI. The point that Rees had just attempted to assassinate an FBI agent did not seem to convince Trinh all that much. Finally had to resort to having people over my head at the Bureau go over her head in the Metro police. By the time I was done Trinh no longer wanted to be my friend, ever. Suited me.

Another hour with the FBI recounting the Rees attack, making up a suitable lie about leaving the scene to check in on my parents and otherwise catching up my place of employment with the day's events. I focused on the Rees attack, rather than the whole day. Did not volunteer to speculate on causes, and no one asked me to. For now Rees's attack was being treated like a single event, unrelated to anything else me and Vann were doing. This also suited me.

Finished up just as my threep ground to a halt. Managed to get to my desk. I would have to schedule for the local Sebring-Warner dealership to pick it up for repair tomorrow. In the meantime I checked the inventory for visitor threeps I could use.

There were none. We had called in reinforcements for the march. Visiting agents were borrowing the five threeps we had on hand. Fine, I thought, and started looking for rentals.

There were none. The march meant that every rental threep in the District, Maryland, and Northern Virginia was rented through Monday. The closest rental threep available was in Richmond. It was a Metro Junior Courier.

"The hell with this," I said, and finally exercised my rich-person privileges. I called up my Sebring-Warner salesman on his personal number and told him that if he could get to his store and have a threep ready for me in forty-five minutes, I would pay full price plus an extra five thousand as a tip for dragging him out of whatever Adams-Morgan singles pit he was currently casting about in.

An hour later I walked out of the D.C. Sebring-Warner dealership in a 325K — a few steps down from the 660XS but at this point it seemed likely I would have it for about a day before I completely trashed it in the line of duty — and took a cab to Georgetown Hospital, calling Vann to let her know I was on my way, and in a new threep.

I found her in the emergency room, arm in a sling, arguing with an orderly.

"We need to have you in the wheelchair until you exit the building," he said.

"I was shot in the shoulder, not the legs," she said.

"It's hospital policy."

"I can't move this arm, but the rest of me works fine, so if you want to try to stop me, see where it gets you. The good news is, you're already at the hospital." She walked off, leaving the annoyed orderly behind.

"Vann," I said.

She looked over at me, taking in the new threep. "Shane?"

"Yeah," I said.

"Prove it."

"I royally pissed off Trinh tonight," I said. "I think she hates me more than she hates you."

"Oh, I doubt that," Vann said. "But if you got her even halfway there I'll buy you a drink."

"I don't drink," I said.

"Good," Vann said. "Then *you* buy *me* a drink. Come on. I know a bar."

"I don't really think you should be hitting the bars tonight," I said. "You have a hole in your shoulder."

"It's a scratch," Vann said.

"A hole in your shoulder from a *bullet,*" I said.

"It was a small bullet," Vann said.

"Fired by someone trying to kill you."

"All the more reason I need a drink."

"No bars," I said.

Vann looked at me sourly.

"Let's go back to my place," I said.

"Why would I want to do that," Vann said.

"Because we have to catch up," I said. "And because there are agents there watching over the place, so you won't be killed in the night. I have a couch you can sleep on."

Vann continued to look unconvinced.

"And we'll stop on the way to get a bottle of something," I said.

"Better," she said.

I entered my town house with my public ID up so that my housemates wouldn't panic when they saw me. Tayla came over and stopped when she looked at Vann.

"They let you out," she said.

"It's more like I didn't let them keep me in," Vann said.

Even without facial expression I could sense disapproval radiating from Tayla, but then she let it go. "You two need to access the news," she said.

"I'm not sure about that," I said.

"They have a video message from Brenda Rees," she said. "It went live on the net just before she shot at Agent Vann." She pointed to the living room. "We have a monitor there for guests."

"I have my glasses," Vann said, but we went into the living room anyway, fired up the monitor to the news channel, which had a copy of Rees's video. In the video she talked about the injustice of Abrams-Kettering, how it was causing suffering among so many of her clients, and how everyone was to blame. "There are no innocents among the non-Hadens," she said. "They allowed this to happen. Cassandra Bell said it, and I believe it: This is a war on a disabled minority. Well, I am now a soldier in this war. And for me the battle starts tonight."

"Do you believe this?" Vann asked me, as we watched the video again.

"Hell, no," I said.

"You caught the reference to Cassandra Bell."

"I did. Another act of violence, ostensibly perpetrated at her behest."

"Anyone killed tonight?" Vann asked.

"Aside from Rees?" I asked. Vann nodded. "No. There were some people who were stampeded and other injuries, and property damage from the grenade. But the only person she shot at was you."

"And you," Vann said.

"I got hit," I said. "But that was because I

was protecting you."

"And that would go against her story anyway," Vann said. "So you and I know she was gunning for me but her story will muddy up the waters. When the morning shows go live tomorrow, they're going to tie this into the Loudoun Pharma attack."

"That sounds about right to me," I said.

Vann didn't say anything to this, but touched the monitor to bring up the latest news. The top story aside from Rees's attack was the shooting at my parents' house. Vann pulled up the story and watched it.

"A burglar," Vann said, after the report ended.

"That's what I told my parents to say."

"Think it will float?"

"There's no reason for it not to," I said.

"How are your parents?" Vann asked.

"Now that they've got their people and responses in place they'll be fine," I said. "Dad's in shock a little. Killing a man ends any thought of him running for Senate."

"A man defending his home doesn't play so poorly in most parts of Virginia," Vann said.

"No, but it's balanced out by the image of a really big angry black man with a shotgun," I said. "Even Mom's ancestors being gun runners for the Confederacy isn't going

308

to make up for that. So I'm pretty sure a party rep is going to come around tomorrow and tell him they would be delighted for him to endorse the candidacy of someone else."

"Sorry."

"It'll be fine," I said. "Eventually. Dad's probably got a week of think pieces and commentary about him and the shooting to get through before he can do anything else. A normal person would be able to get through it in private. Dad has to worry about what it means for his *legacy.*"

"And the 'burglar,' " Vann said.

"A Navajo named Bruce Skow," I said.

"And he's like Johnny Sani."

"As far as we can tell so far, probably," I said. "We'll need to get into his head to confirm."

"Another remote-controlled Integrator," Vann said.

"Looks like," I said.

Vann sighed and then pointed at the liquor store bag I still held in my hand, containing a bottle of Maker's Mark bourbon and a package of Solo cups. "Pour me some of that," she said. "Make it a tall one."

"How tall?" I asked.

"Don't get me drunk," Vann said. "But just short of that would be fine."

I nodded. "Why don't you head up to my room," I said. "I'll bring it up to you in a minute." I pointed in the right direction and then went into the kitchen, which was a characteristically bare Haden kitchen, save for the pallets of nutritional liquid.

Tayla, whose room was on the first floor, saw me go in and followed. "You're getting her a drink," she said.

"The alternative to getting her one here was getting her one at a bar," I said. "At least here I can cut her off if she gets sloppy."

"What she really needs at this point is some sleep, not bourbon," she said, pointing to the bottle.

"I'm not going to disagree with you on that," I said, opening the bottle. "But she's not going to do that at the moment. In which case I might as well make her comfortable because we need to do some work."

"And how are you doing?" Tayla asked.

"Well, you know," I said, opening the Solo cup package. "Today I fought with a ninja threep, saw two women view the last video from a dead relative, had a woman explode twenty feet from me, and watched my dad kill an intruder with a shotgun." I took a cup and poured the bourbon into it. "If I had any sense I'd take this bottle and attach it to my intake tube."

"I've seen people do that, actually," Tayla said.

"Yeah?" I asked. "How does it work for them?"

"About as well as you'd expect," Tayla said. "Haden bodies are sedentary and in general have low alcohol tolerances to start. Our digestive systems are used to taking in nutritional liquids, not actual food and drink. And then there's the fact that the disease changes our brain structure, which for a lot of Hadens increases the propensity for addiction."

"So they're all fucked up, is what you're saying."

"What I'm saying is there's nothing as fucked up as a Haden alcoholic."

"I'll keep it in mind," I said.

"You need sleep too," Tayla said. "Professional opinion."

"I'm not going to disagree with you on that, either," I said. "But for all the reasons I've just outlined, I'm a little wired right now."

"Is it always like this?" Tayla asked.

"My job?"

"Yes."

"This is my first week on the job," I said. "So, so far? Yes."

"How do you feel about that?"

"Like I wish I had decided to be the typical rich kid and been a sponge on my parents," I said.

"You don't really mean that," Tayla said.

"No," I said. "But at the moment I really want to feel like I did."

Tayla came over and rested a hand on my arm. "I'm the house doctor," she said. "If you need help you know where I am."

"I do," I said.

"Promise me you'll try to get some sleep tonight."

"I'll try."

"Okay." She turned to go.

"Tayla," I said. "Thanks for tonight. It means a lot to me that you helped my partner."

"That's my job," Tayla said. "I mean, you saw me help a man who two minutes earlier was planning to bash my head in with a bat. I wouldn't do any less for someone you care about."

CHAPTER TWENTY

"You took your time," Vann said, as I walked into the room.

"Tayla wanted to talk," I said, walking the bourbon over to her. "She's worried about the both of us."

"Seems fair," Vann said, taking the cup. "Both of us survived an assassination attempt tonight. I'm worried about the both of us too." She took a sip from the cup. "Now," she said. "I'm going to tell you a story."

"I thought we were saving story time until after the march," I said.

"We were," Vann said. "But then your friend Tony showed up with his discovery, and then someone tried to put a bullet into my head. So I've decided that sooner is better than later for story time."

"All right," I said.

"This is going to wander a bit," Vann warned.

"I'm all right with that," I said.

"I'm forty," Vann said. "I was sixteen when I got sick. This was during the first wave of infections, when they were still figuring out what the hell to do about it. I lived in Silver Spring and there was a party I wanted to go to with friends in Rockville, but Rockville was quarantined because there was a Haden's outbreak. I didn't care, because I was sixteen and stupid."

"Like any sixteen-year-old," I said.

"Exactly. So me and my friends got into a car, found a way in that didn't have a roadblock on it, and went to the party. No one at the party looked sick to me when we got there, so I figured it wouldn't be a problem. I finally got back home around three and my dad was waiting for me. He thought I was drunk and asked me to breathe so he could smell my breath. I coughed on him like an asshole and then I went to bed."

Vann paused to take another sip out of her cup. I waited for what I knew was coming next.

"Three days later I felt like my entire body had swelled. I had a temperature, I was raspy, my head hurt. Dad was feeling the same way. My mother and my sister felt fine, so my dad told them to go over to her

314

sister's so she wouldn't get sick."

"Not a good idea," I said. They had probably been infected but weren't showing symptoms yet. That's how Haden's spread as far as it did.

"No," Vann agreed. "But this was early days so they were still trying to figure these things out. They left and Dad and I watched TV and drank coffee and waited to feel better. After a couple of days we both thought the worst was over."

"And then the meningitis hit," I said.

"And then the meningitis hit. I thought my head was going to explode. My father called 911 and told them what was going on. They came to our house in hazmat suits, grabbed us, and sent us over to Walter Reed, which is where second-stage Haden's victims were sent. I was there for two weeks. I almost died right at the beginning. They pumped some experimental serum in me that gave me a seizure. I tensed up so hard I ended up breaking my jaw."

"Jesus," I said. "What happened to your father?"

"He didn't get any better," Vann said. "The meningitis stage fried up his brain. He went into a coma a couple of days after we got to Walter Reed and died a month later. I was there when we unplugged him."

"I'm sorry."

"Thanks," Vann said. She took another sip. "What really sucks is that my dad was one of those people who made a big fuss out of wanting to donate his organs when he died. But when he died, we weren't allowed to donate any of his organs. They didn't want someone to get his kidneys and the Haden virus too. We asked Walter Reed if they wanted to use his body for research, and they told us that they already had more bodies for that than they could use. So we ended up cremating him. All of him. He would have hated that."

"What happened to your mother and sister?" I asked. "Did they get sick?"

"Gwen had a low fever for about three days and was fine," Vann said. "Mom never got sick at all."

"That's good."

"Yeah," Vann said. "So, then I spent my next three years being self-destructive and in therapy, because I felt guilty about killing my dad."

"You didn't kill your dad," I said, but Vann held up her hand.

"Trust me, Shane," she said. "Anything you'd say on the topic I've already heard a couple thousand times. You'll just annoy me."

"All right," I said. "Sorry."

"It's okay. Just let me tell the story." Another sip. "Anyway, somewhere in all of this they discover that some of the people who survived the second stage of Haden's without being locked in can integrate — can use their brains to carry around someone else's consciousness. Walter Reed has me on file so they contact me and ask me to come in and get tested. So I do. They tell me that my brain is, in the words of one of the testers there, 'absolutely fucking gorgeous.'"

"That's not bad," I said.

"No," Vann agreed. "And they ask me to become an Integrator. And at the time I'm at American University, ostensibly majoring in biology but actually mostly just getting high and screwing around. And I think, Why not? One, if I become an Integrator the NIH will pick up the rest of my college and pay off half of my existing student loans. Two, when I complete training I'll have a job, which at the time was something that was getting harder to come by, even for college graduates, and it was a job that wasn't going to go away. Three, I thought it'd be something that would make my dad proud, and since I killed him, I figured I owed him."

She looked at me to see if I was going to

317

say anything about her killing her dad. I didn't.

"So I finish up my degree at American and while I'm doing that I get the neural network installed in my head. That gave me a panic attack because for the first few days it was giving me these massive headaches. Just like the ones I got with the meningitis." She motioned to her head in a circular motion. "It's those goddamn wires moving into position."

"I know," I said. "I remember it. If you're a little kid when they install it, you get the joy of feeling it move around as you grow."

"That sounds like a nightmare," Vann said. "They told me when they were installing it that there are no nerve endings in the brain, and I told them that they were high, because what was the brain but one massive nerve."

"Fair point."

"But then the headaches go away and I'm fine. I go in to Walter Reed every couple of weekends and they run tests and condition my network and generally compliment me on my brain structure, which they say is perfectly tuned to receive someone else's consciousness. Which I figure is a good thing if this is going to be my line of work. Then I graduate and I immediately start work on the Integrator program, which is more testing and studying the underlying brain mechanics of how integration works. They're of the opinion that the more you understand it, the better you're going to be as an Integrator. It won't be a mystery or magic to you. It'll just be a process."

"Are they right?"

"Sure," Vann said. "Up to a point. Because it's like everything, right? There's the theory of it, and then there's the real-world experience of it. The theory behind integration didn't bother me at all. I understood the thought mapping and transmission protocols, the concerns about cross-interference between brains and why learning meditation techniques would help us be better receptacles for our clients, and all that. It all made perfect sense, and I wasn't stupid and I had that gorgeous brain of mine."

Another sip.

"But then I did my first live integration session and I literally shit myself."

"Wait, what?" I said.

Vann nodded. "For your first integration session, they have you integrate with a Haden they have on staff. Dr. Harper. It's her job to integrate with new Integrators, to walk them through the process. Everything she does, she explains as she does it. The idea is no surprises, nothing wild. Just simple things like raising an arm or walking around a table or picking up a cup to drink some water. So I meet her, and we shake hands and she tells me a little bit about what to expect, and she says that she knows I'm probably a little nervous and that's perfectly normal. And I'm thinking, I'm not nervous at all, let's just get on with it.

"So she sits down and I sit down, and then I open the connection and I feel her signal requesting permission to download. And I give permission and *Jesus fucking Christ there is another person inside my head.* And I can *feel* her. Not just feel her but feel what she's thinking and what she wants. Not telepathy like I can read her thoughts, but what she's wanting. Like, I can tell that what she really wants is for the session to be over, because she's hungry. I don't know *what* she wants to eat, but I know she *does* want to eat. I can't read her thoughts, but I can *feel* every single one of them. And it feels like I'm suffocating. Or drowning."

"Did you tell them?" I asked.

"No, because I knew I wasn't acting rationally," Vann said. "I knew that whatever I was feeling was an overreaction. So I tried to use all those relaxation and meditation techniques they'd been training us on. I use them and they seem to work. I'm starting to calm down. And as I'm calming down I realize that everything I've been feeling has happened in the space of ten seconds. But fine, whatever, I can handle this.

"Then she tries to move my arm and I just freak the fuck out and my sphincter lets go."

"Because your arm is moving without your intent," I said.

"Exactly," Vann said. "Exactly." She took another sip. "Because this is what I learned about myself that first day: My body is *my body.* I don't want anyone else in it. I don't want someone else controlling it, or trying to. It's my own little space in the world and the only space I have. And to have someone else in it, doing anything *to* it, sends me into a panic."

"What happened then?"

"She immediately breaks the connection and comes over to me and gets me to stop panicking," Vann said. "She tells me not to be embarrassed, and that my reaction is a common one. Meanwhile I'm sitting there in my own shit trying not to rip her little mechanical head off. No offense."

"None taken."

"She says we'll go ahead and take a break, so I can get cleaned up and get something to eat, and then we'll try again. Well, I do go and get cleaned up, but I don't get anything to eat. Instead what I do is go to the nearest bar in borrowed hospital scrubs and have them line up five shots of tequila. And then I down them one after another in the space of about ninety seconds. And then I go back in for the second session and I fucking nail it."

"They didn't notice you being drunk off your ass on tequila," I said.

"I told you that I spent a few years being self-destructive," Vann said. "It wasn't good for my liver, but it was good for being able to drink and still function."

"So in order to integrate, you had to be drunk."

"Not drunk," Vann said. "Not at first. I had to have enough that I wouldn't panic when someone got inside of me. I figured out that if I could make it past the first five minutes I could handle the rest of the session. I was never happy, but I could tolerate the intrusion. And then when it was done I would go and have another couple of drinks to take the edge off."

"You didn't consider just not being an Integrator," I said.

"No," Vann said. "You have to spend a minimum amount of time as a professional

Integrator or else you have to pay them back for everything they paid out for your education and training. I couldn't afford that. And I *wanted* to be an Integrator. I wanted to do the job. I just couldn't do it strictly sober."

"Got it," I said.

"And at first that really didn't matter," Vann said. "I got very good at calibrating just how much alcohol I needed to get through a session. I was never drunk and my clients never noticed. I got good reviews and I was in demand and no one ever figured out what I was doing."

"But it didn't last," I said.

"No," Vann said. Another sip. "The panic never went away. It didn't become more manageable over time. It got worse, and by the end it got a lot worse. So I upped my therapeutic dose, as I liked to call it."

"They noticed."

"They didn't notice," Vann said. "By that time I was very good at my gig. The physical aspect of being an Integrator I could mostly do on autopilot. What I couldn't do as well was put on the brakes. Sometimes a client wants to do something you didn't agree to in your contract. When that happens you need to pull them back. If they fight you on it, you pull the plug on the session and report them. If it's bad enough, or if they pull that stunt on too many Integrators, then the client gets blacklisted and isn't allowed to integrate anymore. It doesn't happen often because there are so few Integrators that most Hadens don't want to jeopardize their chances of using one."

Vann drained her cup.

"You had it happen," I said.

"Yeah."

"What happened?"

"I had a teenage client who wanted to know what it was like to die," Vann said. "She didn't want to commit suicide, mind you. She didn't want to be dead. But she wanted to know what it was like to die. To have that second just before the end when you realized you couldn't escape, and that this was it. She realized that unlike most people, she was in a position to realize her fantasy. All she needed was to push an Integrator at the last minute. Then she would have her moment, and since everyone knew Integrators could stop their clients from doing anything stupid, it would look like it was the Integrator who did it, and that the client was the victim. All she needed was the Integrator to be inattentive just long enough."

"How did she know?"

"That I was the right Integrator for her

plan?" I nodded. "She didn't. She didn't have a long-term contract, so she went into the NIH integration lottery and got who she got. It just happened to be me.

"But the *rest* of it. Well. She *planned,* Shane. She knew what she was going to do and how she was going to do it and had it down so well that when we integrated I couldn't feel what she had planned for me. All I could tell was that she was excited about something. Well, most of my clients were excited about something when they were with me. That was the whole point of using an Integrator. To do something that excited you with an actual human's body."

"How was she going to kill you?" I asked.

"Her stated purpose for wanting an Integrator was that her parents had managed to get her a special event at the National Zoo," Vann said. "She was going to be allowed to hold and play with a small tiger cub. It was a birthday present. But before she did that she wanted to walk around the Mall to look at some of the memorials. So we integrated, we walked around the Mall, and then we went into the Smithsonian Metro station to go to the zoo. We stood near the edge of the platform and watched the train roll in. At the last possible instant, she jumped.

"I felt her tensing, *felt* what she wanted to

do, but my reaction time was too slow. I had four tequilas before we integrated. By the time I could do anything about it we were already in the air and almost off the platform. There was no way for me to do anything about it. I was about to die because a client killed me.

"Then I was jerked back and fell hard onto the platform as the train flew past. I looked up and there was this homeless guy looking down at me. He told me later he'd been watching me because of the way I was pacing and looking down the track for the train. He said he recognized what I was doing because at one point he thought about jumping in front of a train himself. *He* recognized it, Shane. But *I* didn't."

"What happened to the girl?"

"I pulled the fucking plug on her, that's what," Vann said. "Then I had her charged with attempted murder. She said it was me who tried to jump, but we got a court order for her personal effects and records, which included a journal where she described her planning. She was charged and we cut a deal where she got probation, therapy, and was forever blacklisted from integrating."

"You were easy on her," I said.

"Maybe," Vann said. "But I just didn't want to have to deal with her anymore. I didn't want to have to deal with *any* of it. I was almost killed because someone used me to see what it was like to die. Everything my panic attacks were trying to tell me about integrating had just come true. So I quit."

"Did the NIH try to get you to pay back your training and college?"

"No," Vann said. "They were the ones who assigned the client to me. They didn't know the reason I almost died was because my reaction time was dulled by alcohol, and I didn't volunteer the fact. As far as anyone could tell, the problem was that the selection process didn't screen for garden-variety psychopaths. Which was true enough. I promised not to sue, they let me go without a fight, and the selection process was changed to protect Integrators from dangerous Hadens, so I ended up doing some good. And then the FBI tracked me down and said they were looking to build up a Haden-focused division and thought I might be a good fit. And, well. I needed a job."

"And here we are," I said.

"And here we are," Vann agreed. "Now you know why I stopped being an Integrator. And why I drink and smoke and fuck like I do: because I spent years working in a state of alcoholically managed panic, and then someone tried to kill me with my own body. I don't drink as much as I used to. I smoke more. I fuck about the same. I think I've earned all of them."

"I won't argue with you about that."

"Thank you," Vann said. "And now, *this* fucking case. It's every single thing that made my brain scream, come to life. When I almost died, it was on me. I wasn't paying attention and someone took advantage of that inattention to make me do something I wouldn't do. If I had died, at the end of the day it would have been for the choices I made. To drink and to stay in the integration corps.

"But *this*. This is someone taking away the Integrator's choice. It's locking them into their own body and making them do things they wouldn't do. That they would never do. And then throwing them away." She pointed to me. "Brenda Rees. She didn't kill herself."

"No," I said. "I saw her face when her client disconnected. She tried to get away from the grenade. She had no control before that."

"She was locked in," Vann said. "Locked into her own body until there was nothing she could do about what was going to happen. We need to figure out how this is happening. *Why* it's happening. We have to stop it."

"We know who is behind it," I said.

"No, we *think* we know who is behind it," Vann said. "It's not the same thing."

"We'll figure it out."

"I want to share your optimism," Vann said. She held up her cup. "I'm not entirely sure I've had enough of this to do so."

"You might have had enough," I suggested.

"Not yet," Vann said. "But soon. Think maybe a shot more will do it."

I took the cup and walked down the hall toward the stairwell, pausing at Tony's room as I did so. His body lay there, appearing to sleep. His threep was missing. I wondered if anyone remembered to feed Tony today, but then saw his nutrient levels were topped off.

Tayla did that, I thought. It's good to have friends.

I went to the kitchen, poured out a shot of bourbon, and brought it back to my room. Vann was asleep, snoring lightly.

CHAPTER TWENTY-ONE

I woke up at nine thirty and for a moment panicked that I was late for work. Then I remembered that since I had been shot at twice last night, I had been told to take the day off, unless I wanted to talk to the mental health staff. I preferred the day off.

I skimmed through some e-mail, waiting to see if my brain would be willing to collapse back into sleep. No luck. Awake it was, then.

I got into my threep in the apartment and looked around. Vann wasn't on the couch. I assumed that she had headed back to her place. Then I heard her voice downstairs.

She was in the family room, with Tayla and the twins, watching the monitor. On the screen there was a riot. It was happening on the Mall.

"What the hell happened?" I asked, looking at the monitor.

Vann looked over, cradling a cup of coffee. "You're up."

I gestured at the monitor. "Maybe I should have stayed asleep."

"Then when you woke up it would have been worse," she said.

"Someone firebombed a tour group of Hadens," Tayla said.

"Seriously," I said.

Tayla nodded. "The Hadens were grouped up, ready to go to the Lincoln Memorial, and then some assholes drove by and chucked a Molotov cocktail at them."

"Which is less effective on threeps than on human bodies," I said.

"The assholes found that out when the threeps took off after them." Vann pointed at the monitor. "Look, they're showing the video again."

The video was from the point of view of a tourist phone. In the foreground a little kid was whining to her parents about something. In the background, a car swerved toward a group of tightly packed Hadens. A young dude popped up out of a sunroof, lit a Molotov, and flung it at the Hadens.

The tourist now turned his full attention to the flames. Several Hadens were on fire, flapping and rolling to put themselves out. The rest of the Hadens starting running toward the car. Whoever was driving — it was obviously on manual control — panicked, took off with his friend still half out of the sun roof, and rear-ended the car in front of him. The Hadens reached the car, pulled the young man out of the sunroof, and yanked the driver out of the car.

Then the beatdown truly began. By this time one of the threeps hit by the cocktail had made it over to the car. It began kicking the bomb thrower, legs still aflame.

"It would be funny if the entire Mall and Capitol Hill area weren't now on lockdown," Vann said.

"You can't say the dudes didn't deserve it," I said.

"No, they deserved it, all right," Vann said. "It's still a pain in the ass for everybody else."

"Do we need to go in?"

"No," Vann said. "In fact I just got a phone call telling me that you and I are on medical leave until Monday. We're supposed to let Jenkins and Zee follow up on all our stuff."

"Who are Jenkins and Zee?" I asked.

"You haven't met them yet," Vann said. "They're goddamned idiots." She pointed to the screen. "The good news is they'll handle this and all the other penny-ante crap we had to deal with this week so we can focus on the important stuff."

"So we're not doing medical leave after all," I said.

"You can," Vann said. "Personally, I'm kind of pissed off about being shot. I want to take the people who made it happen and screw them right into the wall. And while you were sleeping, Shane, the other shoe dropped."

"What do you mean?" I asked.

Vann turned to Tayla and the twins. "May I?" she asked, and reached up to signal the monitor to switch stories. She flipped through several until she pulled one up, full screen. The image with the story was of the Accelerant logo.

"It's that asshole Hubbard," she said. "He's buying the Agora from the government. The servers, the building, and everything else. He's taking Haden space private."

I was about to respond when a call window opened up in my field of view. It was Tony.

I connected. "Where are you?" I asked.

"I'm at the FBI building," Tony said. "Where are you?"

"I'm at home," I said. "Medical leave."

"Fine," Tony said. "I'm coming to you, then."

"What's up?"

"I'd actually prefer to speak to you about it someplace private," Tony said.

"How private?"

"However private we can make it."

"What is it?" I asked.

"You were right," Tony said. "About me being wrong. But it's a lot worse than that. A lot worse."

"Glasses on," I told Vann.

She put on her monitor glasses. "Hit me," she said.

I pinged her and let her into my liminal space. Then I entered it myself.

There was a threep standing on my platform. It was Vann.

She held out her hands, looking at her representation. "So this is what that's like," she said. Then she looked over to me. "And that's what *you* look like."

"Surprised?" I asked.

"I hadn't actually thought of you having a face before, so, no, not exactly," she said.

I smiled at this, and realized that it was the first time that Vann had ever seen me smile.

She looked around. "It's the goddamned Batcave," she said.

I laughed.

"What?" she said.

"You reminded me of someone just there," I said. "Hold on, I need to bring Tony in." I pinged Tony a door.

He stepped through and looked around. "Spacious," he said, finally.

"Thank you."

"Kind of looks like the Bat —"

"Tell us the bad news," I prompted.

"Right." A neural network popped up above us. "This is Brenda Rees's neural network," he said. "It's a Lucturn model, the Ovid 6.4 specifically. It was a fairly common model from eight years ago, and it's running — well, *was* running — the most up-to-date software for its model. I've done patches for this network a few times, so I'm pretty familiar with its design and capabilities."

Tony pointed to Vann. "You asked me if I thought it would be possible to lock in an Integrator with a commercially available network."

"You said no," Vann said.

"I said I didn't think so," Tony said. "I didn't think so because the code that allowed it to happen in Sani's brain was optimized for a network that was itself optimized for locking in Integrators while giving the client control. Purpose-built software for purpose-built hardware."

"But you were wrong," I said.

"I was wrong," Tony said.

"Why were you wrong?"

"Because I was thinking about Johnny Sani's network incorrectly," Tony said. "I told you that it wasn't a prototype. That it was a release-level brain. Well, it is. But it's also a proof of concept, the concept being that if you knew the hardware and the software *really* well, you could have the client take total control of the Integrator's body. It's not something anyone tried to do — well, that we know about. There's probably some asshole NSA initiative to do just that."

"Focus," Vann said.

"Sorry," Tony said. "Sani showed that it could be done. Now all anyone needed to do was translate that proof of concept into existing, general networks. And to do that you would have to do a couple of things. One, you'd have a deep understanding of the networks you were using. You'd have to know the hardware really well. Two, you'd have to be a complete fucking wizard at programming."

"Hubbard," I said.

Tony touched his finger to his nose. "Lucturn is the second-largest manufacturer of

336

Haden neural networks, after Santa Ana, and Hubbard is famously involved in the design process. The programming forums are full of horror stories about him coming in and tearing up his engineers' early designs for being inelegant."

"And how is he as a programmer?" Vann asked.

"It's how he got into the field," Tony said. "He founded Hubbard Systems to manage corporate legacy computer systems, and then after he got Haden's he started focusing on programming for threeps and networks that were orphaned when their manufacturers got out of the field. He did a lot of that programming himself back in the day. The programming system networks use is called Chomsky. Hubbard didn't invent it, but he did write most of the 2.0 version, and he's on the board of the Haden Consortium, which approves new versions of the code."

"The Haden Consortium," I said.

"What about it," Tony said.

"Hold on," I said. I fished through my e-mail and pulled up one for Tony and Vann to look at. "L.A. finally got back to me about the ninja threep," I said.

"Ninja threep?" Tony looked puzzled.

"I'll explain later," I said. "The point is

the threep's design wasn't a commercial design — it was a low-fee license version that the Haden Consortium offers potential manufacturers in developing countries for use in their countries. You can't buy them or sell them in North America, Europe, or developed Asia."

"So you were attacked by an imported threep," Vann said.

"It could be made here as a one-off," I said. "All you'd need was an industrial 3-D printer and an assembly robot."

"Who has a setup that could handle that?" Vann asked.

"Pretty much any design shop or manufacturer who does full-scale modeling," I said. "L.A. said they would look into it but it would take some time. My point here is that Hubbard's involved with both Chomsky and the threep design that went ninja on me."

"Which could be coincidental," Vann said.

I opened my mouth to respond but Tony butted in. "Hold that thought," he said. "I'm going to tell you why Hubbard's your guy, but I have a couple more things to walk you through."

"All right," Vann said. "Take us to the next thing."

Tony turned to me. "You remember me

telling you that early on the network manufacturers had problems with people hacking
into the networks." I nodded. "So they
made it harder to do. One, they made the
network architecture more complex so it
was more difficult to program for and to
casually hack. But that's a very low-level
measure. Ambitious hackers tend to be top-
flight programmers. So another way it's
done is that all software updates and patches
have to be from approved vendors, who are
identified by a hash they put in the header
of the patch. A patch is downloaded and
the hash is checked. If the patch is verified,
then it downloads and installs. If it's not,
then it's purged and a report is made."

"And that's impossible to get around,"
Vann said.

"Not impossible," Tony said. "But it's difficult. In order to work they have to be
stolen and they have to still be active. When
I do white-hat hacking of these systems, half
my job is getting a verifiable code. That's a
lot of psychological spoofing. Making people
think I'm their boss and need their hash,
finding ways to look over their shoulder
while they're writing code, shit like that."

"How would you do that?" I asked.

"Lots of different ways," Tony said. "One
of my favorites was the time I put a basket

on a remote-controlled toy quadcopter, filled the basket with candy, and then flew the candy into the programmer wing of Santa Ana's headquarters. The quadcopter went from pod to pod, and while the programmers were grabbing at candy, I was grabbing shots of their work screens. I got eight programmer hashes that day."

"Nice," I said.

"Everyone likes candy," Tony said.

"So someone could steal a hash and get into someone else's network," Vann said, dragging us back on point.

"Right," Tony said. "The problem for the hacker is that even when they've got the hash, they're still coming through the front door. Everyone's looking for the stolen or spoofed hash and the malicious code. Which is why every patch is first unpacked and executed in a sandbox — a secure virtual machine. If something malign is in the code, it'll execute there and get caught. And there are other security measures as well.

"The story here is that it's very difficult to get any suspect code into the network in the established route. Even for a brilliant hacker, it's a long walk to a dry well." He turned to Vann. "Which is why I told you that it was very unlikely."

"But then Rees tried to kill me," Vann said.

"Actually that's not the part that convinced me I was wrong," Tony said. "It was the part where Chris said Rees tried to get away from the grenade after intentionally pulling it to avoid being caught. It's possible control was taken by the front door, but if it was there'd be a record of it — patches installed when they shouldn't have been, sandboxes launched to test the patches, a record of the acceptance of the validation of the patch and the hashes of the programmer and company who sent it along. There was nothing out of the ordinary."

"So there's another way in," I said.

"There is," Tony said. "Think about it."

It was Vann who got it. "Fucker did it when he integrated," she said.

"Yes," Tony said. "When a client connects with the Integrator, there's a handshake of information, and then a two-way data stream opens up. This aspect of the network is meant to be a totally separate process from the internal operation of the network, and it is . . . but the code isn't perfect. If you know where to look you can find places to access the network's software. And that's what happened."

Tony zoomed into the network to focus on the nodule that included the receiver for the client data stream. He pointed to a structure. "That's an interpolator," he said. "If there's any short disruption of the data stream, a millisecond or less, the interpolator polls data on either side of the gap and fills in the gap with averaged data. But to do it, the interpolator has to access processing from the network. It's a break in the firewall. And *that's* what Hubbard exploited."

The image changed to a schematic. "Here's what I think he did," Tony said. "First, he handshakes a data feed with the Integrator. Then he *intentionally* introduces gaps into the data stream, long enough to activate the interpolator. Then he uses the interpolator's channel to the processor to feed it an executable file. It does this as long as needed in order to download the file. Then it unpacks and rewrites the network's software.

"It's going directly into the processor, so no sandbox. It's avoiding the verification process, so no need for a hash. It's a small file, so the Integrator's network doesn't have to close the session to execute it. The Integrator never even knows they've been compromised."

"Why the hell hasn't something like this been fixed already?" Vann asked. I could tell she was seriously creeped out by what Tony was telling us.

"Well, think about it," Tony said. "This is a pretty damn big bug, but it's a bug that has a *very narrow* pathway to it. First someone has to know about it. Then they have to have the technical ability to exploit it. Then they need the technical *means* to exploit it — by which I mean that the ability to introduce intentional disruptions into the data stream isn't something your average Haden is going to be able to do in their own head. This needs a specialized instrument *between* the client and the Integrator. And by 'specialized,' I mean that as far as I know it doesn't actually *exist.* It would have to be created.

"No one's patched this bug because up until now it wasn't actually a bug. It was a benign quirk at best. Basically you would have to be a Lucas Hubbard to exploit this."

"But Brenda Rees never integrated with Hubbard," I said. "She integrated with Sam Schwartz."

"Hubbard created the process and tools," Tony said. "Once they existed, they could be used by someone else."

"Sam Schwartz is Hubbard's lawyer," Vann said. "He's in the perfect position to assist him."

"Not a very ethical lawyer," Tony said. "But, yeah. There's no reason Hubbard couldn't hook Schwartz up to his machine and let him have a go at it."

"You seem pretty sure that it's Hubbard," I said.

"You seem pretty sure about it, too, Chris," Tony said.

"I know, but what I want to know is whether you think that because *I* do, or whether you think it because you have another reason to."

"I believe it because you believe it," Tony said. "I also believe it because the scope of what we're talking about here — both for this and for what happened with Johnny Sani — requires resources of either a small country or a very wealthy person. But most of all I believe it because of the code."

"The code," Vann said.

"Yes," Tony said. The schematic disappeared, replaced by lines of code. "How much do you know about Chomsky?" he asked. "The programming language, not the man."

"I don't know anything about either," Vann said.

"Chris?"

"I got nothing," I said.

Tony nodded. "The programming language was called Chomsky because it was designed to talk to the deep structures in the brain. It's a 'deep language' pun. The great thing about Chomsky as a programming language is that it's amazingly flexible. Once you know it — once you *really* know it — you find out there are all sorts of ways to address any problem, or issue, or goal. This is essential for neural networks. They have to be flexible because every brain is different. So the language you program them in has to have the same sort of flexibility. You're keeping up with me so far?"

"It's a little esoteric," I said.

"Which is my *point,*" Tony said. "Chomsky is a language that has to be esoteric, because it's interfacing directly with the brain.

"Now, a side effect of this is, because Chomsky allows so many different ways to tackle any one specific problem, programmers who are truly fluent in Chomsky end up developing their own voice. By which I mean they address goals and parameters in a way that's idiosyncratic to them. If you spend any real time looking at the code, eventually you can tell who wrote it."

"Like someone who writes novels."

"Yeah, precisely," Tony said. "Like one novelist puts in a lot of description while another one is all dialogue. Same thing. And like novelists, some Chomsky programmers are good, some are competent, and some suck. And if you've seen their code before, you can tell which programmer it is from the first line of code."

He pointed to the code on display. "This is the code in Brenda Rees's brain that's variant from the latest point release and patching for the Ovid 6.4," he said. He pulled up some more code. "Here's the code of the software in Johnny Sani's head. It reads the same. Whoever wrote Sani's code wrote Rees's code."

He pulled up a third column of code. "This is code Hubbard wrote back in the day, when he was still pushing out patches and updates at Hubbard Systems," he said. "Believe me when I say that if you ran all of this through the Chomsky equivalent of a semantic and grammatical analyzer, it would light up across the board. All of this was written by the same person. All of it was written by Lucas Hubbard."

"Is that something we can use in a court of law?" Vann asked.

"You'd need a lawyer to tell you that," Tony said. "But if you put me on the stand I would tell you, hell yeah, this is all the same guy."

"Is that enough?" I asked Vann.

"To bring him in?" Vann asked. I nodded. "For what?"

"For killing Brenda Rees, for one," I said. "For Johnny Sani, for another."

"We don't think he killed Rees," Vann said. "We think Schwartz did. We still don't have anything court-worthy connecting him to Sani, either."

"Come on, Vann," I said. "We know this is our guy."

"We go in with what we have and Hubbard's lawyers from Schwartz on down are going to blow our heads off," Vann said. "And I know you don't really need this job, Shane, but I kind of do. So, yes. Hubbard's our man. Let's make *absolutely sure* we can get him." She turned to Tony. "What else you got."

"Two more things," Tony said. "The first is about Rees's code."

"What about it?" Vann said.

"It doesn't bypass her long-term memory," Tony said. "Either Hubbard couldn't find a way to make it work, which is possible because the neural network layout is non-trivially different, or he decided not to waste his time because —" He paused.

"Because he didn't plan on keeping her

after he or Schwartz was done using her," I said.

"Yeah," Tony said. "And now you know why she was carrying around a grenade."

"So she was aware the whole time," Vann said. "Aware and awake and unable to stop her body from doing anything."

"That's right," Tony said. "And no way to get the client out of her head."

"Fuck," Vann said and turned away for a second. Tony looked over at me, confused. *Later,* I mouthed.

"You okay?" I asked Vann.

"If we go in to wheel out Hubbard's body after all this is done, I'm going to need you to watch me very closely," Vann said. "Otherwise I'm going to punt that asshole hard right in the balls."

I grinned very widely. "That's a promise," I said.

Vann turned back to Tony. "What's the second thing," she said.

"Once I figured out how Hubbard hacked Rees's brain I went back into Sani's brain to see what things I missed before because I didn't have context," Tony said. "And I got this." He scrolled very quickly through the code until he came up with a sizable chunk of it.

"What is it?" I asked.

"I didn't know at first," Tony said. "Because it didn't make any sense. What I think is that it repurposes part of the neural network into a relay."

"A what?" Vann said.

"I know, right?" Tony said. "It's a transmitter. It transmits the Integrator's data signal, but not *into* the network. Instead it mimics the network."

"Does it have to be the Integrator's data signal?" Vann asked.

"What do you —" Tony stopped, apparently getting it. "Oooooooh," he said.

"What?" I said. I was the only one in my own liminal space entirely left out.

"Fucking Hubbard," Vann said. "We were asking why Johnny Sani was trying to integrate with Nicholas Bell. He wasn't. He was acting as a goddamned relay station for Hubbard."

I thought about it for a minute. "Then that means that when you were interrogating Bell —"

"It was *never* Bell," Vann said. "It was Hubbard. It was *always* Hubbard. The bastard's been playing us right from the start."

"To get close to Cassandra Bell," I said.

"Yes," Vann said.

"For what purpose?" I asked.

349

"You've been following the news, right?" Vann snapped. "Rumor is, there's a march on Sunday. Imagine what happens to that march when Cassandra Bell is killed by her own brother, who then spouts some sort of anti-Haden bullshit. D.C. is going to burn down to the ground."

"Right, but what point does that serve?" I asked. "Why start a riot?"

"To tank the market," Tony said.

We both turned to him again.

"I told you I follow the sector," Tony said. "It's how I stay employed. The Haden-related companies are already trying to merge or exit the sector because of Abrams-Kettering. Investors are already offloading their stocks. A full-scale riot in D.C. will scare the shit out of these companies and all their investors. They'll flee the scene. And then Accelerant can pick and choose which companies to snap up and which to let die. It'll be lauded for stabilizing the sector when what it's really doing is sniping its competitors in the head. They'll save billions on their merger with Sebring-Warner alone."

"But what's the point?" I said. "Abrams-Kettering is gutting all these companies' profits. There's no gravy train anymore. You said so yourself."

"You know who AOL are, right?" Tony said.

"What?" Vann said.

"AOL," Tony said. "Information services company around the turn of the century. Made billions connecting people online through their phones. A 'dial-up' service. Was one of the biggest companies in the world. Then people stopped using their phone lines to get online and AOL shrank. But for years it still made billions in profit, because even though the dial-up sector had died, there were still millions of customers who kept their dial-up service. Some were old people who didn't want to change. Some were people who kept the service as a backup. Some probably just forgot they subscribed and when they remembered, AOL made it too hard to unsubscribe to bother."

"Lovely story," Vann said. "And?"

"*And,* when all is said and done, there are still more Hadens in the U.S. than people who live in the state of Kentucky. On average another thirty thousand people a year contract the disease and experience lock in. They're not going away. Even a shrunken market can make a lot of money, if you milk it. And Hubbard's the one to milk it."

"Because he's a Haden himself," I said.

"He's one of us."

"That's right," Tony said. "That's what swooping in and saving the Agora is about. Establishing goodwill among Hadens."

"Once he has that, he can roll over every other company, because he's already got every single Haden as a customer," I said. "He'll use the Agora as leverage."

"Right again," Tony said. "And then Accelerant will be doing two things. Using the money he's raking in from Hadens to diversify — even now Haden-related companies are the minority of its portfolio — and getting ready for the day the FDA says neural networks and threeps aren't just medical devices for Haden use only. Because *that's* the real end game. Hubbard's looking to the day when *everyone's* got a threep, everyone's on the Agora, and no one ever has to feel old again."

"That's why Hubbard could spend a billion dollars on something he'd never take to market," I said.

"And why he'll spend a bunch of money now on companies that look like sucker bets," Tony said. "He's not looking at the shrinking Haden market. He's looking at the market that's coming after that. The market he's going to make. The market he's locking in right now."

"You really think that's what happening here," Vann said.

"Let me put it this way, Agent Vann," Tony said. "If you two don't arrest him this weekend, on Monday I'm going out and putting everything I own into Accelerant stock."

Vann stood there for a moment, thinking. Then she turned to me. "Options," she said.

"Seriously?" I said. "We're doing this now?"

"It's still your first week," Vann said.

"It's been a busy week," I said.

"And I want your thoughts, all right?" Vann said. "I'm not just asking you to have a goddamn teachable moment. All this affects *you*. This is *about* you. And people like you. Tell me what *you* want to do, Chris."

"I want to go after the son of a bitch," I said. "Hubbard and Schwartz both."

"You want to arrest them," Vann said.

"I do," I said. "But not just yet."

"Explain," Vann said.

I smiled at her instead and looked over to Tony. "Hubbard's code," I said.

"What about it?" Tony asked.

"Can you patch it?"

"You mean, close the hole in the interpolator?"

"Yeah."

"Sure," Tony said. "Now that I know it's there, closing it up's not a problem."

"Can you do more than that?" I asked.

"Are you going to pay me to do more than that?"

I grinned. "Yes, Tony," I said. "There is payment involved."

"Then I can do whatever you need me to do," he said. "Hubbard's good, but I don't suck either."

"What do you have planned?" Vann asked me.

"So far we've been a step behind Hubbard on everything," I said.

"That's an accurate assessment," Vann said. "Are we going to try to get ahead of him?"

"We don't have to get ahead of him," I said. "But I want us to arrive at the same time."

"And how do you propose we do that?" Vann asked.

"Well," I said. "As our friend Trinh would say, it might require you to be a little sloppy."

CHAPTER TWENTY-TWO

At eleven fifteen I called Klah Redhouse and asked for a meeting with him, his boss, the speaker, and the president of the Navajo Nation, to catch them up on the latest with Johnny Sani and Bruce Skow. The meeting happened at noon.

They were not pleased with my report. Not for how I'd been doing my job, which was not in dispute, but that two of their own had been victimized.

"You are working on this," President Becenti said, in a manner that was not a question.

"Yes," I said. "Johnny Sani and Bruce Skow will have justice. That is my word to you." I waited.

"What is it?" Becenti said.

"You said yesterday that anything you could do to help, you would," I said.

"Yes," Becenti said.

"Did you mean that only within the parameters of the investigation, or would it extend further than that?"

Becenti looked at me doubtfully. "What do you mean?" he said.

"There's justice, and then there's sticking a knife in someone's ribs," I said. "The justice will come no matter what. Like I said, you already have my word on that. But the knife-sticking may come with an extra added benefit to the Navajo Nation."

Becenti looked at the speaker and the police captain, and then back at me. "Tell us more," he said.

I glanced over at Redhouse as I spoke. He was smiling.

At one thirty I was at my parents' house, sitting with my dad in the trophy room. He was in a bathrobe and had a tumbler of scotch, neat, dangling from one of his long, large hands.

"How you doing, Dad?" I asked.

He smiled. "Perfect," he said. "Last night someone broke into my house to kill my kid, I killed him with a shotgun, and now I'm hiding out in my trophy room because it's one of the only rooms in the house that photographers outside don't have a clear shot into. I'm doing great."

"What did the police say about the shooting?" I asked.

"The sheriff came by this morning and assured me that as far as he and his department are concerned, the shooting was justified and no charges are coming and that they'll be returning my shotgun to me later today," Dad said.

"That's good to hear," I said.

"That's what I said, too," Dad said. "They also said the FBI came for the man's body this morning. Does that have anything to do with you?"

"It does," I said. "If anyone asks, the fact that you were about to run for the Senate meant that we had an interest in discovering whether the attacker had any ties with known hate or terrorism groups."

"But it's not really about that at all, is it?"

"I'll answer that for you, Dad, but you have to tell me you're ready to hear it."

"Jesus, Chris," Dad said. "Someone tried to kill you last night in our house. If you don't tell me why, I might strangle you myself."

So I told Dad the entire story, up to my morning visit to the Navajo Nation.

After I finished, Dad said nothing. Then he drained his scotch, said, "I need a refill," and stepped out into the gun room. When he came back in he had considerably more than two fingers of scotch in the tumbler.

"You might want to ease back, there, Dad," I said.

"Chris, it's a miracle I didn't just bring in the bottle with a straw," he said. He took a sip. "Motherfucker was in my house three nights ago," he said, of Hubbard. "In this room. Acting all *chummy.*"

"To be fair, three nights ago I don't think he had planned to have me killed," I said. "Pretty sure that came after."

Dad choked on his scotch on that one. I patted him on the back until he stopped coughing.

"You okay?" I asked.

"I'm fine, I'm fine," Dad said, and waved me off. He set down his drink and looked at me.

"What is it?" I said.

"Tell me what I should do," he said.

"What do you mean?"

"I mean that son of a bitch tried to kill you," Dad said, loudly, forcefully. "My only child. My flesh and blood. Tell me what to do, Chris. If you told me to shoot him, I would go do it right now."

"Please don't," I said.

"Stab him," Dad said. "Drown him. Run him over with my truck."

"They are all tempting," I said. "But none

of those is a good idea."

"Then tell me," Dad said. "Tell me what I can do."

"Before I do," I said. "Let me ask. Senate?"

"Oh. Well. *That,*" Dad said, and reached for his scotch. I picked it up and moved it out of his reach. He looked at me quizzically, but accepted it and sat back. "William came over this morning, first thing," he said, referring to the state party chairman. "He was all concern and sympathy and told me how much he admired me standing up for my home and family, and somehow all that puffery ended up with me being told that there's no way the party could support me this election cycle. And perhaps it was just me, but I think there was the implication I wouldn't be supported in *any* election cycle that might come up."

"Sorry," I said.

Dad shrugged. "It is what it is, kid," he said. "It saves me the trouble of pretending to be nice to a bunch of assholes I never really liked."

"Okay, then," I said. "So. Dad. I need to you do something for me."

"Yeah?" Dad said. "And what is that, Chris?"

"I need you to do a business deal," I said.

Dad furrowed his brow at me. "How did we get to a business deal?" he asked. "I thought we were talking revenge and politics."

"We still are," I said. "And the way it will get done is through a business deal."

"With whom?" Dad asked.

"With the Navajo, Dad," I said.

Dad sat up, uncomfortable. "I know you've been busy," he said. "But I just *shot* one of their people last night. I don't think they'll want to do business with me *today.*"

"No one blames you for it."

"*I* blame me for it," Dad said.

"You didn't shoot him because he was Navajo," I said. "You shot him because he was about to shoot me. He wasn't there because he was a bad man. He was there because bad men were using him."

"Which means I shot an innocent man," Dad said.

"You did," I said. "And I'm sorry about that, Dad. But you didn't kill him. Lucas Hubbard did. He just used you to do it. And if you hadn't, it would be me who was dead."

Dad put his head in his hands. I let him take a moment.

"Bruce Skow was innocent," I said. "Johnny Sani was innocent. Neither of them are coming back. But I have a way you can punish the person responsible for both of their deaths. You'll also get to help out a lot of people in the Navajo Nation in the bargain. Something really good can come out of this thing. You just have to do what you already do better than anyone else. Do some business."

"What kind of business are we talking about here?"

"Real estate," I said. "Sort of."

Three thirty, and I was with Jim Buchold, in his home office. "We're tearing down both buildings," he said, of Loudoun Pharma campus. "Well. We're tearing down the office building, which the Loudoun County inspectors tell me is mostly cracked off its foundation. The labs are already gone. We're just clearing the rubble for that."

"What's going to happen to Loudoun Pharma?" I asked.

"In the short run, tomorrow I'm going to a memorial for our janitors," Buchold said. "All six of them at the same time. They were all each other's friends. It makes sense to do it that way. Then on Monday I'm laying off everyone in the company and then tak-ing bids for buyers."

I cocked my head at that. "Someone wants

to buy Loudoun Pharma?" I asked.

"We have a number of valuable patents and we were able to retrieve a good amount of our current research, some of which can probably be reconstructed," Buchold said. "And if whoever buys the company hires our researchers, there's a chance they'll reconstruct it faster. And we still have our government contracts, although I'm having our lawyers go through those contracts now to make sure they can't be withdrawn because of terrorism."

"Then why sell at all?" I asked.

"Because *I'm* done," Buchold said. "I put twenty years into this company and then it all went up in a single night. Do you have any idea what that feels like?"

"No, sir," I said. "I don't."

"Of course you don't," Buchold said. "You can't know. I didn't know until someone took two decades of my life and turned it into a pile of rubble. I think about trying to build it back up from nothing and all it does is make me feel tired. So, no. Time for me and Rick to retire to the Outer Banks, get a beach house, and run corgis up and down the sand until they collapse."

"That doesn't sound too bad," I said.

"It'll be great," Buchold said. "For the first week. After that I'll have to figure out what to do with myself."

"The night of my dad's party, you were talking about the therapies you were developing to unlock people from Haden's," I said.

"I remember I dragged you into the argument," Buchold said. "Rick gave me crap for that yesterday when he remembered it. Sorry about that."

"It's fine," I said. "I remember that night you also mentioned the drug you were developing."

"Neuroulease."

"That's right," I said. "How far along were you with it?"

"You mean, how long until Neuroulease was on the market?"

"Yes."

"We were feeling optimistic that we'd have enough progress on the drug within the year to apply for clinical trials," Buchold said. "And if those showed promise we were pretty much already guaranteed a fast track at the FDA for approval. You have four and a half million people suffering from lock in. Especially now that Abrams-Kettering's on the books, the sooner we can unlock them, the better."

"What about now?" I asked.

"Well, one of the principal investigators

blew up the company, and with it a whole lot of our data and documentation," Buchold said. "Then he killed himself, and however I feel about *that* at the moment, he was the one who could have most easily reconstructed that data from what we have left. From what we have now, it'll take five to seven years before we're at the clinical trial stage again. And that's optimistic."

"Anyone else as close to it as you were?" I asked.

"I know Roche has a combination drug and brain stimulus therapy they've been working on," Buchold said. "But they're nowhere close to clinical trials with that. No one else is even in the same ballpark." He looked at me sourly. "You want to hear something funny?"

"Sure," I said.

"That bastard Hubbard," he said. "At your dad's party he was tearing into me about Haden culture and how they didn't want to be free of their disease and doing everything short of implying I was encouraging a genocide."

"I remember," I said.

"Yesterday that son of a bitch calls up and makes an offer on Loudoun Pharma!" Buchold said.

"For how much?"

"For fucking not enough!" Buchold said. "And I let him know. He said the offer was flexible but that he wanted to move quickly. And I said to him that a couple of days before he was telling me what a horrible idea our work was, and now he wanted to buy it? Do you know what he said?"

"I don't know," I said, although I had some idea.

"He said, 'Business is business'!" Buchold exclaimed. "Jesus lord. I just about hung up on him then."

"But you didn't."

"No," Buchold said. "Because he's right. Business is business. I have six hundred employees who are going to be out of work in three days, and even though Rick doesn't think I should *socialize* with them" — Buchold rolled his eyes, and looked around to see if his husband was about — "I do feel responsible for them. It would be fine with me if some of them kept their jobs, and the rest had better severance pay than they would have otherwise."

"So you would sell to him?" I asked.

"If no one else steps up with a better offer, I just might," Buchold said. "Why? Do you think I should pass on the offer?"

"I would never tell you how to run your own business, Mr. Buchold."

"What's left of it anyway," he said. "Well, I'll tell you what, Agent Shane. You find me a good reason to keep my options open, and maybe I'll do just that."

"Yes, sir," I said. "I will see what I can do."

Five o'clock, and I was in the liminal space of Cassandra Bell.

It was bare. And by bare, I mean that there was literally nothing in it.

This was not the vast expanse of endless space. It was the absolute opposite, a close, tight darkness. It was like being at the bottom of an ocean of black ink. For the first time I understood claustrophobia.

"Most people find my liminal space uncomfortable, Agent Shane," Bell said. A voice that I could not see and which came from everywhere, although quietly. It was like being inside the head of a very private person. Which, I suppose, was exactly what this was.

"I can understand that," I said.

"Does it bother you?"

"I'm trying not to let it."

"I find it comforting," Bell said. "It reminds me of the womb. They say we don't remember what it is like to be there, but I don't believe that. I think deep inside we always know. It's why children burrow under blankets and cats push their heads into your elbow when they sit beside you. I've not had those experiences myself, but I know why they happen. I've been told my liminal space is like the dark of the grave. But I think of it as the dark from the other end of life entirely. The dark of everything ahead, not everything behind."

"I like the way you put that," I said. "I'm going to try to think of it that way."

"That's the way. Better to light a candle than curse the darkness, Agent Shane," Bell said.

And then she was in front of me, close, a lit candle illuminating her face, the light throwing back the darkness to a breathable distance.

"Thank you," I said, and felt a shudder of relief.

"You are welcome," she said, and smiled, looking younger than twenty years old, although of course here she could appear to be any age she wished.

"And thank you for seeing me on short notice," I said. "I know you are busy."

"I am always busy," she said. Not a brag, or a show of pride, just a fact. She smiled at me again. "But of course I know of you, Agent Shane. Chris Shane. The Haden

Child. So strange, isn't it, that we have not met before this."

"I had that same thought the other day," I said.

"And why do you suppose that is, that we have only now met."

"We ran in different circles," I said.

"Ran in different circles," she said. "And now the image I have is of you and me moving in separate orbits, centered on different stars."

"Same metaphor," I said. "Different description."

"Yes!" Bell said, and gave a small laugh. "And who was your star? Whom did you orbit?"

"My father, I suppose," I said.

"He is a good man," Bell said. Not a question.

"Yes," I said, and thought of him this morning, in his bathrobe, scotch in his hand, grieving for Bruce Skow.

"I know what happened," Bell said. "To and by your father. I am sorry for it."

"Thank you," I said, strangely touched by her manner of speaking. Formal and yet also intimate. "Who was your star, if you don't mind me asking?"

"I don't know," Bell said. "I still don't know. I am beginning to suspect it's not a person but is an idea. And that's why I'm strange, and also gives me my power."

"Maybe," I said, as diplomatically as possible.

She caught it, smiled, and laughed at me. "I don't mean to be obtuse or intentionally bizarre, Agent Shane, honestly I don't," she said. "It's just that I am terribly bad at small talk. The longer it goes on the more I sound like a refugee from a commune."

"It's all right," I said. "I live in an intentional community myself."

"Kind of you to empathize with me," Cassandra Bell said. "You are better at small talk than I am. That is not always a compliment. This time it is."

"Thank you," I said.

"You did not come to make small talk with me," she said. "As well as you make it."

"No," I said. "I came to talk to you about your brother."

"Have you," she said. "I would like to tell you a story of my brother, if you will hear it."

"Sure," I said.

"He was a little boy when I was born and he knew that I was held within myself," she said. "And so he would come to me, and kiss me on my forehead, and sing to me for hours. Can you imagine. What other seven-year-old boy would do such a thing. You have no sisters or brothers."

"No," I said.

"Do you miss them?"

"I can't miss what I never had," I said.

"Which is not true at all," Bell said. "But I have put it poorly. I mean do you feel that you have missed out by not having siblings."

"I think it would have been interesting to have siblings," I said.

"Your parents had no more after you."

"I think they were worried that if they did, they would neglect one or the other of us to focus on the other," I said. "And that the one who was neglected would have eventually become resentful. It's hard to have one child be a Haden and one not. I would imagine." I paused.

"You have a question about me and my brother," Bell said.

"I wondered if you ever integrated with him," I said.

"Oh, no," Bell said. "Altogether too intimate, I should think. I love my brother and he me. But I have no desire to be inside of his head, and I don't believe he wants me in his. Both of us in the same head at the same time! We would become our parents."

"That's an image," I said.

"I have never integrated. I am enough in my own head. I don't wish to be in someone else's as well."

I smiled at this. "You should meet my partner," I said. "She was an Integrator who didn't like people being in her head."

"We would be like magnets," Bell said. "Either rushing together or pushing apart."

"Another interesting image," I said.

"Tell me about my brother."

"When was the last time you spoke to him?"

"That's not telling me of my brother, but I'll allow it," Bell said. "We spoke the other day. He wishes to spend time with me Saturday afternoon."

"And will you?"

"Wouldn't you make time for your family?" Bell asked. "I know how you would answer so you don't have to."

"I would make time for them," I said, answering anyway. "Will you meet him here?"

"Yes, and also he will be with my body," Bell said. "He still likes to sing to me, to my ears."

"Will anyone else be there?"

"He is family."

"So, no."

"Agent Shane, now is an excellent time to

stop making small talk," Bell said.

"We believe your brother has had his body taken over by a client," I said. "This client has considerable technical skill and has been able to change the programming of your brother's neural network in order to trap him and use the body for his own purposes. We believe he means to use your brother's body to kill you and then kill your brother as well. It will look like a murder-suicide."

"And you believe this why?"

"Because he's taken over other bodies," I said. "In the same way. He and an associate have both done it. The end result has been three dead Integrators."

Cassandra Bell looked very solemn, the light from the candle suddenly guttering and flickering before resuming a steady glow. "You believe he is possessed already, then."

"Possessed," I said, and I realized that it simply hadn't occurred to me to think of what happened to Johnny Sani or Bruce Skow or Brenda Kees in that way. "Yes. He is already possessed."

"For how long?"

"We believe since last Tuesday morning at least."

"Why has it taken you this long to tell me of it?"

"We didn't know it was possible until yesterday," I said. "We didn't think it affected your brother until today. It shouldn't have been possible. And because it shouldn't be possible we didn't pick up on it until now."

"Is he dead?"

"Your brother? No."

"I know his body isn't dead," Bell said. "I mean *him.* My brother's soul."

"We don't think so," I said. "We believe strongly that he is alive, but locked in. Unable to speak or communicate to the outside world. Like . . . well, like us. But without a threep or liminal space or an Agora. And with his body at the whim of another, doing things he would not choose to himself."

"He would not choose to murder me," Bell agreed. "You say you strongly believe that he is alive."

"Yes."

"Describe the strength of that belief."

"Strong as iron," I said. "Strong as oak."

"Iron rusts. Oak burns."

"We can't be certain," I said. "But from what we know, the person possessed still exists. The person I saw possessed like this still existed after her client left."

"You said they all died."

"She died," I said. "Her client pulled the

pin on a grenade before he left."

"Who are these people?" Bell asked.

"We'd rather not say," I said. "For your own protection."

Cassandra Bell's candle brightened immensely even as the darkness sucked in more tightly around me. "Agent Shane," she said. "Do not confuse me for a child. I am not damaged, nor am I incapable. I am bringing hundreds of thousands of us to announce ourselves to the world. I could not do this if I were a coddled *thing*. I do not need *protection*. I need information."

"It's Lucas Hubbard," I said.

"Oh," Bell said. The candle returned to its original state. "Him."

"You know him."

"With the exception of you, Agent Shane, I know almost everyone of importance." Not a brag, just a fact.

"What is your opinion of him?"

"Now, or before I learned that he's enslaving my brother in his own body?"

I smiled at this. "Before."

"Intelligent. Ambitious. Able to speak passionately about Hadens when it is convenient and advantageous for him to do so, and when not, not."

"Standard-issue billionaire," I said.

Bell fixed me with a stare. "I would imagine you of all people would know not all billionaires are poor humans," she said.

"In my experience, there are few much like my father," I said.

"A pity," Bell said. "When will you rescue my brother?"

"Soon," I said.

"There are whole paragraphs lurking behind that single syllable," Bell said. "Or perhaps you merely meant to say 'soon, but not yet.' "

"There are complications," I said.

"I won't ask you to imagine the terror of being locked in, Agent Shane," Bell said. "I know you know it all too well. What I would ask you is why you would willingly inflict it on anyone else for a second longer than you had to."

"To save others from that same fate," I said. "And to punish Hubbard in a way more complete than mere capture. And to keep your brother safe."

Bell looked at me, stony. "If we move on him this second, we have enough to charge him for and punish him for," I said. "But he's not stupid. He's almost certainly planned for the contingency of being caught. He's rich and he's got more lawyers than some countries have people. He'll tie things up for years, cut deals, and introduce doubt. And the very first thing he'll do is cover his tracks however possible. That includes getting rid of the single person who can account for every moment of Hubbard's movements over the last week."

"My brother," Bell said.

"Your brother," I said. "Hubbard's smart, but his intelligence and ambition are also his blind spot. He believes he's covered every angle and every contingency. But we propose that there are a couple of angles he can't see."

"Because they are in his blind spot."

"Yes."

"Promise me my brother," Bell said.

"I promise you I will do everything I can to save him," I said. "I promise we will do everything we can."

"Now tell me how you plan to capture Hubbard."

"He intends to kill you," I said.

"So you say."

"I think we should let him try."

CHAPTER TWENTY-THREE

Samuel Schwartz was not in the least pleased to see us on a Saturday morning but invited us in nevertheless. He sat us in his home office, in front of a desk festooned with pictures of two small children. "Yours?" Vann asked.

"Yes," Schwartz said, sitting down behind his desk.

"Adorable," Vann said.

"Thank you," Schwartz said. "And to forestall the next set of questions, Anna and Kendra, ages seven and five, by way of seminal extraction and in vitro fertilization, the mothers are a married couple of my acquaintance, one of whom was a law school classmate, yes, the children know who I am and yes, I am an active part of their life. In fact I need to be at a soccer game almost immediately. I assume you're here about Nicholas Bell."

"Actually, we're here about Jay Kearney,"

Vann said.

"I've already talked to your fellow FBI agents about Jay," Schwartz said. "I'll tell you what I told them, which is that at no point in our professional or personal relationship did Jay ever reveal or even hint at his plans or his association with Dr. Baer. And as for my whereabouts that evening" — Schwartz nodded toward me — "your associate here can confirm my presence at Marcus Shane's home that evening. We were at the dinner table when the Loudoun Pharma bombing happened."

"Our labs tell us Kearney — or Baer — created a car bomb made out of ammonium nitrate," Vann said.

"All right," Schwartz said. "And?"

"It's probably nothing but I'll note that Agrariot is an Accelerant company. They make dehydrated and frozen food, cattle feed, and fertilizer."

"Accelerant is a multinational conglomerate that wholly owns or has significant investment in nearly two hundred different companies, Agent Vann," Schwartz said. "You are correct that it's probably nothing."

"Agrariot does have a warehouse in Warrenton," Vann observed. "Right down Route 15 from Leesburg. And it's missing several pallets of fertilizer from its inventory. I checked yesterday."

"Then I hope you informed those associates of yours more directly involved in the investigation," Schwartz said.

"We have," Vann said.

"I understand Accelerant made an offer on Loudoun Pharma," I said.

Schwartz turned to me. "This is the first I heard of it," he said. "You might not give credence to rumors."

"I don't know that it's a rumor if it comes directly from the CEO," I said. "I spoke with Mr. Buchold yesterday afternoon."

"Mr. Buchold was indiscreet," Schwartz said. "There have been discussions, but nothing serious."

"I also recall at dinner Lucas Hubbard being pretty negative about what Loudoun Pharma was doing," I said. "Interesting that he would be considering buying the company now, especially after it's been turned into a crater."

"Lucas is interested in keeping jobs in Loudoun County," Schwartz said. "Loudoun Pharma has products that fit into our portfolio."

"Sure," Vann said. "And one that you'd probably like to keep off the market."

"Neuroulease," I said, helpfully.

"That's it," Vann said. "Don't want a bunch of Hadens unlocked. That'd cut into the profit margins of a whole bunch of Accelerant's companies. And you need them cranking out revenue for the next several years at least."

"I'm afraid I don't know much about Neuroulease," Schwartz said, rising. "Now, as I said, I have a soccer game —"

"Do you know much about Salvatore Odell, Michael Crow, Gregory Bufford, James Martinez, Steve Gaitten, or Cesar Burke?" Vann asked.

"I don't know these men," Schwartz said.

"They're the janitors killed when Loudoun Pharma went up," Vann said. "They only just managed to get them dug out the other day. They're doing the memorial ceremony for them today."

"Right now, just about," I said.

"That so," Vann said, to me, and then turned back to Schwartz. "Our med people tell me that a couple of them died when the building blew up, but the rest survived the explosion. They died from being buried under four stories of concrete. Pressed them flat. Crushed."

"Memorial is closed casket," I said.

"It would be," Vann said.

"I'm very sorry to hear that," Schwartz said.

"Are you," Vann said.

"I think that's all the time I have," Schwartz said.

"How close are you to Lucas Hubbard?" I asked.

"What do you mean?" Schwartz said.

"I mean, I'm remembering at dinner the other night when Lucas asked you a question and you blanked out on the answer," I said. "Hubbard reached over to reassure you after you blanked and patted your hand. I'm not a slavish follower of gender roles, but that seemed pretty 'not guy' to me. You don't strike me as the sort to need reassurance, and Hubbard doesn't strike me as the sort to offer it to you. You're his corporation's chief lawyer, not his girlfriend."

"I think you're reading too much into it," Schwartz said.

"And there was the moment I was talking to you about your threep, and you looked at me like you had no idea what I was saying," I said. "Hubbard answered for you then, too. I remember you reading us the riot act when we had Bell in the interrogation room. I don't think it's like you to let someone else speak for you."

"Maybe it wasn't him not speaking," Vann said.

"Maybe not," I said, looking at Schwartz.

"You and I did speak," Schwartz said. "I remember very clearly in your father's trophy room we spoke about the fact I was using a woman Integrator."

"Brenda Rees," I said.

"She's dead now," Vann said.

"Yes," I said.

"Opened fire at a café and then blew herself up with a grenade."

"I was there for it," I said.

"So was I," Vann said, and motioned to her arm, in its sling. "She shot me."

"Me too," I said.

"It's strange," Vann said.

"Being shot?" I asked.

"Yes," Vann said, and pointed at Schwartz. "But I was more thinking about Mr. Schwartz here having two Integrators blow themselves up in the same week."

"That *is* strange," I said.

"I mean, what are the odds?" Vann asked me.

"Pretty slim, I'd say."

"I'd say pretty slim too," Vann said. "Maybe not as slim as these Integrators being eaten by bears or falling into a wheat thresher. But still, overall, pretty remarkable coincidence."

"Agent Vann," Schwartz said. "Agent Shane. We are d—"

"She says you weren't there," I said.

"What?" Schwartz said, distracted.

"Brenda Rees," I said. "She told me that you weren't there at dinner. She says you were gone."

"Right at the time Jay Kearney was doing his thing," Vann said.

"Jay Kearney was integrated with Dr. Baer," Schwartz said. "Baer said so on that recording of his."

"Well, no," I said. "Kearney's *mouth* said it, and we assume that Baer was speaking it because Baer was in the background. But we have an alternate theory."

"It goes like this," Vann said. "You integrate with Kearney and go to Baer's apartment. He's expecting Kearney. You drug Baer so he passes out, make the video, shove a knife into his temple, position the threep to make it look like suicide, and then take a quick trip to Loudoun Pharma with Kearney."

"And are back with us in time for dessert," I said. "If we had dessert. I wasn't there for that part."

"No, because Loudoun Pharma blew up," Vann said.

"You just accused me of murdering Baer," Schwartz said.

"Yes," I said.

"And the six janitors," Vann said.

"And Jay Kearney," I said.

"Eight total," Vann said.

"I'm done speaking to you two," Schwartz said. "I'm not going to say any more to you without a lawyer. If you plan to arrest me, do it now. Otherwise, get out of my house."

"Mr. Schwartz, one more word," Vann said.

Schwartz looked at her, impassive as only a threep can be.

" 'Interpolator,' " Vann said.

"What did you say?" Schwartz said.

"Oh, I think you heard me just fine," Vann said.

"I don't know what the word means," Schwartz said.

"We're past that point, don't you think, Mr. Schwartz?" Vann said. "You know perfectly well what that word means. And you know what it means that *we* know it. It means that you are fucked, sir. *Magnificently* so."

Schwartz was silent again.

"Options," Vann said, and ticked up a finger. "Door number one. You maintain your right to remain silent and your right to an attorney. Good for you. I applaud your stand. We arrest you for those eight murders we've mentioned plus the murders of Bruce Skow and Brenda Rees. We'll also be charging you with the kidnapping of Kearney and Skow and Rees. Not to mention the attempted murders of me and Agent Shane, here. Plus a whole other grab bag of miscellaneous charges which I won't go into but I imagine that you are already running down a list of in your brain, because you are a lawyer. We go to trial, you lose, your body goes into a federal Haden detention center, and you get to speak to other human beings one hour a week, forever."

"We're fine with that option, by the way," I said.

"Yes we are," Vann said. She ticked up another finger. "Door number two. You *talk.*"

She put her hand down. "Make your choice. You have five seconds, after which we assume you're going with door number one."

"Which we're fine with," I said again.

"Yes we are," Vann said.

Schwartz sat down and waited until the count of four, maybe four and a half. "I want a deal," he said.

"Of course you do," Vann said.

"Full immunity," he began.

"No," I interrupted. "You don't get that."

"You're going to prison, Schwartz," Vann said. "You better get used to that. What we're discussing now is where, how long, and how bad it will be."

"Full immunity or nothing," Schwartz said.

" 'Nothing' works for us," I said.

"Mr. Schwartz, I don't think you fully appreciate what I meant when I said you are magnificently fucked," Vann said. "It means that we have more than enough to bury you. Forever. And we will. Forever. But the fact of the matter is, you're not the person we really want. You're not the main attraction. I'm pretty sure you know who we're talking about, here."

"But if we can't get him, we'll be happy to take you," I said.

"It's true," Vann said. "And let's be honest, Schwartz. *He'll* be happy to let us take you, too. You of all people should know how many lawyers he has and how good they are. The very second he learns we bagged you is the second all of it — *all* of it — gets shoved onto you. I can see the press release now."

"He'll be shocked and disturbed at the allegations and will pledge to cooperate fully with the authorities, which means us," I said.

"And you know what," Vann said. "At that point we might just decide to cut our losses and go with what we have. We'll still look good, and honestly it'll be a nice object lesson for you on the subject of blind loyalty to a man who'll be happy to throw you to the dogs."

Schwartz was silent again. Then, "What are you looking for from me?"

"All of it, of course," Vann said. "Dates. Plans. How you used Accelerant's various companies to further your goals. Who else is involved. What the end game was. What both you and Hubbard were planning to get out of it all."

"Why you chose Sani and Skow," I said.

"That's right," Vann said. "You have the upper echelons of the Navajo Nation ready to run you down with a car. You picked the wrong guy to mess with when you picked Sani. It's probably just as well we'll be putting you away for a while."

"How long?" Schwartz asked. He was entirely defeated now. "How much time are we talking about here?"

"Are you asking for a specific number of years?" I asked.

Schwartz turned to me. "I have children,

Agent Shane," he said.

"You're missing that soccer game, Mr. Schwartz," Vann said, surprisingly gently. "You'll be missing high school graduation too. Depending on what we get from you now, we can work on having you out to walk one of them down the aisle."

CHAPTER TWENTY-FOUR

Nicholas Bell entered Cassandra Bell's second-floor apartment and entered the living room, which was in fact where Cassandra Bell lived, the bedroom of the apartment being used as storage and as a lounge for her caregivers. Cassandra's morning caregivers had left for the day. Her afternoon caregivers would not come to the apartment for another hour. Nicholas walked over to the living room's major feature: a cradle, in which lay a young woman. She looked, as all Hadens did, as if she were sleeping.

"It's good of you to come see me, brother," Cassandra said. "I haven't seen you at all this last week." Her voice was carried by a speaker next to her cradle, into which was also embedded a small camera, which she could use to see within the apartment. Cassandra preferred a simple real-world presentation. Which may have been why Nicholas paused when he saw the unfamiliar shape in the room. A threep.

"A gift from an admirer," Cassandra said, following Nicholas's gaze. "Not someone who admires me enough to know that I don't use nor have I ever used a Personal Transport. But one of my caregivers knows someone who needs one. It's waiting for her to come take it."

Nicholas nodded and smiled and took his small backpack from his shoulder. He unzipped it and reached inside.

"Why, brother," Cassandra Bell said. "Did you bring me a gift?"

"Yes," Nicholas said. He took the large kitchen knife he had drawn from the backpack and thrust it into the young woman in the cradle, driving it deep into her abdomen.

Two more hard, deep thrusts into the belly, pushing upward. A rough jab downward, piercing the left upper thigh — a thrust in search of the femoral artery.

The flesh sliced open, pale.

Three thrusts making a sloppy triangle of cuts just below the sternum. One vicious slash on the left side of the neck and a matching slash on the right, opening up the arteries taking blood to the brain, and the veins drawing it away.

Nicholas Bell dropped the knife to the

floor, and stepped back, breathing heavily. He stared at the ruined body, as if something about it puzzled him.

Such as: The body he had stabbed eight times now had not one drop of blood coming out of it.

"Brother," Cassandra Bell whispered. "It didn't work."

I launched myself from the chair I was sitting in and tackled Nicholas Bell, who went down rolling and squirming.

He managed to get out of my grip and scrambled to his backpack. I rolled up and saw him, gun in hand, aiming at me.

"Oh come on," I said. "I just got this threep."

The crash behind us — the sound of FBI agents breaking down the door to get at Nicholas — distracted Nicholas just enough for me to run at him, but not enough for him to break his aim. He fired, and the bullet took me in the shoulder, spinning me.

Nicholas turned and fired three shots into the sliding glass door separating the living room and the balcony, and then ran into the shattered glass, hands up to protect his face. The glass tore away in a sheet and then Nicholas was through and stumbling over the balcony.

"Fuck," I said, and followed him.

That's when I learned the shot Bell took at me had affected the movement of my right arm. I tumbled over the balcony railing and fell hard onto the concrete walkway underneath. If I had been in a human body, I'm pretty sure I would have been dead or paralyzed.

But I wasn't.

I stood up, scanned around, and saw Bell thirty yards ahead, limping but moving surprisingly fast. His gun was still in his right hand.

"What the hell just happened?" Vann said, in my head.

"He jumped out of the balcony," I said. "He's running on Ninth Street. Headed toward Welburn Square. I'm going after him."

"Don't lose him again," Vann said.

"Again?!?" I said, and then went running.

Bell's limp had gotten worse when I caught up to him just short of Welburn Square. I jumped him and we both went down on the redbrick sidewalk. I grabbed at him with my one good arm. He kicked it off and pistol-whipped me with the butt of his gun.

This did not work as well as he wanted it to. I had turned down my pain sensitivity. He turned the gun on me and I rolled away.

Bell took off again, limping, cutting across the central circle of the grass in the square, scattering passersby when they saw his gun.

I went after him again, tripping him short of Taylor Street. He turned as he stumbled, and fired at me, hitting me in the hip. My left leg collapsed under me. I looked up to see Bell give a small grin of triumph and then run out into Taylor Street —

— on which he was immediately struck by a car. Bell splayed dramatically across the hood of the automobile and then collapsed on the road, clutching his leg.

Vann got out of the driver's side, walked over to Bell, ascertained that he was not in immediate danger of death, and handcuffed him.

Two minutes later all the other FBI agents had caught up to us. Vann walked over to me, still down on the sidewalk. She sat down next to me and pulled her e-cigarette from her jacket pocket.

"That's the third threep you've ruined in two days," she said.

"Fourth," I said.

"I don't want to tell you how to do your job," she said. "But I will say that if I were your insurer, I'd drop your ass."

"You hit our suspect with a car," I said.

"Oops," Vann said. She sucked on her

cigarette.

"You could have killed him."

"I was going five miles an hour," Vann said. "And anyway it was an accident."

"You're not supposed to be able to get into accidents like that anymore," I said.

"It's amazing what you can do when you disable autodrive," Vann said.

"We promised Cassandra Bell we wouldn't hurt her brother," I said.

"I know," Vann said. "It was a risk. On the other hand, that asshole just shot my partner. Twice."

"It wasn't Bell who shot me."

"That's not the asshole I was talking about." She put her cigarette away.

"I'm curious about a number of things," Vann said, to Bell. They were sitting across the table from each other in one of the Bureau's interrogation rooms. Vann had a manila folder in front of her. "But I'll tell you what I'm curious about right this second. It's that you're here in an FBI interrogation room, under arrest, and you have neither affirmatively invoked your right to remain silent or asked for your lawyer. You should. You should do both."

"Yes," I said. I was standing behind Vann. I was in one of the threeps the FBI used for visiting agents. The agent who had been using it half an hour before was currently stewing in Chicago because I had interrupted her work. She could stew for a while longer. "Although if I were you I wouldn't try to call Sam Schwartz."

"Why not?" Bell asked, looking up at me.

"We arrested him this morning on charges of murder and conspiracy, relating to the Loudoun Pharma bombing," I said. "Won't his boss be surprised."

"Hubbard's in the clear," Vann said. "Everything points to Schwartz alone. Not the best sort of extracurriculars to have, though." She turned back to Bell. "Now. Would you like to remain silent?" she asked. "When you answer, keep in mind that the minute you were out of your apartment and on the way here, we executed a warrant to search your residence and belongings. Which is to say we've already found the video you made confessing to the murder, and also, your suicide."

"Which explains the gun," I said. "Stabbing's fine for your sister, but you wanted your own end to be quick and mostly painless. But I suppose me rushing you scrambled your plans a bit."

"So," Vann said, again. "Do you want to remain silent? Do you want a lawyer?"

"You have the video," Bell said, to Vann. He motioned up to me. "Your partner saw the attack. What would be the point?"

"To be clear, you're waiving your right to silence and to an attorney," Vann said. "I really need you to say 'yes' if that's in fact what you want."

"Yes," Bell said. "It's what I want. I intended to kill my sister, Cassandra Bell. That was my goal."

"Well, that makes our lives a lot easier," Vann said. "Thank you."

"I'm not doing it for you," Bell said. "I wanted people to know my sister is dangerous."

"Is this covered in your suicide note?" Vann asked. "Because if it is, if it's all the same we can just skip ahead to us taking you in and putting you in federal detention while you await sentencing."

"Well, there is that one thing," I said.

Vann snapped the fingers of her left hand. "That's right. I *did* have one more question for you, Nicholas."

"What is it?" Bell asked.

"How long are you going to keep this up?" Vann asked.

Bell looked at her uncertainly. "I don't know what you mean by that."

"I mean, how long are you going to keep

pretending to be Nicholas Bell, Mr. Hubbard?" Vann asked. "I ask only because Shane and I have a bet going on here. Shane thinks you're only going to keep this up until we get you into detention. After all, you do have a life and a multinational conglomerate to run, and now that you've confessed as Bell and admitted guilt, the hard part is done."

"That's right," I said. "When the real Bell surfaces and backtracks in detention, no one will believe him. They'll think he's begun to regret his decision and is maybe hoping for some sort of psychiatric ruling."

"That's a fair call," Vann said. "But I said no. You've come too far with this to half-ass it now. I think you're committed to this all the way through the sentencing and housing. It's only once the door slams shut on Bell in a six-by-nine cell that you'll know for sure you've gotten away with it. So you have to stick with it, just like you've stuck with it this entire week. Yes, that means Accelerant doesn't have you at the helm. But maybe when Bell's asleep you can sneak out and leave a note saying you're on vacation for a couple of weeks. They can get along without you."

"Legal might have a problem," I observed.

"They've got a lot of lawyers," Vann said.

"They can work around."

"Neither of you are making any sense," Bell said.

"He's sticking with it," I said.

"Well, he has to, right now," Vann said. "But let's mix things up. Mr. Bell, I have a picture for you." Vann opened the manila folder, pulled a picture out of it, and slid the photo over to Nicholas Bell.

"Meet Camille Hammond," she said, to him. "Twenty-three years old, and a resident of the Lady Bird Johnson Haden Care Facility in Occoquan, which is where the NIH stores Hadens with other severe brain disorders, who have no family or other means of support. More accurately, Camille *was* a resident, until Wednesday evening, when she died of a persistent pneumonial infection. Unfortunately common in people in her situation."

Bell looked at the picture but said nothing.

"The NIH wasn't too thrilled with us when we asked if we could borrow her for today's festivities," Vann continued. "But then, they also didn't want to see Cassandra Bell brutally murdered by her own brother on the eve of the largest civil rights march on D.C. in a decade, either. So in the end they decided to help us."

She leaned in across the table to Bell.

"So here's the thing I want to know," she said. "You came into that room to murder your sister. Someone you knew your entire life. I'm a little confused how you managed *not* to recognize that the woman you stabbed eight times was not the same woman that you had known for twenty years."

Bell looked up and stayed silent.

"You know what, don't answer that," Vann said, and looked back to me. "Tell them to bring in Tony."

I sent the message with my inside voice. A minute later Tony was in the room with us.

"Tony Wilton, Lucas Hubbard," I said, by way of introduction. "Lucas Hubbard, Tony Wilton."

"If it was a week ago, I'd say it was an honor to meet you," Tony said, to Bell. "As it is, I can still say I admire your skill at coding."

"Tony," Vann said. "If you would be so kind as to catch up Mr. Hubbard on your latest adventures."

"So, that thing you did where you downloaded code into the processor through the interpolator really was some genius-level work," Tony said. "But it's also *really* dangerous, because, well" — Tony gestured at

Bell — "for obvious reasons. So last night I wrote a patch that would block that pathway, and the NIH, which can still dictate mandatory patching, put it at the top of their priority queue. Right around the time you entered Cassandra Bell's apartment, it started going out to every Integrator in the United States. And after they're patched, it'll go into the general queue for Hadens, too. I mean, there's no way that you could exploit it with a Haden like you do with an Integrator. But then we didn't see *this* coming with the Integrators until you exploited it. Evil but brilliant. So we decided better safe than sorry."

"I'm not understanding anything you're telling me," Bell said. "What is an interpolator?"

Tony looked over to me. "He's really committed to this," he said.

"What choice does he have?" I said. "If he drops out now, the real Nicholas Bell surfaces and spills everything."

"Which reminds me," Tony said, and turned back to Bell. "I'm sure you of all people are aware that patches to neural networks can be general or they can be tailored to be very, very specific. As in, a patch for one single neural network."

Bell looked back at him, blankly.

400

"Okay, since you're pretending not to understand any of this, I'll make it really simple," Tony said. "In addition to coding a very general patch last night, I also coded a *very* specific patch, for the neural network here." Tony tapped the top of Bell's head, lightly. "It does two things. One of them deals with control of the data stream."

"Pay attention," Vann said, to Bell. "This is good."

"Usually during integration either the Integrator or the client is able to stop the data flow — if the client is done with the session or the Integrator's had enough of the client," Tony said. "Right now you've managed to disable Bell's ability to kick you out of his head."

"That doesn't seem fair," Vann said.

"Right," Tony said. "So the patch I just had automatically downloaded into Bell's network removes your ability to cut the data stream. You've got Bell trapped in his own head. And now I've got *you* trapped in the same place. Go ahead, try to cut it."

"Oh, he's not going to do *that*," Vann said. "You're bluffing to try to get him to leave Bell's head."

"Huh," Tony said. "I hadn't thought about that. Fair call."

"He'll find out soon enough," I said. "He

had Nicholas Bell trying to kill his sister." I tapped my head. "I have it right here. When the door of that six-by-nine cell slams shut, he'll be in there with Bell."

"So that's the first thing about the patch," Tony said. "The second thing is something I think you're going to *really* like."

"Hold that thought," Vann said. Tony silenced himself. Vann turned to Bell. "Anything to say yet, Mr. Hubbard?"

"I honestly don't know what you are going on about," Bell said, pleadingly. "I'm very confused."

"Let's aim for some clarity," Vann said, and nodded to me. "Our next guests, please."

Another minute, and May and Janis Sani came into the room. Vann got up to give May her seat. Janis stood behind her grandmother, hand lightly on her shoulder.

"This is him?" May asked, looking at Vann.

"It is," Vann said. "On the inside at least."

"I don't know these two ladies," Bell said.

"And that's the first true thing you've said all afternoon," Vann said.

"Lucas Hubbard, May and Janis Sani," I said. "Their last name may sound familiar because you used Johnny Sani, their grandson and brother."

"This is insane," Bell said.

"I think we've done enough of the preliminaries," Vann said. "And I'm getting tired of the bullshit. So let's get right to it." She put her foot on Bell's chair and spun it back and out from the table.

"We lied to you about Schwartz," she said, to Bell. "We've got him on murder and conspiracy, but he's cut a deal with us. He's told us the whole story of your play to dominate the Haden market. His version of the story doesn't look good for you at all. We're ready to hit Accelerant with a battalion of forensics geeks. I've got twenty more at your house waiting for me to tell them to go in. We have almost more warrants on you and your companies than we have people to serve them. Almost."

Vann kicked Bell's chair, lightly. It jumped a fraction of an inch, and Bell with it.

"But you are still here playing your idiotic game of 'I'm not Hubbard.' It's time to stop playing that game," Vann said. "So here's what we're doing now. You stop pretending to be Bell." She pointed to May and Janis Sani. "You can start by telling the two of them what really happened to Johnny Sani. They deserve to know.

"Or, you can keep pretending to be Bell, in which case, here's Tony to tell you what happens next." She looked over to Tony. "Tell him about the *other* thing your patch does," she said.

"It flips the script," Tony said.

"A little more technical, please," Vann said, looking at Bell. "I think he can keep up."

"When a client uses an Integrator, the Integrator steps back and lets the client's consciousness drive the body," Tony said. "The Integrator assists but is supposed to hold back." He gestured at Bell. "With your variation of it, the Integrator's consciousness is pushed back entirely. It's disconnected from any control of the body at all. The patch I've introduced into Bell's body reverses that. It gives the *Integrator* complete physical control while relegating the client to the background, unable to do anything but watch."

"The client experiences lock in," I said.

"That's right," Tony said. "Now obviously it makes no sense to do this in the usual client-Integrator relationship. But then" — he looked down at Bell — "this isn't the usual relationship, is it."

"Bell gets his life back and Hubbard is trapped inside, forever," I said.

"And that's not even the good part," Vann said. She got in very close to Bell. "Here's the really good part. Bell is a known Integrator for Hubbard now. So why not just . . . let that *roll*?"

"Have him say he's Hubbard?" I asked.

"Have him *be* Hubbard," Vann said. She looked up at Tony and me. "We back off on the warrants, let Schwartz take the fall, and install Bell at the head of Accelerant. And then he starts dismantling the company. Sells it off, piece by piece. And with the profits from the sales, he invests in Hadens. Starting with your dad's new thing, Chris."

"Oh, right," I said. I leaned in on the table, toward Bell. "My father just reached a deal with the Navajo Nation to fund a nonprofit competitor to the Agora," I said. "The Navajo have an immense server farm. More than enough room for the entire Haden nation. Staffed by Navajo techs. Affordable and accessible. And technically not in U.S. territory. We're announcing it tomorrow at the march. To make the point that the Haden community has another option besides being strip-mined by someone trying to corner the market."

"Just think," Vann said. "Cassandra Bell announcing it, Marcus Shane standing on one side, Lucas Hubbard on the other. Coming together for every Haden. And then Hubbard dismantling his company, a piece

405

at a time, to keep funding the goal. Until there's nothing left."

"It's a dream," I said, standing back from the table.

"Yes," Vann said.

"A more than slightly unethical dream."

"More unethical than bombing competitors, attacking federal agents, and planning to assassinate a Haden activist?" Vann asked.

"Well, no," I admitted.

"Then I'm *fine* with it," Vann said. "And the only people who will ever know are in this room right now. Anyone have a problem with it?"

No one said anything.

"Then these are the options you have, Hubbard," Vann said, returning to Bell. "Admit who you are, and tell May and Janis what happened to Johnny Sani. You're guilty but your company will survive. Keep doing what you're doing and we flip the script. Bell gets his life back from you and then takes over your life. And you watch everything you've ever done fall apart. Make your choice."

Bell sat there, silent, for more than a minute.

Then.

"At first it was more a thought experiment than anything else," Hubbard said. And it was definitely Hubbard. Even cuffed to a chair the swagger was there. "I had written the code and modeled the network, designed for a client to integrate full-time. There was no point to it other than curiosity.

"But then Abrams-Kettering came along and the business model I'd been working on was changing. Other businesses started to panic but I knew there were opportunities there. They just needed to be directed. In a way that was effective but untraceable, and not reproducible. If I used the network I designed, I knew I could manipulate people and events in ways that other businesses couldn't. And in a way that couldn't be traced back to me.

"It was Sam who pointed out that Medichord had access to Navajo Nation medical records, and that those records weren't part of the U.S. national health database. We could find a test subject there who would be otherwise invisible — no records elsewhere, nothing to track. We found two. Johnny and Bruce. We moved on Johnny first. He was . . ."

Hubbard stopped, realizing how what he was about to say would sound to Johnny Sani's family.

"Say it," Vann said.

"He was mentally deficient," Hubbard

said. "Easy to fool. Easy to control. We set him up in California through a Chinese company Accelerant had a minority stake in. Our contacts with him were through one-of-a-kind threeps. Everything untraceable even though Johnny wasn't smart enough to figure it out. Overcautious. We kept everything small as possible. Only Sam and I knew everything.

"When the network was installed we tested it first for a few minutes at a time, then an hour or two. We became comfortable using Johnny for more things. Driving him on simple tasks. A little corporate spying. Some bits of sabotage. Nothing really significant. Simply testing the capabilities.

"We figured out that Johnny was limited. Not in his brain — that didn't matter when I was driving him. But the same lack of identity that attracted us to him limited him. Having no identity makes it harder to move in our society, not easier.

"With what we learned from Johnny, we started working on commercial network models. We own Lucturn, and we had the database of networks to work with. I came up with the interpolator method to hack into the networks and leave a door open. All we had to do was wait for the right opportunity.

"Then Abrams-Kettering passed and the walkout and march were planned. It was the right opportunity to destabilize the market and pick off companies we wanted.

"I knew Nicholas Bell was an Integrator. I'd known people who used him. And I knew that when Abrams-Kettering passed, he would be looking for a long-term contract. But I didn't want to approach him directly. I had one last job for Johnny Sani. I drove him out to D.C. and used him to contact Bell, posing as a tourist. I used him to get into Bell's mind.

"When I was in Bell, Sam was supposed to link right in and take over Johnny. But Sam got distracted for a couple of minutes. Johnny came to, looked around, grabbed a love seat, and ran at the window with it, and pushed it out into the street. Then he came back, grabbed a glass, and smashed it against the dresser. I thought he was going to use it on me. I put up my hands.

"He yelled at me, telling me that now someone would come up to see what was happening. He wanted to stop being used. He wanted to know what he was being used for. He said he wanted to go home."

Hubbard paused again.

"Keep going," Vann said. "If you won't

say it, Bell will. It's all coming out, Hub-bard."

"I laughed at him," Hubbard said. "I knew Sam was coming to link to him and then that would be the end of it. So I told him that what he was being used for was to make me very rich. He wanted to know if he'd ever been made to hurt people. I told him that he didn't remember it anyway so he shouldn't worry about it.

"Then he said to me, 'I know you're a bad man and I know you won't let me go home so now I'm going to make trouble for you.'

"And then he cut his throat."

May and Janis stared at Hubbard stonily. I remembered Klah Redhouse telling me how they tried not to show too much grief.

"I'm sorry —" Hubbard said, looking at May and Janis.

"Don't you dare," Janis spat. "You're not sorry Johnny is dead. You were going to kill someone today. You're sorry you got caught. But you did get caught. You got caught because Johnny stopped you from getting away with what you were doing. He made trouble for you, just like he said. My brother was slow but he could figure things out if he took enough time. He figured you out. And now look at you. My brother is ten of you."

Janis helped May up out of the chair. The two of them left the room without looking back.

"You saw him cut his throat, but then you panicked, didn't you," Vann said, after they left. "You actually left Bell's body for at least a couple of minutes."

"Yes," Hubbard said. "I left but Sam told me to go back in. He said if Bell told anyone about his experience that they would figure out what we had done, and sooner or later it would come back to us. I had to stay with Bell until the thing was done." He snorted. "He said he'd come up with a cover story that would last through Saturday, and that would be long enough. For all the good it did either of us."

"You were gone just long enough for Bell to give us a clue," Vann said. "He was confused just enough by what was happening to let us know something was seriously wrong. Thanks for that."

Hubbard smirked ruefully and looked up at Vann. "Now what," he said.

"Now it's time for you to go get arrested for real, Mr. Hubbard," Vann said. "Go back to your body. Do it now."

"You need to swap out the patch," Hubbard said.

"About that," Tony said.

"What about it?" Hubbard asked.

"We lied to you," Vann said. "There was no patch."

"There was a general patch that closed the interpolator back door," Tony said. "That was true. So if you backed out you wouldn't have been able to come back in."

"But we knew you wouldn't do that," Vann said. "So we decided to press our luck."

"There was no script-flipper either," Hubbard said.

"If we had that, we would have led with that," I said. "And then we would have made you watch your company burn."

"Now, go, Hubbard," Vann said. "My colleagues are waiting for you. You've got a lot to answer for."

Hubbard left, which was not noticeable. Nicholas Bell surfacing was. He shook himself, almost knocking over his chair, and sucked in his breath. *"Jesus,"* he said.

"Nicholas Bell," Vann said.

"Yes," Bell said. "Yes. It's me."

"Nice to meet you," Vann said.

"Hold still," I said, gently putting a hand on his shoulder. "I need to get you out of these cuffs." I undid him. He shook out his arms and rubbed his wrists.

"Mr. Bell," Vann said.

"Yes," he said.

"What Hubbard said about Johnny Sani," Vann asked.

Bell nodded. "It was true," he said.

"I'm sorry you had to watch that," Vann said.

Bell laughed, shakily. "It's been a long week," he said.

"Yes," Vann said. "That it has."

"I hate to say this," I said, to Bell. "But we need to have you answer some questions. We need you to tell us everything you saw or heard while Hubbard had control of your body."

"Trust me, I intend to tell you everything I know about that son of a bitch," Bell said. "But there's something I really would like to do before I do that. If I can. If you don't mind."

"Of course," Vann said. "Tell us what you would like to do."

"I'd really like to see my sister now," Bell said.

CHAPTER TWENTY-FIVE

Vann pointed at the stage in front of the Lincoln Memorial, where the speakers for the Haden march stood. "Your father looks pretty good up there," she said, nodding toward Dad, standing next to President Becenti and Cassandra Bell, held in a portable cradle.

"He looks like an ant," I said. "Which for my father is pretty impressive."

"We could get closer to the stage if you want," she said. "The rumor is, you know a guy."

"I do," I said. "But I think we're fine where we are."

Vann and I stood at the periphery of the crowd, far down the Mall from the stage and the speeches.

"No riots," Vann said. "I wouldn't have put money on that yesterday morning."

"I think the Hubbard thing took the air out of those sails," I said. News of Hubbard's and Schwartz's arrests was significant enough to escape the news dead zone of a late Saturday afternoon. We made sure that everyone had as much information as they wanted on the details. Saturday night in D.C. was no more filled with incident than most Saturday nights. Sunday was Sunday.

"We dodged a bullet," Vann said, agreeing. "In a general sense. You took several."

"Yes," I said. "If I have learned anything this week, it's to invest in economy threeps. I can't afford this sort of attrition."

"Yes, you can," Vann said.

"Well, yeah," I said. "I can. But I don't want to."

We walked the Mall, her in her sling and me in a borrowed threep. She glanced back toward the stage. "You could have been up there," she said. "Standing there with your father. You're still famous enough that you could have given his deal with the Navajo even more credibility."

"No," I said. "Dad's got credibility to burn, even after this week. And I don't want that life anymore. There's a reason I'm an FBI agent, Vann. I want to be useful for something else other than as a poster child."

"The Hadens could still use a poster child," Vann said. "Abrams-Kettering still takes effect at midnight. Things are going to get harder from here. A lot harder."

"Someone else can do that job," I said. "I think I'm better at doing this job."

"You are," Vann said. "At least this week you were."

"They're not all like this, right?" I said. "The weeks, I mean."

"Would it be so bad if they were?" Vann asked.

"Yes," I said. "Yes. It would."

"I did say I was going to ask a lot of you," Vann said. "On that first day. You remember."

"I remember," I said. "I'm not going to lie to you. I kind of just thought you were trying to scare me."

Vann smiled and patted my shoulder. "Relax, Shane," she said. "It gets better from here."

"I hope so," I said.

"Excuse me," someone said. We looked over and there was a threep, standing with a few other people. It pointed to Vann. "You're that FBI agent. The one that arrested Lucas Hubbard."

"Yes," Vann said. "One of them."

"How cool!" the threep said, and then motioned at the group. "Would you mind? If we got a picture?"

"No," Vann said. "Be happy to."

"Awesome," the threep said. Then it and the group began to crowd around Vann. One of them handed me a camera.

"Would you mind?" she asked.

"Not at all," I said. "Everybody crowd in." They crowded in.

"You're loving this, aren't you," Vann said.

"Just a little," I said. "Now. Everyone say 'cheese.'"

ACKNOWLEDGMENTS

As always, I think it's important to acknowledge the people behind the scenes at my publisher, Tor Books, who make such an effort to getting my books to you. This time around, these include Patrick Nielsen Hayden, my editor; Miriam Weinberg, his assistant; Irene Gallo, art director; Peter Lutjen, cover designer; Heather Saunders, interior designer; and Christina MacDonald, copy editor. Also Alexis Saarela, my publicist, and of course Tom Doherty, publisher of Tor.

It's also important to thank Ethan Ellenberg, my agent, and Evan Gregory, who handles my foreign sales. They do a frankly fantastic job for me, and I'm lucky to have them.

Thanks also to Steve Feldberg at Audible and to Gillian Redfearn at Gollancz.

Many thanks to friends and readers who have cheered me on and/or been there as welcome distractions when I needed to be distracted. This list is very long, so rather than list it out, assume that you're on it. Thanks, y'all.

I really mostly just want to thank my wife, Kristine Blauser Scalzi. I wrote this book in 2013, which was in many important ways a really amazing year for me (I won a Hugo for Best Novel in it, for *Redshirts,* as just one salient example), but also very, very stressful. Simply put, she was the one who had to put up with me. That she did so with love and patience and encouragement instead of strangling me, throwing my remains into a wood chipper, and then pretending she had never been married to me at all is a testament to the fact that she is, in fact, the single best person I know. I love her more than I actually express in words — an irony for a writer — and am every day genuinely amazed I get to spend my life with her.

I try to let her know how much I appreciate her, as often as I can. This is me letting the rest of you know, too. You have this book because of her.

— *John Scalzi, 11/29/13*

ABOUT THE AUTHOR

John Scalzi is one of the most popular and acclaimed SF authors to emerge in the last decade. His massively successful debut *Old Man's War* won him science fiction's John W. Campbell Award for Best New Writer. His *New York Times* bestsellers include *The Lost Colony, Fuzzy Nation,* and *Redshirts,* which won 2013's Hugo Award for Best Novel. Material from his widely read blog *The Whatever* (whatever.scalzi.com) has also earned him two other Hugo Awards. He lives in Ohio with his wife and daughter.

TELL THE WORLD
THIS BOOK WAS

Good	Bad	So·so

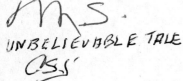

UNBELIEVABLE TALE